To My Girl,
Thank you for
on my first book!
thing!

# Dedicated
# 2
# Bmore City

Nigel Ali

GH99 Publishing
Atlanta, GA

## Nigel Ali Bio

Nigel Ali was born and raised in Baltimore City. At an early age, Nigel Ali found a passion for writing. He was first introduced to the art of expression through poetry which later turned into hip-hop music and then matured into novels. Like many fatherless children in Baltimore City, Nigel Ali was forced to become a man at an early age and he had a front row seat to the dark side of Baltimore City. He is no longer that young man standing on the corner with a nothing to lose attitude. He is now a husband and a father of three beautiful children. No more risking his freedom for crumbs, Nigel Ali is dedicated to leaving a better path for his children.

Nigel Ali writes from a unique, unapologetic, raw perspective and he credits that to the streets of Baltimore City. Nigel Ali gives his readers enough detail to allow their imaginations to run wild, but leaves enough speculation to allow them to paint their own picture. In 2013, Nigel Ali formed GH99 Publishing with one goal in mind, to put Baltimore City on the literary map. From the booth to the block and finally to the bookstore, informing people that writing is the new cool.

Dedicated to Bmore City
Published by GH99 Publishing

Copyright © 2013 by Nigel Ali

Cover Design by Gregory Goodwin
Proofreading & Typesetting: Rahiem Brooks
Editing: Locksie Locks

ISBN 9780615790671
LCCN 2013949102
All Rights Reserved

PRINTED IN THE UNITED STATES OF AMERICA

[September 2013] First Edition

# ACKNOWLEDGMENTS

First and foremost, I want to thank God for being patient with me and loving me through all of my faults and sins. I have been blessed beyond my wildest dreams even when I didn't see it. I thank him for loving me when I took things for granted and I thank him for giving me an opportunity to change my life and hopefully those around me. I realize that anyone who is reading this not only knows me, but really supports me, so it is very important that I speak to you on this. If we cried tears, argued, fought each other or side by side, then you know how important you are to me. If you've ever had a cup of GH99, then you know how important you are to me. If you ever stood on the corner of Monument and Luzerne, then you know how important you are to me. If you ever attended Woodlawn High school, then you know how important you are to me. Class of 92 – Beyond we're all Warriors at the end of the day. I pride myself in keeping it 100 with the people I call friends and it feels good to get that love back. To those of you who pre-ordered your copy, you have no idea how much that means to me. You took a chance on me, you took a moment out of your busy day to support me and I will never forget those individuals because when I started to second guess myself, you gave me the confidence to push on. To each of you who invested in me blindly, I want you to know that I will forever hold those moments close to me and I will find a way to give it back and show my appreciation, you've got my word.

I want to also thank Mr. Rahiem Brooks and Ms. Locksie Locks for taking a hungry author and molding me into a sharper individual, but I know I'm not done growing yet. I'm looking forward to building a stronger relationship over the years with them. I also would like to thank Gregory Graphics for his artwork and A.D.E.D for video editing. I'm anxious to see where my next project will go with these types of professionals in my corner.

I'm not going to fill this up with shout-outs so I'll just throw a couple of phrases out there and those that know, know what I'm talking about. Havsumm, Red Cup, 3rd Ave, The Square, Roc, Pop Shop, Owe Willy, Rumors, Warrior. To my squad, we've been patient and humble for a long time, we've kept it a 100 when the world was keeping it 50, it's time to cash in these stripes. Musvah.

Dedicated
2
Bmore
City

# CHAPTER 1

A poster of a red Porsche 911, a Mercedes Benz and a silver BMW are taped onto the small bedroom wall. His mother calls it junk, but to Carlos, it's called inspiration. He walks over to his dresser and presses play on the CD player. While getting dressed, Wu-Tang Clan blasts out of the speakers setting the mood to match his mindset. Carlos opens his dresser drawer, reaches to the back, and grabs a beat up, small black book and opens it. Written in pencil are names, dates and dollar amounts. The names with checks beside them represent the people who he has collected money from. With his index finger, he scrolls down to the name Fat Gary, and there is no check beside his name. *It's payday big man,* he thinks to himself.

At an early age, Carlos Strickland was always an ambitious kid. In middle school, he would sell candy, shovel snow in the winter and cut grass in the summer. It is now the year 1994, he is 15-years-old and his days of slaving for pennies are over. Carlos never had a traditional relationship with his mother, Loretta. Loretta has been an alcoholic for as long as Carlos can remember. She never made him a home cooked meal, punished him or even asked about school. A mother's love was something that Carlos never truly felt, so he

1

filled that void by chasing money. In his freshmen year in high school, Carlos attempted to sell candy, but he quickly realized that wasn't going to buy him the things he needed – so he started selling weed. In the tenth grade, he was not making a lot of money, but for a 15-year-old, he was doing well.

While the rest of the students rushed to class to avoid being late, Carlos would shoot dice in the school auditorium with the seniors. He had a knack for fitting in and the troublemakers at Woodlawn High School quickly embraced him.

Now standing at five-foot-ten with brown skin, Carlos has a charm that most girls can't resist. But beneath the good looks and gift for gab, he can be extremely cold – especially when it comes to money.

While staring into his closet, he hears a knock at the front door. He rushes downstairs and opens it. It's Kendrick Rumsfeld. Kendrick and Carlos have known each other since elementary school, but Kendrick is slightly different from Carlos and the difference started at home. Kendrick's mother, Amy, is very protective. She doesn't allow Kendrick to wear name brand clothes, and he has to be in the house when the neighborhood lights come on. Carlos, on the other hand, wanders around like an undisciplined puppy because he is.

Kendrick and Carlos didn't grow up with the same family values, but the one thing they had in common was basketball. In Heraldry Square apartment complex, the basketball court was where everyone hung out. Kendrick's ability on the basketball court was what drew them close, and they have been inseparable ever since.

Even though Carlos is only a year older than Kendrick, Kendrick looks up to him. Carlos possesses a certain type of independence that Kendrick yearns for and he would do anything to get Carlos' approval.

Heraldry Square is a community zoned for section eight residents. Most families living in the area are being raised by single mothers who don't have time to monitor their children's whereabouts. Needless to say, the neighborhood is wild, but Amy tries her best to keep Kendrick trouble free.

Once inside of the bedroom, Carlos closes the door and locks it. He opens up his closet revealing hundreds of dollars worth of clothes. The things that Carlos has in his room, Kendrick's mother would never allow. Carlos' walls are filled with posters of his favorite rappers, cars, and Jet magazine beauty of the month. Kendrick walks over to Carlos' window and sees a blunt inside of an ashtray on his nightstand.

"Go ahead, light it up," Carlos offers.

"In here?"

"Yeah, nigga."

Even though Kendrick is in Carlos' home, just the thought of smoking in the house is terrifying. All he can envision is his mother kicking open the door and giving him the ass-whipping of a lifetime. Kendrick places the blunt back into the ashtray. "Nah, I'm cool."

"Good, more for me." Carlos grabs the blunt and lights it up. Afterwards, he gets dressed and unlocks his bedroom door. "Take a ride wit' me."

"Where we going?"

"Just come on."

Whenever Carlos asks Kendrick to take a ride, somehow it always ends with Kendrick sitting in the car while Carlos visits some fully developed, fast ass teenager. The last time Kendrick took a ride with Carlos, he was out past his curfew and grounded for three days. Kendrick hates the unexpected, but can't tell the person he admires *no,* so he agrees.

Inside the car, Kendrick notices Carlos mumbling and staring at his little black book, which he playfully tries to snatch from Carlos' hand.

Carlos raises his fists. "What da fuck is wrong witchu?"

"Damn, I'm just playing with you."

"I ain't," Carlos replies, tossing the black book into the glove compartment. "If I lose this book, I lose my money."

While driving, Carlos lights up another blunt and inhales deeply. Some people smoke weed to relax and use the high to remove themselves from reality, but Carlos smokes to feel sober. He will never admit it, but being a chronic smoker helps him deal with the damage his mother caused.

Carlos exhales a cloud of smoke. "You know you want some."

"You smoke too much."

"Nah, nigga, you don't smoke enough," Carlos says laughing. "Ya momma will whip that ass."

Carlos parks in front of a department store, then turns and stares at Kendrick with bloodshot eyes. "I need you to go inside and –"

"Hold up, you asked me to take a ride witchu, but you ain't say shit about helping."

"C'mon, Kendrick! All you gotta do is, go inside and look for a dark skin nigga named Fat Gary who works at the register. Trust me, you won't miss him. He owes me four hundred dollars. Can you handle that?"

"What do I get for helping?"

Carlos grins. "You get a ride home. Just go in there and handle this shit for me."

Kendrick opens the passenger door and walks inside. He scans the store and sees Fat Gary. What Carlos failed to mention is Fat Gary is the size of college football linebacker. "Damn," Kendrick mumbles. The closer he gets, the smaller he becomes. He walks to line four and to avoid looking suspicious, he grabs a bag of bar-b-que potato chips and places them on the conveyer belt. "You got something for Carlos?"

"Do I know you?" Fat Gary responds with an attitude.

"Nah, Carlos sent me."

Fat Gary reaches into his pocket and gives Kendrick three twenty-dollars bills.

*I know this nigga ain't just give me sixty dollars.* At this moment, Kendrick knows this is going to be a problem. "Carlos said you owe him four hunned, this ain't —"

Fat Gary can smell the fear seeping through Kendrick's pores. "Tell Carlos come in here and get the rest himself."

Kendrick always picked his battles wisely and going to war with a six-foot-four, three hundred pound man is not going to work out in his favor. Instead of arguing, he pays for his chips, walks out and gets inside of the car.

"Yo, why you ain't tell me that nigga was a giant?"

"You get the money?" Carlos asks.

"Next time, can you at least –"

"Did you get the damn money?"

Kendrick pulls out the three twenty dollar bills. "This is all he gave me." Kendrick leans back in his seat. "He basically said 'fuck you'." Kendrick chuckles. "Shit, if I was his size, I wouldn't pay ya little ass either."

"You think this shit is funny?"

Kendrick stutters, "Nah, I'm just saying if I was as big as –"

"I heard whatchu said, Kendrick."

When it comes to respect, Carlos has learned that you must protect it at all costs, even if it means deadly force. He positions himself in the seat and sits in silence. Reaching under his seat, he grabs his black nine millimeter and places it in his lap. This is the first time Kendrick has seen a real gun and he becomes nervous.

"C'mon, Carlos, it ain't this serious. I ain't going to jail over four hundred dollars."

Carlos removes the clip. "I ain't gonna kill him. I'm just going to teach his big ass a lesson." He checks his watch and stares at the front entrance of the store. The more time that passes, the angrier he becomes. "He gets off in about ten minutes. We are gonna wait right here for his ass."

The sight of Carlos' gun changes things. If Kendrick could walk away, he would, but the last thing he needs is to show Carlos that he is scared. Kendrick bites his nails watching the clock on Carlos' dashboard and each minute that passes, he becomes more afraid.

Fat Gary walks out, and Carlos looks at Kendrick one last time before opening the driver's door. "You ready?"

*I can't believe this shit,* Kendrick says to himself, but what comes out of his mouth is, "Yeah."

Kendrick reluctantly gets out of the car and follows behind Carlos. Clearly outsized, Carlos fearlessly stands face to face with Fat Gary. "Where's the rest of my money?"

"You better watch who you talking to lil' nigga. I ain't got it."

Fat Gary bumps Carlos' shoulder almost knocking him to the ground. Carlos reaches behind his back, grabs his gun and hits Fat Gary across the head as hard as he can. If Fat Gary wasn't a giant, a blow like this would have knocked him out, but instead it just pisses him off. Fat Gary turns around, but before he can defend himself, Carlos hits him again. Kendrick pulls Fat Gary's shirt over his head and punches him repeatedly in the face. Goliath falls to the ground and curls up like a newborn baby. While being kicked by Kendrick, Fat Gary pulls Carlos to the ground, but before Fat Gary can literally pound Carlos to death, Kendrick grabs a jagged rock and bashes Fat Gary across the head leaving him unconscious in a puddle of blood.

Carlos steps back, picks up his gun and kicks him square in the face. "Dontchu ever short me again."

Kendrick shouts, "Let's go, Carlos."

"Hold up."

With all his might, Carlos rolls Fat Gary over onto his back. He reaches into Fat Gary's pockets, pulls out two one hundred dollar bills and kicks him in the ass one last time before running back to the car. Kendrick has seen Carlos get into many fights and with each altercation, Carlos seems to be getting closer to shooting someone.

After swerving recklessly through traffic and running stop signs, Carlos pulls up in front of Kendrick's house.

Still frazzled by the fight, Kendrick looks over at Carlos. "I can't believe that shit happened. Whatchu gonna do about Fat Gary?"

Carlos grabs his gun. "One bullet will chop his big ass down to size. I don't care how big you are, ain't nobody bitching me. Period."

"Is four hundred dollars worth killing someone?"

Carlos turns down the radio. "It ain't the money, Kendrick, it's the respect. If I let it happen once, it'll happen again. Besides, I can't afford to take no shorts. My mother lost her job again and everything is on me now."

Kendrick opens the passenger door and walks towards his house. He looks back and sees Carlos sitting in the car as if he has nowhere to go. Kendrick yells, "You hungry?"

Carlos smiles; he hoped that Kendrick would ask that. Carlos walks inside and instantly he feels the difference. He looks around and sees family pictures everywhere. He takes a deep breath and smells chicken frying and it puts his soul at ease. To Kendrick, this is just dinner, but to Carlos, a hot plate of food from your mother is a symbol of love.

Amy peeks out from the kitchen. "Hey, Carlos, I haven't seen you in a while. How's your mother?"

"She's fine."

"Are you hungry?" Amy asks checking the biscuits.

"We both are," Kendrick replies.

"Well wash them hands, cause ain't no telling where y'all nasty fingers have been."

Carlos and Kendrick sit down at the table and Amy serves them a plate of fried chicken, macaroni and cheese, broccoli, and perfectly buttered biscuits.

Carlos' eyes widen. "Oh my God. Is this how you always cook, Ms. Amy?"

"No, sweetheart. We just got our food stamps, so I went to the market. But, every Sunday, me and Kendrick have dinner together. You're more than welcome to join us."

"Now I see why he always running home when the neighborhood lights come on. Your food is delicious."

Amy smiles. "Thank you."

If Kendrick didn't invite Carlos into his home, Carlos would have done what he does almost every night, which is carry his mother to bed, fix a sandwich and smoke himself to sleep. It's been awhile since Carlos visited Kendrick's home, but as he watches how close Kendrick is with his mother, Carlos has a newfound respect for him. After dinner, Kendrick walks Carlos to his car.

The street lights come on, and Carlos looks up and jokes, "You better getcha ass in that house before you get in trouble."

"Whatever, nigga," Kendrick replies.

"I see a lot of potential in you, Kendrick. Your mother is wonderful, but she's struggling like the rest of us and you can help her."

"How?"

"Sell weed with me."

"We almost died tonight."

Carlos bursts out laughing. "Stop being so dramatic. Trust me, there's enough money to go round."

The time has finally come for Kendrick to get rid of his tag-along image and be equal to Carlos, but after tonight he wonders if the consequences are worth it. Kendrick thought his answer to this type of question would be a simple, "Yes," but now Kendrick understands the magnitude of this decision, and his urge to 'fit-in' overrides what he feels.

"Yeah, I'm down."

"Cool, I'll see you tomorrow and tell your mother thanks for dinner."

*　*　*

The next morning, loud music startles Kendrick and he almost falls out of the bed. "What the hell," he complains, digging crust out of his eye. He places his feet onto the cold wood floor and walks to the window. He lifts the curtain and sees Carlos' car. While struggling to open his window he mumbles, "What did I get myself into?" After numerous attempts, Kendrick pulls up his bedroom window and yells, "Come around front."

Carlos bangs on the door screaming, "Yooooo. Let me in."

Kendrick runs downstairs and unlocks the door, then turns around and walks back to his bedroom dragging his feet. "What the hell you want? It's early as shit."

Carlos follows Kendrick smirking behind his back. "I thought you was gonna be at church."

"I pretended like I was sick. If she could, my mother would have me in church every damn day." Kendrick flops onto his bed. "I love her, but she's crowding me."

"Well get dressed. I really like how you handled yourself with Fat Gary, and I appreciate you inviting me over for dinner last night. I needed that. I wanna pay you back."

"You ain't gotta do that."

Carlos walks over to Kendrick's closet and opens it up. "Look at this shit! Where you get your clothes from, the flea market?"

Kendrick wants to say 'no', but actually almost everything in his closet was purchased from the flea market. Carlos continues to laugh throwing Kendrick's outdated clothes onto the floor.

"Whatchu doing? Pick that shit up."

Carlos continues to snatch Kendrick clothes off the hangers. "I'm saving your life. If we're gonna be partners, the first thing you need to do is get new clothes," Carlos says laughing uncontrollably.

"How am I supposed to do that?"

Carlos reaches into his pocket and pulls out a wad of cash. "I gotchu."

Carlos is a firm believer in the phrase, "If you look like money, you'll make money" and right now, Kendrick's outfit is looking like he couldn't find two pennies under his sofa. Carlos walks over to Kendrick's bedroom door and notices a fluorescent sticky note and snatches it off. He looks at Kendrick. "You gotta be kidding me." Carlos reads it aloud trying his best to impersonate Ms. Amy, "Dear Keddy, clean your room. I already washed your clothes." Carlos balls up the note and basketball shoots it into the trashcan.

Kendrick's room is normally neat, clean and in order, but in a matter of minutes – Carlos manages to completely destroy it.

"Your mother washes your clothes?" Carlos snickers. "That is the saddest shit I have ever heard. I feel like I'm six years old. Let's get outta here before I need my diaper changed," he says laughing.

\* \* \*

After leaving Kendrick's house, Carlos drives them to Mondawmin Mall where all the dope boys shop.

They walk inside of Footlocker and Carlos walks over to the sales clerk. "Gimme those Jay's, size ten." The sales clerk returns and Kendrick's eyes light up with joy. He sits down, takes off his old beaten up shoes and puts on the most expensive pair of shoes he has ever touched. Carlos sits down next to him. "What a man puts on his feet says everything about that man."

"I never had a pair of Jay's." Kendrick takes off the shoe and looks at the price tag. "Damn, now I see why. These shoes cost two hunned dollars."

"If they didn't, everybody would have them. When you look like money you attract money, you feel me?"

Kendrick puts the shoes on his feet and looks at himself in the mirror. Kendrick always thought that only a certain few could wear nice clothes. As he stares at his reflection, he can see the potential that Carlos has been talking about. Kendrick's mother doesn't buy him name brand clothes for a reason. She doesn't want Kendrick to lose focus on school trying to keep up with the Joneses, but it's too late. Kendrick has now had his first taste of being cool.

For the next few hours, Carlos purchases Kendrick a few more items from name brand stores. Kendrick has never felt more alive. Kendrick thinks that Carlos is just being a good friend. He is naive to the fact that Carlos is grooming him to want the finer things in life, and it's working. After leaving the mall, Kendrick leans back in the passenger seat feeling the best he has ever felt. Up until this moment, he never understood what it felt like to look good.

While driving, Carlos passes Kendrick the blunt. Kendrick rarely smokes, but this is obviously a rare occasion. He inhales and coughs so hard that his eyes water. "Gotdamn," he says trying to catch his breath. "How much of this shit do you got?"

"That's the last of it."

Kendrick is so high and mesmerized by his new Jay's that he isn't even paying attention to where he is going. Twenty minutes later, the car stops, Kendrick looks up, and they are parked in front of a house on Calvert Street. Carlos inhales the blunt. "I need you to go in there and pick up some more shit for me. This is how you're gonna keep new clothes on your back and help your mother, you feel me?"

The last time he was asked to get out of the car, Kendrick had to go to war with a giant. He has no clue of what to expect, but he has come too far to walk away. Carlos reaches under his seat and gives Kendrick his gun. On a normal Sunday, Kendrick is sitting in the third row of his church watching his mother sing in the choir. This Sunday, he is sitting in the car, high, with a gun two inches away from his hand. *I can't do this.* Unfortunately, this moment of clarity doesn't stop him from gripping the gun handle. Kendrick instantly feels the power and evil it possesses. Carlos watches with enjoyment as Kendrick slowly wraps his fingers around the handle. He squeezes it tighter and drops it onto the middle console.

"What are you doing, Kendrick?"

"I can't man, it's Sunday."

"It's not even loaded."

"I don't care."

"Look, just put it on your hip. If they see it, they'll know you mean business." Carlos gives Kendrick a wad of cash. "Get in and get out." Carlos reaches inside the ashtray, grabs the blunt and passes it to Kendrick. "You need to hit this shit. Trust me, it'll help."

Kendrick takes the blunt and inhales as much as he can. He exhales and the high takes him to the next level.

*You can do it,* he repeats to himself before picking up the gun and putting it into the back of his jeans. Kendrick takes the money, walks up the cracked stone steps and knocks on the door. *I don't know what the hell is about to happen, but I'm ready for whatever.* The door swings open and an older man named Charles greets him.

"Come inside," Charles says, stepping aside to let Kendrick in.

*What the hell?* Kendrick was expecting to walk into a house full of young thugs drinking and shooting dice. Instead, the house looks homely, decorated with antique furniture and family pictures hanging on the wall. Kendrick stands in the foyer. *Did I just walk into a time machine?* Wearing slippers, Charles slides his feet into the kitchen.

"You thirsty, young man?" he asks, looking back over his shoulder at Kendrick.

"Nah, I just came to handle this business and leave."

Charles walks around the corner out of Kendrick's sight. "Calm down young man, I just had surgery on my back and –"

Kendrick isn't listening to Charles' rambling. He nervously looks around waiting for someone to attack him. Even though there are no bullets in his gun, Kendrick puts his hand behind his back and grips the handle. "Where are you?"

"Just a second gotdammit."

Minutes later, Charles returns with a gift bag containing three pounds of weed and places it on the floor. Kendrick has never participated in a drug transaction and he never thought his first would be with

15

a sixty-something year old man. He takes the bag, gives Charles the money and stands uncomfortably in the foyer.

Charles pulls his glasses down to the bridge of his nose and looks Kendrick in the eye. "I don't have to count this, do I?" Charles flips through the money. "I see Carlos gotchu doing his leg work, huh? We have something in common."

"We do?"

"You work for Carlos and I work for my nephew. I'm too old to be selling this shit. Carlos and my nephew do business together; I'm just the middle man, just like you."

Kendrick pokes out his chest. "Sorry, grandpa, but I ain't no middle man. Me and Carlos are partners."

Charles grins. "There's no such thing as partners in this game." After an awkward silence, Charles stares at Kendrick. "I remember when I was your age, young and stupid," he says, escorting Kendrick to the door. "Never get greedy, son, there's never enough."

"Enough of what?"

Charles opens the door. "You'll see."

"I'll see what?" Kendrick repeats to himself as he slowly walks down the stone steps.

Carlos pops the trunk, and Kendrick sits the gift bag inside. But before closing it, he looks at Charles' front door one last time. "I ain't no fucking middleman," Kendrick mumbles before closing the trunk and getting inside of the car.

"Well?" Carlos asks.

"Well what? He was old as shit. And why'd you tell me to take the gun? He wasn't no damn threat."

"It's not him I'm worried about. It's his nephew, Andre, that can't be trusted. Besides, I want you to get used to carrying it."

"Hold up, if you don't trust Andre, why would you send me in there with an empty gun?"

"If the gun was loaded and you were in danger, would you have pulled the trigger?"

Kendrick pauses. "Nah."

"Then what's the difference?"

Kendrick reaches behind his back, grabs the gun and puts it under the passenger seat. He is stumped because Carlos is right, an empty gun is the same as a loaded gun in the hands of a scared nigga. Kendrick is a scared nigga.

While Carlos drives bobbing his head to the sounds of music, Kendrick continues to replay his conversation with Charles. While staring out the passenger window, he realizes that if he is going to be Carlos' partner he needs to grow some balls.

Carlos stops at a red light, reaches into the glove compartment, pulls out his black book and flips through the pages.

"Let me see that shit."

Carlos gives Kendrick the book. Kendrick flips through the pages and is amazed at how many of his classmate's names are scribbled in it.

"My name better not be in here," Kendrick replies.

Carlos smiles, but he is dead serious. "The 'X's mean they haven't paid yet," Carlos says.

With his index finger, Kendrick scrolls down the list, looks to the right and sees an 'X' placed next to the name Anthony. "Who's Anthony?"

"That's not important. Did he pay?"

"Nope."

Carlos smirks. "It's time to go to work." Carlos leans far back in the seat. "Aye, Kendrick, reach under my seat and grab my CD book." Carlos lights up a cigarette. "I like to hear music when it's time to pick up my money."

Kendrick reaches under the seat, grabs the CD book and scrolls through Carlos' CD collection. He expected to see a bunch of hardcore hip hop, but to his surprise, Carlos' CD book is filled with Miles Davis, Donny Hathaway, and Marvin Gaye. Carlos has always been a secretive person, but ever since Kendrick became his "partner" he is finding out that he doesn't know Carlos as well as he thought.

"Whatchuwanna hear?" Kendrick asks.

"Marvin Gaye, of course."

Kendrick slides the CD inside of the CD player and presses play. He watches Carlos' attitude change as the sound of Marvin Gaye's voice sets the mood. When Carlos was a child, every Friday night, his mother would play Marvin Gaye's "Trouble Man" album. Whenever he hears Marvin's Gaye's songs, he remembers picking his mother up from the floor, placing the top on her bottle of cheap liquor and tucking her in the bed.

Carlos bobs his head, busts a U-turn in the middle of street and drives towards Anthony's neighborhood. Kendrick can see Carlos transforming into a money-collecting thug, but while doing it to the smooth sounds of Marvin Gaye seems like a contradiction. Carlos pulls into Anthony's apartment complex and spots Anthony walking down the street.

Carlos yells, "Aye Anthony."

Anthony doesn't even look as he takes off running and cuts through the alley. Carlos looks at Kendrick. "Whatchu waiting for?"

"C'mon, Carlos. You can't be for real!"

"We're partners right? That's our money getting away. Hurry up, I'ma circle round."

Kendrick looks at his shoes. "I just got these damn shoes."

"Without money, we can't buy shoes. Go get his ass."

Kendrick takes a deep breath, opens the passenger door and runs at top speed. While chasing Anthony through the alley, all he can think about are the permanent creases he will have in his new two hundred dollar pair of Jay's. After jumping fences and running through trashy backyards, Kendrick stops to catch his breath. Moments later, Carlos pulls up at the end of the alley.

"Do you see him?" Carlos yells.

Kendrick is breathing so hard, he can barely talk. Bending over resting his hands on his knees, he tries to catch his breath. He looks down at the ground and sees a large black mark across the tip of his shoe. His brand new shirt is soaked in sweat and he smells like he's been wrestling a bear. "Fuck," he yells, trying to rub out the black mark.

"C'mon," Carlos orders.

Kendrick jogs to the car, gets inside and closes his eyes. "You shoulda brought me the shoes he had on," Kendrick says sarcastically. "He was running fast as shit. How much did he owe you?"

Carlos pulls out his black book, and scrolls down the list. "Eighty dollars."

"What? My shoes cost more than that. I fucked up my outfit for eighty dollars? I can't believe –"

Carlos abruptly pulls over and places the car in park. "This is what I do, and if you wanna be a part of this shit, you play your fucking role."

Kendrick mumbles, "Charles was right."

"Whatchu say, nigga?"

"Nothin."

"I ain't pulling off until you tell me whatchu said."

Kendrick sighs, "Charles said there ain't no such thing as partners, and right now, I don't feel like no fucking partner."

Carlos turns down the radio. "Kendrick, we've known each other for a long time, but this ain't about friendship. This is about money. I have a role and you have a role, but if you can't do what I asked you to do, then maybe this isn't for you."

"Look at my fucking shoes. I don't see any marks on yours. All you do is sit in the car and give out orders."

"Aight, the next time you drive." Carlos looks over at Kendrick. "We cool?"

Kendrick continues to rub out the black mark on his tennis, "Whatever," he mumbles.

"Let's get something to eat, my treat."

"You damn right it is."

Carlos drives to the Cheesecake Factory in Downtown Baltimore. The sun sits high and the weather is perfect for some snow crab legs. Carlos walks out onto the deck overlooking the tourists and Kendrick follows. He turns his chair to face the skyline and puts on his sunglasses to enjoy the beautiful scenery.

The server walks over and her beauty gets Carlos' attention, but Kendrick is so consumed with fixing the mark on his tennis, he doesn't even look up.

"How can I help you?" she asks smiling.

Carlos gently grabs her wrists. "You can start by giving me your phone number."

"I have a boyfriend."

Carlos grins. "I have a girlfriend, so we got something in common."

Kendrick should have been taking notes, but that stain on his tennis shoes irritates him worse than an unreachable itch in the middle of his back. Carlos eventually convinces the cute waitress to give him her number. She takes their order and he watches her switch out of sight.

"She fine as shit. I'ma bust her 'lil ass wide open." Carlos taps Kendrick. "Did you see her?"

Kendrick looks up. "See who?"

Carlos shakes his head. "Wassup witchu? It's beautiful outside and all these girls walking around, but all you can think about is a pair of fucking shoes." While Carlos continues to scold Kendrick, Carlos sees another attractive girl in the distance. "Aye, come here for a second," he yells. She walks over and Kendrick can sense that Carlos is about to do something. "What's your name?" Carlos asks.

"Melanie."

"Melanie, do you think my friend is cute?"

Melanie smiles. "He's kinda cute."

Melanie extends her hand, but Kendrick freezes. He begins to sweat and he nervously sits up in his chair placing his dirty tennis shoes further under the table. He grabs Melanie's petite hand and shakes it.

"Hi," Kendrick says struggling to give Melanie good eye contact. Kendrick can feel Carlos judging his every move and the longer it takes him to strike up a conversation, the dumber he feels.

"Aren't you gonna tell me your name?" Melanie asks.

Kendrick's knee shakes and his inner thoughts cripple his ability to conduct a normal conversation. *Tell her your name you idiot.* Every second that passes, Kendrick's mouth becomes dryer. He peeks over and that silly smirk on Carlos' face is a clear sign that he enjoys watching Kendrick fall out of the sky.

"Uh…Kendrick. My name is Kendrick," he mumbles.

Melanie frowns up her face and snatches her hand away. "I'm sorry, I have to go," she says walking away.

Kendrick can hear everyone who witnessed his poor display of 'game' snickering and he wishes his two hundred dollar Jay's had wings so he could fly home. This moment is, by far, the most embarrassing eight seconds of his life and there is nothing he can do about it. He blew it with Melanie and he did it in front of

22

Carlos. As soon as Melanie leaves, the voices in his head stop, his heart stops pounding and he finally relaxes.

Carlos bursts out laughing. "I fucking knew it."

Kendrick wipes beads of sweat off his forehead. "Knew what?"

Before Carlos can respond, the waitress returns with two plates of crab legs. Kendrick doesn't waste time cracking open his snow crab legs, but he can sense that something is on Carlos' mind.

"You're not hungry?" Kendrick asks dipping his crabmeat in hot butter.

Carlos looks Kendrick up and down. "I knew it. I just didn't wanna believe it."

"Why you keep saying that shit? You knew what?"

Carlos blurts out, "You a virgin, ain't you?"

*Shit, he knows.* Kendrick keeps his calm and forces a smile to appear on his face. "Nah."

Carlos playfully takes a sniff. "I can smell a virgin from a mile away and the way you handled Melanie was the worst shit I ever saw."

"She wasn't that cute anyway."

Carlos pulls his chair closer to Kendrick. "I've known you since the sixth grade and I've never seen you wit a girl, ever. As a matter of fact, I haven't seen you look at one girl since we been out here."

"Whatchutrynna say?"

"You know what I'm saying. You a gotdamn virgin." Carlos stands to his feet and playfully yells, "I'd like to make a public announcement –"

"Chill out, Carlos."

Instead of embarrassing Kendrick any further, Carlos sits down and finishes his food. After eating, Carlos and Kendrick watch the sun set forming a beautiful purple, pink and silver skyline over the city. Carlos stares at the tall luxury Zenith condominiums overlooking the Harbor waters. His top of the world view is only a few hundred yards away and he can feel it getting closer. Carlos takes off his shades and leans on the rail. "Mark my word, one day I'm gonna live in the Zenith and I'ma keep a bad bitch in my bed." Carlos looks over at Kendrick. "Whatchu want outta life?"

Kendrick jokes, "I want some clean shoes."

"You're thinking too small, Kendrick, and I think I know why." Carlos takes one more look at the Zenith condominiums. "C'mon, I got one last stop to make and don't worry, this ain't business, this is recreational," he says with that signature sneaky grin on his face.

*   *   *

If hell had an entrance, it would be called Baltimore Street. Hookers parade back and forth wearing skimpy clothes, while hustlers and junkies conduct transactions in pockets of darkness. Critters dart back and forth from one trashcan to another, while strip club owners stand outside trying to convince customers that they have the baddest bitches on the strip. Carlos circles the block multiple times looking for something or someone.

Kendrick can't believe these types of places are even allowed to conduct business on a Sunday night. Normally, by this time, he would be waiting in the carwatching his mother kiss, hug and talk to everyone in the church. On this Sunday, he is literally behind the gates of hell.

"Where are we?" Kendrick asks staring out of the window.

Carlos laughs. "You've never been to the block? Damn you a momma's boy."

Carlos drives slowly with his windows down. He sees a hooker standing on the corner wearing a black mini skirt, heels and a glittery long sleeved shirt. She is clearly from a different decade. Carlos pulls up next to her. "Aye, come here."

The worn out hooker steps closer with a half-lit cigarette in her left hand. She walks to the passenger side and leans in close enough for Kendrick to smell her cheap perfume and nicotine scented hair. "I'm Shae, whatchu boys need?"

Carlos reaches into his pocket and pulls out his money. "It's my boy Kendrick's birthday, so I want you to take care of him."

"It ain't my birthday."

"Yes it is."

"No it's not, nigga."

"Look, I don't care who birthday it is. Sixty to fuck and twenty-five for head," Shae says licking her lips.

Carlos gives Shae sixty dollars. She takes the money and stuffs it into her dirty garter belt. "Happy birthday, sweetie," she says, running her finger tips down Kendrick's face, "I'm gonna make your birthday very special."

Kendrick stutters. "I'm s…sorry ma'am, but it's not my birthday."

"C'mon, sugga."

While Shae sings happy birthday, Kendrick shoots Carlos a look as if he wants to kill him. There is no way that he is going to get out of this and each second that passes, he is looking more and more like a virgin.

"You scared."

"I'm not scared," Kendrick says under his breath.

"Prove it." Carlos demands.

Shae opens the passenger door. "Honey, you won't be disappointed."

The pressure that comes from his so-called best friend and a hooker is indescribable. Kendrick can't believe that he is being forced to have sex with a filthy prostitute. Ever since Kendrick reached puberty, Amy drilled into his head the dangers of having sex outside of wedlock. His hormones are raging just like any other teenager, but his mother's strict rules about sex trained him to wait until he is married. While Kendrick is caught between defying his mother's religious beliefs and getting Carlos off his back, Shae is growing impatient.

"C'mon, baby," Shae says, tapping the tip of her heels against the pavement. "This pussy got money to make."

Kendrick thinks of one last excuse. "I ain't got no condoms."

Carlos reaches into his pocket and pulls out a pack of Lifestyles. "Now you do."

Kendrick forces a smile. Losing his virginity to a prostitute is not what Kendrick planned. He takes a deep breath, steps out of the car and looks around in awe. The block is an open market for every type of illegal activity known to man. The homeless, hustlers, pimps and scumbags, parade up and down the street signaling each other with hand gestures and secret looks. As he tries his best to fit in, he wonders to himself, *What are these people doing here?* Kendrick has never seen this side of Baltimore City and he is clearly out of his element. He follows Shae into a dark alley where he steps over the scattered trash and syringe needles. *Where is she taking me?*

Shae escorts him further into the alley to where she takes care of her customers, but someone beat her to the spot. Another prostitute is sucking an older white man's dick. Kendrick stands in shock because the white man is clearly out of place. Kendrick watches as the white man forces the prostitutes head up and down, as his wedding ring shines in the dark.

Shae interrupts, "Aye, get the fuck outta here Tee-Tee, this is my spot." Shae looks at the white man. "Robert?"

Shae is clearly jealous of Tee-Tee. Shae used to have the perky breasts, white teeth and coke bottle figure. When Tee-Tee first started working on the block, Shae wanted to show Tee-Tee how to become a good prostitute, but this is the third time Tee-Tee has brought one of her tricks to Shae's spot and enough is enough.

Robert is one of Shae's loyal tricks. He is a short, oval shaped, piece of shit husband who is verbally abused by his wife, so he comes to the block where his money is king and his ego is stroked. Robert's fetish for black pussy has him in a tight spot and he wishes he stayed his fat ass home and ate his wife, Gertrude's, overcooked turkey dinner.

"I'm sorry, Shae," Robert begs, placing his little dick back into his white drawers.

"Oh, so my pussy not good for you anymore, huh? How 'bout I tell your wife that you come see me two times a week? You white piece of shit."

While Shae and Robert argue, Tee-Tee rises to her feet and faces Kendrick. Carlos has been trying to get Kendrick to look at a girl all day, but Tee-Tee is the first to catch his eye. Tee-Tee is only seventeen years old, but her abused body sings a different story. Kendrick has always been attracted to girls with lighter skin, but Tee-Tee's dark chocolate complexion and curvy figure is breathtaking. Kendrick blocks out Shae and Robert, undresses Tee-Tee with his eyes and wishes Tee-Tee was the one taking his virginity instead of Shae's old ass. *How does someone so young and pretty end up sucking dick in the back of an alley?* He wants to speak, but is afraid that Shae will beat Tee-Tee's ass.

All Robert wants to do is get into his compact car and go home. Robert's face turns as red as a stop sign and he tightens his belt. He straightens his tie and tries to bribe his way out of trouble. He reaches into his brown slacks, and pulls out his wallet. "Look, Shae, there's no need for you to be upset; there's enough money for both of you. Here." Robert hands Shae a fifty-dollar bill.

"This ain't enough."

Robert sighs and hands her another fifty-dollar bill.

28

Shae lights up another cigarette. "I can't stand you muthafuckers. You think you can just go to the next girl and treat me like yesterday's trash? Why, because she younger than me? She can't do what I do."

"You're right, and I'm sorry." Robert pleads. "Can't nobody do it like you. I —"

"Shut up, Robert."

Shae snatches Robert's wallet and cleans him out of everything and tosses his wallet down the alley. "If I see you on this block again, I'm telling your ugly wife how small your dick is," she yells.

Kendrick never thought that he would see a white man controlled by a black prostitute. Kendrick is learning more about life in this dark alley than any classroom can teach. Kendrick wants to leave, but he didn't know this side of Baltimore City existed and he is mesmerized by its ignorance.

Shae walks over to Tee-Tee and points her finger in Tee-Tee's face, "Bitch, are you crazy?" Shae shouts. "I've been sucking dick in the alley before you knew how to spell your own name."

"I'm sorry, Shae," Tee-Tee pleads. "I wasn't gonna stay long. I promise I —"

"Pay up." Shae slaps Tee-Tee in the face and snatches her purse. She turns over Tee Tee's purse and dumps all of Tee-Tee's things to the ground. Kendrick watches as Shae ruthlessly takes the money that Tee-Tee earned for the night.

"That's all I got," Tee-Tee cries.

"Bitch, do I look like I care? Now pick that shit up and get outta here," Shae yells.

Tee-Tee grabs her scattered change from all over the alley and puts her make-up, a pack of condoms and a broken mirror back into her purse. Between Tee-Tee and Robert, Shae has already made enough for the night. Shae notices how Kendrick is staring at Tee-Tee, so Shae grabs his wrist and pulls him further into the alley. With an attitude, she backs Kendrick into a corner, spits out her gum, drops to her knees and unfastens his belt buckle.

Shae reaches inside of boxers and wraps her cold hands around his dick. "Don't worry, baby, I know what I'm doing."

A flickering sign flashes every other second from the bar across the street, and all Kendrick can think about is catching every disease known to man. He can't believe he let Carlos talk him into this shit, but if he admits to being a virgin, he'll never hear the end of it. Every other second, the flashing sign gives Kendrick just enough light to see Shae's battered face and eroded teeth. Kendrick cringes. Everything about this situation turns him off, from the needle marks on her arm, to the sounds of her cheap bracelets moving up and down.

"Wait," he says grabbing her cold hands.

"What's wrong, honey?"

"I...I can't."

"But it's your birthday."

Kendrick shakes his head. "It's not really my birthday."

Shae stands up and steps back and looks Kendrick up and down. "You must be gay."

Kendrick stuffs his dick into his boxers. "I ain't gay."

"Well if you're not gay, what's the problem?" Shae lights up another cigarette, "Oh I get it... you wanna fuck Tee-Tee, huh?"

Kendrick doesn't respond.

"No refunds, sweetheart, so make up ya mind."

"Keep the money."

"Well fuck you, and that little ass dick," she says switching out of sight.

Mentally and physically exhausted, Kendrick leans up against the wall confused. He can't believe the type of lifestyle that Carlos lives, but he is intrigued. He looks up at the dark clear sky and he can feel his mother's presence around him. Kendrick checks his watch and walks out of the dark alley towards Carlos' car.

"What happened?"

"Whatchu think?" Kendrick lies, "I fucked her."

Carlos walks over to Kendrick, places his nose close to Kendrick's shoulder and playfully takes a deep sniff. "You still smell like a virgin to me."

"Fuck you," Kendrick yells before opening the passenger door and getting inside.

They drive in silence and Kendrick just stares. His mind is so cluttered that he just wants to go home and sleep. When they arrive at Kendrick house, his front porch light is on which means he missed his curfew.

"Shit," Kendrick shouts. "My mother is going to kill me. I'm late."

Carlos shakes his head. "If you gotta curfew, how you supposed to make money? I'm not trying to tell you what to do, but money don't sleep and damn sure don't have a curfew."

"I hear you, Carlos, but I can't just do whatever I want like you." Kendrick opens the passenger door and prepares to face his punishment. "I'll see you tomorrow."

After dropping Kendrick off, Carlos drives off still listening to Marvin Gaye. On the outside, he may appear to have it all together, but he wishes that his mother instilled the same values that Amy instilled in Kendrick. People admire Carlos' freedom to do whatever he wants, but to Carlos, he feels neglected. Within minutes, he pulls in front of the house, parks the car and stares at the front door. Before going inside, he grabs a small blunt in his ashtray and lights it.

Carlos smokes the blunt to his fingertips, opens the car door and walks toward his home. The closer he gets to the front door, he can hear the sounds of Marvin Gaye and he knows his mother is throwing another party with herself and a bottle of cheap liquor. He opens the door and there she is, sitting in the chair asleep with a lit cigarette hanging from her mouth. Carlos removes the cigarette and turns off the radio.

"The party's over, ma." He softly taps her on the knee. "Ma, get up," But she doesn't budge. After numerous attempts, Carlos picks her up and carries her up the steps like a groom carries his bride. He lays her on top of the bed and kisses her on the forehead. "Goodnight, ma," he says cutting off her bedroom light.

* * *

After a few weeks of selling weed with Carlos, Kendrick understands his role as Carlos' right hand man. Whenever Carlos arranges to buy product from a stranger, Kendrick is there holding an empty gun behind his back. Carlos tries to convince Kendrick to keep it loaded, but he refuses. Kendrick is still hopping out of the passenger side of the car chasing down Carlos' debts, but he is making enough money to replace all the shoes he damages. Having Kendrick on the team allows Carlos to venture off and earn a thousand dollars a week, but Carlos will never let Kendrick know. He's only paying Kendrick two hundred dollars per week, which is crumbs, but to Kendrick it's a fortune. Carlos knew exactly what he was doing when he recruited Kendrick. Carlos could have paid Kendrick fifty dollars a week and Kendrick would have been just as happy, but most importantly, just as loyal.

Every time Kendrick gets paid, he places half of his money into a shoebox. Every night before he goes to bed, instead of falling to knees and saying his prayers, he looks inside of his shoebox. The more Kendrick learns about the hustle, he realizes that old ass Charles was right. There is no such thing as partners; there's a boss and then the help, but even Kendrick can admit that he is not yet experienced enough to be anything else, so he's content.

There are many rewards to hustling with Carlos, but there's also a flip side. Kendrick is living a double life.

He hides his new clothes and shoes in the back of his closet and waits for his mother to go to work before he gets dressed. Amy can feel that something is different about her son, but she believes it is just another phase of puberty. Amy has kept such a tight grip on Kendrick that she tends to forget that he is no longer her baby, but a curious, horny, young man.

At home, Kendrick paces his bedroom floor. He looks around his room and for the first time, he feels out of place. Everything about his room screams, 'mama's boy' from the freshly folded sheets on his dresser, to the lime green fluorescent sticky note that reads, "Clean your room, love mommy" on his door. He pulls his chair to the window and cracks it just enough to hear the night but instead of crickets, he hears the sounds of his friends enjoying freedom. "This some bullshit," Kendrick mumbles. "Why I gotta stay in the house?" He rests his forehead against the window and envisions himself on the other side, when his phone rings.

Kendrick answers, "Whatup, Carlos?"

"I know it's passed your curfew, but I want you to come to the Regal Begal with me tonight."

"But it's Tuesday."

"Trust me, you don't wanna miss this shit."

The Regal Begal is not a bar or club, but a small three-bedroom home in Heraldry Square and Timothy is the host. Whenever Timothy's parents go out of town, his place turns into the hangout for all the cool kids, troublemakers, freaks and wannabe divas.

The Regal Begal has the same slogan as Las Vegas; and what happens there definitely stays there. The Regal

Begal is a "B.Y.O.E." event: meaning, Bring Your Own Everything, drinks, weed, and most importantly, your own piece of pussy. Kendrick walks over to his closet, reaches in the back and grabs his best shit. After getting dressed, he tries to creep downstairs but the squeaky hallway gives him away. Amy sits up in bed and mutes the television. Kendrick stands still hoping she will mind her business, but that never happens.

"Where you going, boy?"

Kendrick thinks of a lie, but he was never good at it. She always found a way to get the truth, but as long as she doesn't get out of the bed and see that he is dressed in clothes she didn't purchase, he has a chance to escape.

"I'm just going out front to get some air. I can't sleep."

Strangely, Amy doesn't ask him a thousand questions, but turns back and un-mutes the television. "Get some air and get back in this house, you hear me, Kendrick?"

"Yes, ma, I hear you."

Kendrick reaches the bottom step, quietly unlocks the front door and stands outside. Moments later, he sees a champagne-colored Acura Legend pulling into his complex.

*Who's that?* Kendrick wonders.

The Acura Legend parks and the passenger window rolls down. "Whatchu waiting for?" Carlos yells.

Kendrick turns around to face his front door. *Fuck it, I'm not staying in the house.* He runs to the car as his mother opens the front door wearing a purple robe and bright orange house shoes.

"Kendrick, you better get your ass back here," she shouts.

Kendrick ducks down in the passenger seat. "Drive."

Carlos speeds down the street laughing so hard that he almost hits a row of parked cars. "What the hell did your mother have on? Damn, now I see who you get your fashion from." Carlos continues to laugh. "That was the funniest shit I've ever seen. She's gonna kick your ass tonight. You might as well live it up."

"I'm tired of her treating me like a baby."

Carlos just shakes his head. "You gotta put your foot down." Carlos smiles pretending to love the freedom that he has. "I can do what I want."

Kendrick runs his fingers across the cherry wood dashboard. "How can you afford this?"

Carlos laughs. "It's a rental."

"Whatchu get it for?"

Carlos pulls up at a red light and stops next to a car full of girls. He turns up the radio and nods his head to the music while the girls try their best to get his attention. The light turns green, and Carlos slams on the gas leaving skid marks in the street.

Carlos smiles. "That's why I got it." He looks over at Kendrick, "Bitches love money and I love bitches, you feel me?"

Thirty minutes later, they arrive at Timothy's house, and Carlos does a secret knock on the door. Seconds later, Timothy opens the door holding a camera. "Who's dis?" Timothy asks.

"My boy, Kendrick."

"You not supposed to bring strangers to the Regal Begal, you know that." Timothy gives Kendrick a stern look. "You better not break my shit and you better not run ya mouth."

Carlos pushes by Timothy, while Kendrick takes in the scene around him and he can't believe his eyes. Every girl who is somebody at Woodlawn High School is in arms reach. In school, these girls pretended to be holier than thou, but here at Timothy's party, they are taking shots of hard liquor and lifting their tops for the camera's red dot.

Kendrick stands in the middle of the living room when a voluptuous girl pushes her plump breasts up against his back and screams, "The new guy has to take a shot."

A crowd gathers around Timothy's living room table and one of his guests brings over four shots of Vodka and places them on the living room table.

The friendly, drunk, big-breasted girl grabs Kendrick's hand and leads him to the living room table. "Don't be scared," she says jumping up and down.

"What the hell is this?" Kendrick asks.

Timothy walks through the crowd of people and puts his arm around Kendrick's shoulder. "This is the alcohol test. Everyone in here had to take it. If you can swallow these four shots without throwing up, you good, but if not, I'm kicking your ass out my house. Can you handle that?"

Kendrick looks over at Carlos. He hoped that Carlos would jump in and save him, but rules are rules.

"Whatchu waiting for?" Carlos whispers, "You're already in trouble, so you might as well get fucked up."

Kendrick stares at the four shot glasses, and just the thought of drinking this much alcohol makes him gag, but he can't bitch out now. This moment can make or break his reputation. He reaches for the first glass, closes his eyes, and swallows. He then takes down the other three. Kendrick gags, but he manages to force down the combination of alcohol and vomit. He raises the last shot glass in the air, slams it on the table and everyone cheers. Kendrick passes the alcohol test.

Carlos pats Kendrick on the shoulder. "I knew you could do it. How do you feel?"

Kendrick can barely keep his eyes open and his mouth begins to water as the urge to throw up increases, but he controls it. "I'm cool."

"Look around, Kendrick, what do you see?"

"A bunch of bad bitches."

"You're still thinking small. These are our customers. Our customers don't care about curfews, and we have to always be available to supply their need." Carlos passes Kendrick a cigarette. "It's time you leave the nest." Carlos exhales a cloud of smoke. "Don't you wanna make more than two hundred dollars a week?"

"Hell yeah."

"Then you gotta become a vampire; look around you, Kendrick. You think these people in here are running home when their streets lights come on?"

Kendrick scans the room and sees something in each one of their eyes that he doesn't possess called, "I don't giva fuck" and Kendrick needs to get with the program.

A few weeks ago, Kendrick was a 'nobody' wearing old clothes. Now he stands in the middle of Timothy's home with the who's who.

Kendrick yells over the loud music, "Why you ain't tell me about this before?"

"Because the Regal Begal got one rule."

"Whatchu talking 'bout? I passed the alcohol test."

Carlos grins. "There's one more rule."

"What's that?"

"No virgins allowed."

"I keep telling you, I ain't no virgin."

Carlos smiles."Whatever, nigga."

Kendrick looks around the room and sees Ebony. Ebony is stunning, her legs are firm and her ass is perfectly shaped for her petite frame. Her hair is pulled back into a ponytail showing her slanted eyes and beautiful dark skin. It's no secret that Ebony is out of Kendrick's league.

Kendrick continues to stare in awe. "What is Ebony doing here?"

Carlos laughs. "Don't be fooled, she's the biggest freak in here. Watch this."

Kendrick watches Carlos walk over to Ebony and move his hands down her back. Ebony giggles and Kendrick wishes he could make her laugh like Carlos. Carlos pulls Ebony away from the crowd and whispers into her ear, "You ever had sex with a virgin?"

"Um…no, that don't sound like fun," she answers.

"Ahh c'mon, Ebony, don't every girl want to be remembered forever?"

Ebony steps back and places her hands on her curvy hips. "I'm already unforgettable, you should know," she pauses, "hold up, you brought a virgin to Timothy's party? I'm telling." She tries to walk away, but Carlos grabs her wrists.

"Chill out, Ebony. I want my boy's first time to be with someone beautiful and I thought of you."

Ebony loved to have her ego stroked. "Aww that's sweet, who is it?"

Carlos whispers, "Kendrick."

"Oh my God. Kendrick is a virgin?"

Carlos begs, "C'mon, Ebony, do it for me."

Ebony rolls her eyes. "What's in it for me?"

Carlos reaches into his pocket and pulls out three bags of weed.

"Are you serious?"

Carlos knew this wasn't going to be easy so he raises the stakes. "What if I take you shopping?"

Ebony perks up. "Now you're talking. I saw these Prada shoes that I –"

"Whoa. Prada?"

"Yeah nigga, Prada. I ain't no cheap thrill and I know how the 'knock-offs' look so don't try it." Ebony opens her palm, "I don't trust you, give me the money now."

A few minutes with Ebony just cost Carlos four hundred dollars, but he'll pay almost anything to get Kendrick his first piece of pussy. Ebony has had sex for less, so this should be a piece of cake. She takes the money, leans in closer and whispers, "Tell him to come upstairs."

Carlos walks over to Kendrick. "It's on. Ebony is upstairs waiting for you."

Kendrick looks like he won lottery. "For real? This better not be a joke, Carlos. I'm not in the mood right now."

"I'm serious. She's upstairs right now waiting for you."

Kendrick waits for Carlos to say "syke" but Carlos keeps a straight face.

"You're serious?"

"If you don't, I will," he says handing Kendrick a condom.

Kendrick nervously walks up the steps and maneuvers through crowds of people kissing and fondling each other. He gets to the top of the steps and hears a sweet, soft voice calling his name. He checks his breath, and clutches his dick from excitement.

"I'm in the bathroom," she says.

The upstairs hallway is pitch black, so Kendrick feels his way to the bathroom, turns the knob and peeks in. Ebony grabs his hand, closes the door and backs him into the sink. The last time Kendrick was this close to a female, she had on a bad wig, cheap shoes and yellow teeth, but not tonight. This is exactly how Kendrick envisioned losing his virginity. With his back against the sink, he has no idea of what to say or do.

"It's kinda cute how shy you are," she says, running her fingers through his hair.

"I ain't shy."

41

"Shhh, Carlos told me everything." She seductively runs her hands along his cheeks, down his neck, and along his chest. "It's ok," she says nibbling on his neck.

Kendrick has never been touched like this before. Her fingernails send chills down his back and he can't wait to see what her pussy feels like. Ebony lifts his arms up into the air and slips his shirt off over his head. Normally, Ebony would sit back and let the man do all the work, but she wants to leave an everlasting stain in Kendrick's memory. She pecks his chest and bites his nipples sending shocks up his spine.  She then falls to her knees and unzips his pants, reaches in, and pulls his dick through the slit in his boxers. She drops to her knees and kisses the head of his dick and he jumps from pleasure.

"You like that?"

"Yes."

"How bad do you want it?" she purrs.

Kendrick voice cracks, "You have no idea."

"Yes, I do."

Ebony thrusts his dick into her mouth and Kendrick tries to hold onto anything his fingers can grasp. Kendrick has only seen this type of shit in porn movies, but never in a million years did he think it could happen to him. The slurping sounds echo throughout the bathroom and his body shakes, until his eyes roll into the back of his head.

Ebony stands up and the tips of their noses touch. He can smell his own dick on her lips, but he kisses her anyway. Ebony steps back and waits for Kendrick to do the rest, but he stands as stiff as a mannequin.

"You gotta condom?"

Kendrick has never put on a condom. He tries opening the package but his hands are shaking, so using his teeth, he rips the package and pulls it out. After a few failed attempts, he finally finds the lubricated side of the condom and pushes it over the head of dick, but it pops. Kendrick is afraid that if he tells her, she won't sleep with him – so he lies.

"It's on."

Instead of checking to see if Kendrick's dick is protected, Ebony faces the wall, arches her back, and lifts her skirt. "Put it in."

Kendrick grabs his dick and presses it up against Ebony's butt. Ebony flinches. "Whoa. Not there."

"Oh, I'm sorry. I –"

Every second that passes, Kendrick can feel his inexperience ruining the moment. Tired of waiting, she reaches underneath her legs and grabs his dick.

"Where's the condom?"

"Uh…" Kendrick looks for the perfect excuse, but Ebony makes it easy for him.

"It's ok, I'm clean."

Kendrick doesn't care; he has the hottest girl bent over holding his dick. Ebony could have said she was HIV positive and Kendrick would have talked himself into going raw. She grabs him at the base of his dick and softly rubs it against her clit.

"I got it nice and wet for you."

No words can describe the feeling of his dick being slowly stroked against warm, wet flesh. If Kendrick never sleeps with another woman again, he has enough memories to masturbate for the rest of his life.

Ebony arches her back further. "I want you to go slow, ok?"

Kendrick has no idea what slow means and it is too late to ask questions. The head of his dick finally breaks the first level of Ebony's pussy and the rest follows. He squeezes her hips and thinks about all the porn videos he has seen. Ebony moans and it builds his confidence so he pumps faster.

"Fuck me."

"Huh?"

"Fuck me."

"I thought you said to go slow?"

"Just do it." Ebony bounces back on Kendrick's dick.

Kendrick follows orders and Ebony screams louder, "Yes!"

A minute later, Kendrick's dick begins to pulsate, *Not now, please not now. Hold on just a few pumps, hold on man.*

Kendrick thinks of anything to prolong the inevitable, but he can only coach himself for so long. He squeezes Ebony's hips tighter and his knees begin to tremble.

"Are you about to cum?"

Kendrick moans. "Huh?"

"Are you 'bout to cum?" Ebony asks again.

"Um…," he moans still pumping.

Kendrick wants to stop, but he can't. It's as if her pussy has a magnetic force that pulls him in.

"You better not cum inside me."

"Huh?"

Ebony pushes Kendrick out and he squirts cum all over his shoes and pants. His face looks like he sucked a lemon and his body jerks from shock. Ebony can't help but laugh. Kendrick leans up against the bathroom door breathing heavily. Once the blood returns back to his brain and his legs regain strength, he doesn't know if he should be embarrassed, proud, or grateful. He is not sure if he should ask for her number or just pull up his pants and leave.

Ebony cuts on the bathroom light, wipes herself with a warm rag, and fixes her hair in the mirror. "You were ok for a virgin," she says, putting on her lipstick.

"Can we do it again? I –"

"Sorry, Carlos is going to need four hundred more dollars."

Kendrick is slightly disappointed that Ebony was paid, but the feeling of no longer being a virgin is priceless.

Ebony opens the bathroom door and Carlos is standing there with a huge smile on his face holding two shot glasses filled to the rim.

"How long have you been standing there?" Kendrick asks.

Carlos smiles. "The whole damn time. Here, let's toast."

Kendrick takes the shot glass. "What we toasting to?"

"You're no longer a virgin," he screams nudging Kendrick. "It's about fucking time."

Kendrick swallows the shot. "I told you I ain't no virgin."

Carlos smiles. "Not anymore, now let's get this money. Are you a vampire?"

"What?"

"Are you ready to stay up all night and chase this money?"

"Yeah."

Carlos is so high he can barely stand. "Say it again, are you a muthafucking vampire?"

Kendrick yells at the top of his lungs, "Yeaaa!"

Kendrick completely forgets about how much trouble awaits him. He never understood how some of friends could rebel against their parents, but now he does. As he stands on the second floor of Timothy's home surrounded by rebellious teenagers, he realizes that getting into trouble isn't that bad and enjoys the rest of the night. He is now an honorary member of the "Regal Begal" and officially, a part of the in-crowd.

# CHAPTER 11

Inside of the police station locker-room, Officer Miles is shining his steel toe boots when the Sergeant walks in to make an announcement.

"Ok, listen up. I want everyone to get familiar with our newest member of the police force. This is Officer Miles."

The officers in attendance clap and give Miles a warm welcome, but in the back of their minds, they are hoping they are not paired up with the rookie.

The Sergeant looks around the room and points. "Officer Buckner, I want you to take the rookie out for a spin."

"Shit." Officer Buckner mumbles under his breath.

Officer Buckner is an out of shape, fifty-six year old black man who has clearly abused his free donut privileges. He grew up in Baltimore City and after twenty-seven years on the police force, he has built good and bad relationships with people in the community. In his career, Officer Buckner has locked up hundreds of inner city kids, but after watching the city shut down recreational centers and stop neighborhood development funding, Buckner had an epiphany. He decided to never do the cities dirty work again.

At the police station, Officer Buckner acquired the name "Stop-N-Go," because he was always last to arrive at a crime scene and the first to leave. Officer Buckner and Officer Miles have only just met, but Officer Buckner can see it in the rookie's eyes that he would give a "jay-walking" ticket to a blind man. Officer Buckner walks over with a fake smile and they share an awkward handshake.

"Everybody calls me Buck."

"Nice to meet you. I'm Timothy."

Buck shakes his head. "We call each other by our last names, so I'm calling you Miles. C'mon, you ready?"

*That's what they called my father.* Miles eagerly slides his gun on his hip. "I'm ready to put these bad guys where they belong."

"Yeah, ok."

Miles grew up on the Southside of Baltimore in a poor white neighborhood. He comes from a strict military background. His father and his grandfather both served in the military and later became police officers. When Miles was fourteen years old, his father was gunned down on duty by a young black teenager in a botched robbery. To this day, Miles has the newspaper article of his father's killing taped to his bedroom door. His family never truly recovered from the loss of his father, and Miles watched his mother fall apart. At age twenty-four, he still prays for the day that he will avenge his father's death. Miles isn't too pleased to be paired with a black officer.

Miles jogs to the driver's side of the police car and opens the door.

"Aye, rookie, have you lost your mind? I'll drive."

"Sorry."

While Buckner drives, Miles stares out the passenger window looking for his first arrest when a white two-door coupe zooms past them. Miles checks the speedometer. "He's going seventy-five miles per hour. That's twenty miles over the speed limit."

Buckner grins. "And?"

"He's breaking the law."

"Before you became a cop, did you ever drive twenty miles over the speed limit?"

"Probably."

Buckner chuckles. "Congratulations, you solved your first case." *This is going to be a long fucking day.*

Buckner drives down Liberty Road and Miles notices an elderly white lady waving her hands wildly standing in front of her car. "I think she needs our help. Looks like her car broke down."

Buckner looks over at Miles. "I don't get paid to change tires, rookie," he says passing the lady.

"She was old enough to be your mother."

"If my mother was alive, she would be ninety-six," Buckner laughs. "That old white lady ain't look a day over sixty-five, so she'll be alright."

"I bet if she was black you would have helped."

"Don't make this a race issue, rookie. They don't pay me to change tires."

Miles stares at Buckner. Miles was raised to believe that a police officer's job is to protect and serve. As they drive by the elderly white lady, Miles watches her from the rear view mirror until she fades away. Every time Miles points out illegal activity, Buckner looks for a reason not to investigate. After patrolling the area for hours, Buckner pulls into the police station, cuts off the engine and looks at Miles. "Today was a good first day."

Clearly frustrated, Miles opens the passenger door, *Whatever you say.*

Moments later, Miles stands in front of his locker and undresses. He remembers the exciting stories that his father and grandfather shared about their first day on the job. His first day was nothing like he expected. Miles takes a deep breath, exhales and removes his gun, then unbuttons his pants and lets them fall to the ground. He can feel everyone looking at him, but he tries to ignore it. He looks up and sees Buckner surrounded by the other officers laughing and pointing in his direction.

For Buckner, today was just another day on the job. While getting undressed, Buckner jokes, "I can't believe the Sergeant paired me with Robocop," Buckner yells. "Aye, rookie, there's a cat stuck in the tree, he needs your help." Everyone in the locker room bursts out laughing, and all Miles can do is deal with the rookie hazing.

* * *

After three weeks of patrolling the streets of West Baltimore and making no arrests, Miles is beginning to wonder if his partner is a real cop. Each day at one-thirty in the afternoon, Buckner drives outside of their

50

jurisdiction to Edmondson Village shopping center for lunch. This shopping center has a reputation for two things, the best chicken box and the biggest vials of dope.

Whenever they pulled into the shopping center, Miles thought it was very bizarre how no one ran. Instead, the hustler's continued to sell their dope as if they knew Buckner wasn't going to do anything, and they were right. Miles takes in the scene, *I'm putting an end to this.* He hops out of the patrol car and pulls out his baton. "Let's go, clear this front, no soliciting. Move sir, move. You can't just sit here. "

Buckner shakes his head from embarrassment while Miles talks to the residents as if he has been waiting to chastise black people all his life. Instead of backing up his partner, Buckner walks into Lake Trout and stares at the menu. As Buckner orders his food, a skinny kid wearing braids strolls up and stands beside him sweating as if he just ran a mile.

"Everything alright?"

"Yeah."

While Buckner talks to the young hustla, Miles stands in the doorway of the store and sees the skinny kid giving Buckner a knot of money. Miles clears his throat; Buckner turns around and looks him in eyes. The skinny kid leaves, and Buckner grabs his food and walks outside.

"What the hell was that, Officer Buckner? I know what I saw."

Buckner places his food on the hood of the patrol car. "Aye, rookie, we've been riding together for three weeks."

"And we haven't made one fucking arrest. Instead, you're taking knots of money from some skinny ni–"

"You was gonna say nigger, wasn't you?" Buckner interrupts.

Officer Miles turns red from embarrassment. "I know what I saw."

"Look, you got two options, you can either turn me in, or I can show you how to make a living. You think they're gonna believe some rookie over me?"

Confused and still in cop mode, Miles stands in a combat position yelling at the residents, "Clear this front, gotdamit."

"Aye, rookie, tell me what that says on the side of our police car."

"Baltimore County Police Department, why?"

"We're in the city you asshole, outside of our jurisdiction. Now put that damn nightstick away. Let's take a walk." Buckner escorts him to the end of the shopping center. "The minute you put that police uniform on, you become a piece on a ruthless board game. Look around you rookie, this is what makes the world go round. Do you see any chemical plants around here?"

"No, what's your point?"

"The same people that we work for are the same ones putting this shit in these communities. Everybody's hands are dirty."

"Not mine."

Buckner laughs. "Oh really? I used to be just like you. I woke up early and put on my uniform with pride. I thought that every time I put someone in jail, I was making the world a better place. I have yet to see the world change and I've been putting people in jail for over two decades." Buckner stops at the end of the walkway and faces him. "A police officer has a lot of power on the streets, but in the big scheme of things, we're pawns just like the rest of these miserable muthafuckas. I lost partners that were just like you, and they all died thinking they were making a difference."

A breathing hard Miles steps in Buckner's face. "My father did make a difference and one of these muthafuckas took his life."

With his index finger, Buckner pokes Miles in the chest. "I knew your father, and he was a great officer, but he wasn't stupid."

Miles looks shocked. "You knew my father?"

"How do you think your father was able to keep a roof over your head and clothes on your back?"

"Because he worked hard."

Buckner grins. "You're right, your father was a hard worker, but he also got his hands dirty."

"Watch your mouth, Buckner. I might not turn you in, but I will beat the –"

"I don't mean to be disrespectful, but every cop wearing a uniform has gotten their hands dirty; it's part of the game. You didn't just become a police officer, you became part of a brotherhood. We are worth more than an American flag draped over our caskets."

Miles thinks back to the day his father was buried and he remembers watching his father's casket being lowered into the ground covered by the American flag. In broad daylight, Buckner reaches into his pocket and pulls out the cash that the young skinny hustler handed him. "This is a thousand dollars, take it."

*This must be a setup*. He looks around waiting for someone to jump out and confirm this is a test, but nothing happens. "You're serious?"

"Take it, it's free money. Your father wouldn't turn down free money."

Everything that Miles was taught about being a police officer comes crashing down. He has seen many movies about good cops turning bad, but he never thought that he would become one. "This isn't right." Miles mumbles under his breath.

"Well, turn me in or take the money."

Miles reaches behind his back and places his hands over his cuffs. He looks down at the cash and just the thought of taking this money and betraying the oath makes him ill. *My first arrest can't be a cop. No one will trust me.* Miles takes a deep breath, exhales and removes his hand from the cuffs. "I can't take you in."

"Then take the money."

Miles looks Buckner in the eyes and opens his palm. "You better not say a word."

Buckner puts the money in Miles' hand and squeezes it firmly. "Now, we're partners."

Buckner pretends to be a caring older cop, but underneath it all, he's just a greedy bastard using Miles' skin color to apply pressure on those he extorted.

Buckner has been doing this long enough to know that a white officer is extremely intimidating on the streets. Buckner has been planning this from the moment he laid eyes on Officer Miles.

For the next few months, Buckner teaches Miles the extortion business. Miles witnesses Buckner take money and drugs from the neighborhood hustlers and the term, 'stealing candy from a baby' has never been clearer. Miles learns that most drug dealers will do anything to avoid jail time and most don't put up a fight. Miles is surprised that Buckner has built a working relationship with the dealers who he extorted. *It must be a black thing,* Miles wonders. *There is no way they are going to let some scrawny, red-headed, poor, white-trash cop take their money without a fight.* On a bad night, he watched Buckner collect up to three thousand dollars. The hood became Buckner's personal ATM and everyday Miles becomes more intrigued.

Buckner is playing with Miles' mind like brand new Christmas toys. He didn't know Miles' father, and it was all bullshit to persuade Miles to keep his white ass mouth shut. Buckner knows that he is taking a risk with the rookie, so just in case Miles grows a conscience, Buckner has been secretly recording their conversations. Being in the extortion business has taught Buckner all the sleazy tricks to place people in a lose/lose situation.

One Tuesday afternoon, they sit parked in a wooded area pretending to monitor the speed limit. Buckner sleeps while Miles counts the number of cars breaking the speed limit. He has been a cop for a month and a half and all he has done is collect paychecks. A huge smile appears on his face and he mumbles, "I'm the fucking law." In the middle of Miles' realization that he is 'the man', the dispatcher interrupts loudly awakening Buckner.

"Officer Buckner, I need you to report to Milford Mill Road. There has been a —"

Buckner turns off the dispatcher, "I ain't tryna hear that shit."

Miles nervously shakes his leg. He has been waiting for the right time to express how he feels and there's no better time than now. "I'm ready to start making my own money."

"We all think we're ready until that moment comes. Do you even know what extortion is?"

"It's an unlawful way to obtain money, property, and services from a person, entity, or institution, by force."

"You sound like a damn dictionary. Ain't no rulebook to this shit, you learn as you go. Once you expose yourself as a dirty cop, you belong to the streets."

"So how'd you know when you were ready?"

Buckner looks Miles in the eyes. "I didn't, I just did it." Buckner turns on the ignition and pulls out of the wooded area. "I'm hungry." While Buckner drives, Miles bombards him with questions and Buckner gives the rookie all the information he can handle. "If you think you're ready, the first thing you need to do is find a snitch. Every hood has one, so you find yourself a good snitch and you'll make more money than you can count." Buckner cuts his eye. "A corrupt cop and a snitch is a match made in scumbag heaven."

"How do I find a snitch?"

Buckner laughs. "Damn, I keep telling you there are no rules to this shit. When you're ready, you'll know, trust me."

*Trust you, yeah right.* Miles snickers.

Miles learns from Buckner that it is best to extort outside of his jurisdiction. For a couple of weeks, Miles watches a group of hustlers on North Avenue and now he is itching to make a move. All alone with nothing but his thoughts, Officer Miles turns onto Braddish Avenue. When Miles' police car is spotted, the lookout boy standing on the roof yells, "CAW, CAW," at the top of his lungs to let everyone know that a cop is in the area. Miles doesn't have much time and he is out of his jurisdiction, so he puts black tape over his badge number, takes a deep breath, cuts on the police lights, and pulls up to the corner store. At this moment, he realizes that without Buckner, he is just some white cop.

He opens the car door and rushes the young man. "Up against the wall," he screams pushing the young man's face into the brick.

"What's your name?"

"Get the fuck off me. You're outside your jurisdiction. What I do?"

Miles grinds his face into the brick wall. "What's your fucking name?"

"Ow. Skeeter, my name is Skeeter."

Officer Miles turns Skeeter around and stares him in the eyes. He reaches into Skeeter's pockets and pulls out three knots of money.

The chaos causes a scene and a crowd begins to form. Officer Miles has to move quickly. He grabs Skeeter's wrist and awkwardly pulls it behind his back. Skeeter resists and Officer Miles slams his face onto the hood of his police car. Everyone who witnesses this excessive force from a white cop, stare with hate. Officer Miles yells at the spectators while forcing Skeeter inside the backseat. His adrenaline rushes, and he can't believe he actually did it. He got his first unlawful arrest and it feels damn good. He drives eight blocks to a vacant parking lot, counts the money and places it in his pocket.

"I know whatchu are."

Officer Miles adjusts the rear view mirror to see Skeeter's face. "What am I?"

"You ain't no fucking cop."

"So let's talk business."

Skeeter chuckles. "You must have lost ya damn mind. All y'all the same, you ain't protecting and serving shit. I hate cops like you." Skeeter spits through the steel cage. "I rather die, than talk business with a crooked cop."

Miles wipes the spit from the back of his head. "I hope you can run fast, nigger."

"You got whatchu want, you fucking pig, so just let me go."

While Skeeter continues to call Officer Miles every racial slur in the book, Miles drives across town to Cherry Hill – an area known for drugs, violence and a dislike for outsiders.

Skeeter is all too familiar with dirty cops leaving black men stranded in a war zone to be killed and he'd rather go to jail than to be left stranded in unknown territory. With his feet, Skeeter violently kicks the inside door handle hoping that he acts stupid enough to get locked up. Any other cop would have taken Skeeter to jail for spitting on him, but not Miles. Miles needs niggas like Skeeter on the street so he can continue to collect.

The police car comes to a stop and Skeeter goes wild. "I ain't get'n out, fuck you. You're gonna have to drag me out."

"No problem."

Officer Miles opens the back door and pulls Skeeter to the ground. "Don't move." Miles un-cuffs his wrists and kicks him in the ass. "Good luck getting home, you porch monkey."

"Fuck you."

Miles tips his hat. "Nah, fuck you and have a nice day sir." Miles speeds off and his adrenaline is pumping so much he can barely think. "I fucking did it. I am the law," he screams at the top of lungs.

* * *

Days after taking Skeeter on a road trip he'll never forget, Officer Miles rides around Baltimore County when he spots a white Ford Expedition with chrome twenty-four inch rims swerving down Security Boulevard. He pulls up behind the truck and follows it four blocks before cutting on his police lights and forcing the truck to pull over. He walks to the driver's side and knocks on the window.

"License and registration, sir."

The driver is obviously under the influence of drugs and alcohol and nervously fumbles around for his wallet. He rolls down his window and Officer Miles can smell the liquor on his breath. In the passenger seat, sits a beautiful girl wearing a short dress and heels. Officer Miles takes his license and insurance information and then goes to his car to run the driver's credentials.

A moment later, Officer Miles flashes his light in the young woman's eyes. "What's your name?"

"Sasha."

Officer Miles looks at the driver's identification. "Antoine, right?"

"Yes, sir."

"You know your license is expired, right?"

"Uh, I didn't –"

"Have y'all been drinking?"

With blood shot eyes and slurred speech Antoine lies, "No, sir."

While deciding if he feels like wasting his time writing a traffic ticket, Officer Miles smells the aroma of marijuana.

"I need you both to exit the car. I need to search your vehicle, sir."

Antoine isn't the brightest bulb, but he knows an officer is supposed to ask permission. After careful thought, he envisions slamming on the gas, but he doesn't have the courage. He tries to talk his way out of going to jail.

"Sir, I was going to get my license renewed but –"

"Get out the fucking truck."

Antoine and Sasha exit the vehicle and he places them both in cuffs and sits them on the curb. While Miles checks the vehicle, the brisk wind runs up Sasha's skirt and she tries her best to keep warm. This is Antoine's third strike and if Miles finds his stash, he is facing fifteen years without parole. Miles reaches under the driver's seat and pulls out a black nine-millimeter pistol. He walks over and dangles the gun in Antoine's face.

Antoine cries, "I didn't know that was there. It ain't mine."

Miles walks back to the truck and reaches further under the seat. He sees a crumbled up brown bag and opens it. Inside are ecstasy pills and three ounces of exotic weed. He walks back over to them, "Do you have any idea how much trouble both of you are in? Whose drugs are these, and you better not lie?"

"They're hers."

*You fucking coward,* Sasha thinks as she wipes away her tears. She looks over at Antoine and his eyes say, *"Please don't tell on me, please."* Sasha knows that a gun and drug charge will put Antoine behind bars for a long time, so she bites the bullet. "It's mine."

Miles kneels down and runs his hands across her face. "Are you selling this shit, or using it?"

Sasha mumbles, "Both."

Miles stares off into space while Sasha and Antoine prepare to take a ride to jail. Before calling for the paddy wagon, he walks back to the police car and gets inside.

"Thank you, Sasha. I can't afford to have both charges. This is your first offense, so you'll probably get probation."

The more Antoine talks, the angrier she becomes. Sasha has only been dating Antoine for a month. She was simply getting a ride home and now she has a criminal record. Prior to this, Sasha thought Antoine was a real nigga, but as she stares at him nervously rocking back and forth she sees that he is just the opposite.

"I swear I'm going to make this up to you."

"Are you fucking serious?"

Moments later, Miles' car door opens and he walks over to them. He leans up against Antoine's truck and stares awkwardly. "Antoine, I pulled your police record, and this is your third strike. Luckily for you, Sasha, this is your first offense, but these are very serious charges."

"That gun ain't mine. I didn't –"

"Did I ask you to speak?"

Antoine drops his head. "No, sir."

"I could use two people like you." Miles kneels down. "You got two options, I can take both of you to the precinct and you can face the weapon and drugs charges, or you can work for me."

Antoine perks up as if he has been waiting to hear these words all his life. "I would shake your hand, but I'm wearing cuffs," he says smiling. "I'd rather work for you."

"I had a feeling you'd say that." Miles looks at Sasha, "What about you beautiful?"

Sasha can see right through Officer Miles and everything about him screams 'snake'.

"No thank you," Sasha responds.

Miles steps back. "You ungrateful little bitch. If you don't work for me, I'm charging the both of you with the gun and the drugs."

"C'mon, Sasha." Antoine begs. "Don't do this to me."

"Listen to Antoine, sweetheart. When I'm done with you, you'll be wishing you worked for me."

Sasha's eyes fill up with tears and roll down her face. Sasha knows she is stuck. She looks Miles in the eyes and shakes her head.

"That's not good enough, Sasha. I need to hear you say it."

"Yes."

"Good, I'm going to hold onto the gun and drugs for a little insurance policy. If you ever try to fuck me over, I will make sure that you spend the rest of your life in jail." Miles walks behind Antoine and places the key into his handcuffs. "Once I take these cuffs off, you belong to me."

Antoine can't believe he just escaped fifteen years in prison, so as he stands to his feet he assures, "Whatever you need just ask, I'm your guy."

Miles walks over to Sasha, but before removing the cuffs, he places his mouth next to her left ear and whispers, "You belong to me." He removes the cuffs and Sasha stands to her feet. "I have all the information I need on you two, so don't try anything funny. I'll be in touch."

In shock, Antoine and Sasha watch the dirtiest cop they have ever met walk away. When Miles drives off, Sasha slaps Antoine in the face.

"What was I supposed to do, Sasha?"

"Be a real nigga and take your charges. That's what you supposed to do."

"I ain't going to jail."

"So you're gonna work for a cop now?"

In a threatening manner, Antoine steps in Sasha's face and grabs her arm, "We both work for a cop now, right?"

* * *

The next day, Miles drives to his favorite liquor store on Reisterstown Road. He parks and walks inside. Today is Miles' day off, and he's dressed casually appearing to be a regular, taxpaying resident. He purchases a six pack of beer and leaves. Before getting into his car, he notices a young black kid leaning up against the pay phone. Miles can spot a drug dealer from a mile away and this kid definitely fits the description. Miles walks over to the young ambitious hustler.

"Whatchu need? I got dimes, quarters and –"

"I need a partner."

"A partner? Get the fuck outta here, white boy. You look like the police."

Miles grins. "I am."

"Stop playing with me, white boy. Either buy something or get the fuck outta here."

64

Miles pulls out his badge and the young hustler panics. "I ain't got shit on me. I'm just outside minding my business. I'm waiting for a ride and –"

"Calm down. If I wanted to arrest you, I would've done it by now."

"So whatchu want?"

"I want you to pay me for allowing you to sell drugs."

"You're extorting me?"

"If I catch your ass out here tomorrow, I'm taking you to jail," Miles turns around to walk away.

"Hold up, what's in it for me?"

Miles opens the car door. "Freedom." He gets inside and turns on the ignition, but before he pulls off, the young hustler walks over and taps on the passenger window.

"Look, man, I'm not making a lot of money. I'm too smart to be standing out here selling dime bags, but if you can find me a supplier – someone with some real weight, I can make some things happen."

It never occurred to Miles to supply the people he extorts and form his own drug distribution ring. He likes how the young man thinks and is impressed. "What's your name?"

"Sean."

Miles takes Sean's phone number and drives off. Inside the car, Miles' mind races with ideas on how to corner the drug market. Minutes later, he pulls up to his home and walks inside. He sits down at his living room table and stares at a picture of his father hanging on the wall. *I'm sorry, pops, but I'm sure you understand. It's all part of the game, right?*

Days later, Miles picks up his phone and dials.

"Hello."

"Is this Sean?"

"Yeah."

"Where are you?"

"You know where I am."

Moments later, Miles pulls up in front of the liquor store and flashes his headlights. Sean runs over and gets inside. "You said you need a supplier right?"

"Hell yeah."

"You ever held a gun before?"

Sean lifts up his shirt showing his forty-five caliber. "I can handle myself."

"Good, have you ever robbed anyone before?"

Sean grins. "Whatchu think?"

"If you do this right, I'll make sure you won't have to stand outside that liquor store again."

Sean replies with confidence, "Don't worry about me."

At 1:27 in the morning, Miles and Sean park in the distance as they watch Skeeter and his crew run their operation.

Normally, Miles would just snatch Skeeter off the block, take his money and drop him off in Cherry Hill like before – but not tonight. Tonight, Miles wants the product so he can give it to Sasha, Antoine, and Sean to distribute.

An hour later, Miles notices a suspicious gray Cadillac Seville. Skeeter walks over to the car and conducts a transaction. Minutes later, another black man quickly tosses two blue book bags in the back seat.

"I can't believe they're dumb enough to do this in the open. That's the drugs, I know it." Miles declares.

The Cadillac pulls off and Miles follows, trailing four cars behind it. He grows anxious because he doesn't have a lot of time before he gets spotted. If he was on duty, he would have just turned on his police lights and took what he wanted, but he can't hide behind his badge. One wrong move can put both of them in a casket, but Miles is too determined to quit.

While Miles continues to follow behind the car, Sean lowers his hat to cover his face. Sean looks at Miles and cannot resist asking, "Are you sure you're a cop?"

Miles pulls out his badge and shows him. "I didn't get this from a damn dollar store. Why you ask?"

"You don't think or act like one."

"You'd be surprised how many cops think and act like me." He makes another right turn. "Stop asking me silly questions and pay attention."

The Cadillac pulls into a gas station and Miles parks in the distance. They watch the men exit the car and walk inside. "Go," Miles orders.

Sean looks confused. "What?"

"Those idiots left the car running. Go take it."

"Take what?"

"The damn car!"

*This white boy is crazy.* Sean musters up enough courage to commit grand theft. He opens the driver's side door, jumps in and slams on the gas before the men leave the store. Sean breathes heavily, *Oh shit, I can't believe I just did that.* He looks in the back seat and he can smell the potency of the product. "That's some good ass weed."

Twenty minutes later, Miles pulls into an apartment complex with Sean following. Using his shirt, Sean wipes down the steering wheel and gear shift, snatches the book bags and jumps inside of Miles' car. "That was the craziest shit I ever did." Sean rubs his hands together. "When do I start?"

Officer Miles looks inside the bag. "Just be ready when I call."

For the next couple of weeks, Miles continues to rob multiple crews. He tracks and watches their operations so much that he knows when they change shifts so each heist becomes easier. Miles manages to steal close to sixty pounds worth of weed, which is more than enough to resell because it is all profit. One Saturday afternoon while at home, Miles decides it is time to call his first meeting.

"Hello?"

"Sean, meet me at my place." Miles hangs up and calls Antoine.

"Antoine?"

"How are you doing, sir? I just wanna thank you again for –"

"Antoine, you don't have to kiss my ass. Meet me at my house in ten minutes."

"I'm on the way."

\* \* \*

Sasha sits in the nail salon getting her toes done when her cell phone rings. She picks up the phone and looks at the number. *Shit.* She lets the phone ring until it stops, but Miles just calls again. *What does he want?* After Miles' fourth attempt, Sasha finally answers, "Hello?"

"I called you four times." Miles grits his teeth, "Look, I need you to meet me at my house in ten minutes."

"I'm getting my toes done. I can't be there in ten minutes."

Miles bangs his fist onto the living room table. "You wanna getcha toes done, huh? Well how about I pick you up and take you to the precinct? I'm sure they would love to do your feet down there."

Sasha looks down at her half-done toes and sighs. *I hate this muthafucker.* Sasha taps the nail technician. "I'm sorry, but I have to go." With six of her toes painted hot pink and the others untouched, Sasha stomps to her car and drives off. In exactly ten minutes, she pulls up in front of Miles' home and sees Antoine's truck and instantly feels sick. She walks up the steps and stands in front of Miles' door. *I can't believe I'm about to walk in a crooked cops house.* Unsure of what to expect, she takes a deep breath and knocks on the door. Miles answers and she rolls her eyes.

"Come inside."

*Whatever, pig.* Sasha looks around and the first thing she sees is Antoine and some other guy sitting in the living room. Sasha doesn't want to get comfortable like

69

Antoine and this other guy, so she stands with her hands folded giving everyone as much attitude as she can deliver.

Miles walks into the living room holding a bottle of Vodka and four cups. "I think it's time we all meet." Miles places the cups onto the living room table and pours a shot. "Antoine and Sasha, this is Sean."

Antoine looks at Sean from head to toe. The moment that Miles freed him from those cuffs, Antoine wanted to become Miles' right hand man. Antoine doesn't know Sean, but he can sense that they'll be competing for the same spot. While Antoine and Sean get to know more about each other, Sasha continues to look uninterested. Miles raises his glass. "Let's toast."

Antoine and Sean raise their glasses, but Sasha just stares. *Look at these niggas, I can't believe this shit.*

"Pick up your glass, Sasha." Sasha hesitates and Miles steps closer. "I said pick up the damn glass. All of our lives are about to change."

Miles' plan works to perfection and the weed is split between Antoine and Sean. They supply the streets with the best product, and their competition is forced to lower their prices. Within two months, Antoine and Sean manage to sell the weed that Miles stole. When the product was gone, Miles robbed more hustlers and his reputation grew. Miles became so reckless that the streets gave him the nickname Snatch-n-Grab because he snatched hustlers off the block and grabbed everything they had. Miles didn't care. The money was good and the power was even better.

* * *

Weeks later, Miles is home when he sees a shadow standing at his doorstep. He grabs his gun, looks through the peephole and sees Buckner wearing a blue tailored suit, white shirt, red pinstripe tie, rust colored shoes and dark shades. Miles is a little skeptical, but he opens the door.

"Everything alright?"

Buckner doesn't crack a smile. "Get dressed. I'll be in the car."

Miles closes the front door and from his peephole, he watches Buckner walk back to his car. *What the hell is he doing here?* The way that Buckner is dressed, Miles can't help but think about a scene from his favorite movie, Casino, when Joe Pesci was led to believe he would become a "made man" but instead, he gets a bullet to the back of the head.

Miles walks into the kitchen and discreetly pulls the curtain to the left to see if there are any unfamiliar cars parked out back. He runs upstairs and opens his closet. While staring at his clothes, his mind races with every possible scenario and they all end with him dying. He gets dressed, reaches under his mattress, grabs his unregistered three-eighty pistol and places it in his coat pocket, just in case he has to shoot his way out of trouble. He takes a deep breath and mentally prepares himself for what could be the worst night of his life.

Inside of the car, Miles tries to lighten the mood, but Buckner drives in complete silence until they arrive at a luxury condominium building overlooking the Baltimore Harbor's dirty black waters. Buckner gives the valet twenty dollars and walks towards the elevator.

"What have you done?" Buckner asks fixing his tie.

"That's the first thing you said to me since I got in the car. What the hell is going on?"

Buckner looks Miles in the eyes. "I don't know. I got a call to come down here and bring you."

"A call from who?"

"Carter."

"Who the hell is Carter?"

Buckner doesn't answer. They step inside of the elevator and Buckner presses the number four. The elevator ride is short, but long enough to make Miles worry. The elevator doors open and Buckner speed walks down the hallway as if he is late for his own wedding. They stand in front of Suite 487, but just before he knocks, Miles stops him.

"Tell me something, Buckner. I don't like surprises."

Buckner knocks, and a black man wearing a sweat suit answers. The guy looks familiar, but Miles doesn't have time to figure it out. Miles extends his hand, but the black man frowns up his face as if he wants to slap the shit out of him. They step further inside the condominium and Miles recognizes more faces, but he doesn't know from where. He tries to appreciate the nice condominium, but everywhere he turns, one of the guys is giving him the look of death. Miles reaches into his pocket and grips his hand over his gun before following Buckner onto the balcony.

"It's about fucking time," a well-dressed Puerto Rican man yells.

Miles doesn't know what to think, but this gentleman is obviously in a position of serious power. Why he is hanging out with thugs is the question that rattles Miles' mind. Miles nervously walks over, fixes his posture and extends his hand. "My name is –"

"I know who you are; my friends downstairs call you Snatch-n-Grab." Carter yells, "Skeeter, there's someone here to see you."

Miles looks at Buckner, *You set me up*. At this moment, he loses all trust in Buckner and if he makes it out of this situation alive, Buckner is going to pay. Miles' mouth becomes dry and he feels the urge to vomit. He is aware of his nickname in the streets and reality hits him like a ton of bricks. Every guy in this luxury condominium, he either robbed or extorted for cash and drugs. All of a sudden, the thought of being on a balcony four floors up isn't so pleasant. This may be the last time he gets to see the Baltimore skyline.

Clutching his fists, Skeeter walks onto the balcony and stares Miles in the face. "Small world, huh?"

Miles nervously bites his lip knowing an apology won't get him out of this one. Carter, the well-dressed Puerto Rican, lights up a cigarette, takes a long drag and exhales. "Either you know what's going on, or you're a stupid muthafucker, so which one is it?"

Miles waits for Buckner to save him, but Buckner keeps his head down. While Buckner pretends to be

73

invisible, Miles looks over the balcony to see how bad the damage will be if he jumps.

Carter faces Miles. "Every game has rules. You never snatch a drug dealer off the corner before doing the proper research. Every time you took from them, you took from me." Carter reaches into his pocket, pulls out his police badge and tosses it onto the pool table. "You thought you were the only one? Half the force is in the extortion business."

"I'm sorry, I didn't know."

"I expected you to say that."

Carter pats Miles on the shoulder. Unfortunately, this type of pat on the shoulder is not for doing a good job. This pat on the shoulder says, "You'd better make this right, or else."

Now that Carter has made his point, it's time to talk business. Carter is only five-foot-seven, 175 pounds, but everything about him screams dangerous.

"Roughly, how much do you think you took from my boys?"

Miles knows this is a trick question. He mumbles, "I don't know."

Carter calmly places his gun against Miles' stomach. "I want it all back, with interest." Carter grins. "No one is exempt from extortion, not even the extorters; but I'm sure by now, you understand that."

With his hands in the air Miles pleads, "I can make this right. I'll give you the cash that I got and I'll work the rest off for you."

Carter puts his gun away and grins. "You got a lot of balls, rookie, but how are you going to handle the interest?"

"I can do it, let me earn your trust."

"You wanna earn my trust? I gotta hundred pounds I need you to take off my hands. Can you do it?"

Miles knows if he gives the impression that he can't handle the terms of the agreement, he is a dead man. Miles has never sold or seen that much weed in his life, which further lets him know that Carter intends to kill him, but he agrees to Carter's conditions.

* * *

The next day, Miles orchestrates another meeting at his house. He pulls out his chair and sits at the head of the table. "I gotta shipment of a hundred pounds so I need everyone to be on their 'A' game."

Antoine shouts, "I'm ready. Give it all to me, I can handle it."

Sean laughs. "You must've lost ya fucking mind. What makes you think you can sell a hunned pounds?"

Antoine teases. "Nigga, you still in high school. I was doing this shit when you couldn't even leave the porch."

Sean stands to his feet. "Fuck you."

"Nah, fuck you."

Sasha sits in silence. She can't believe she is witnessing two idiots arguing over which one will work with a dirty white cop. While Antoine and Sean argue, Sasha looks down at her phone.

Miles bangs his fist onto the table, and restores order like a slave-masters whip.

"Both of y'all shut up. We don't have a lot of time, so I need everyone's participation." Miles cuts his eye at Sasha. "I got something real special for you."

Sasha looks up. "I bet you do."

Miles is tired of Sasha's attitude and he can't afford any mistakes. He walks over to her. "You think you're too cute to get your hands dirty?"

Sasha rolls her eyes. Miles grabs her throat and squeezes until her face turns red. "You think I give a fuck about you?"

While Antoine and Sean watch how ruthless Miles handles her, Sasha tries to pry his fingers from around her throat. Miles pushes her out of the seat and she falls violently to the ground hitting her head on the wood floor.

Miles kicks her in the ass. "Get up."

Scared out of her damn mind, Sasha gasps for air. Completely shocked, she struggles to stand to her feet and face Miles. Sasha's "I-don't-giva-fuck" attitude has been shattered and Miles finally has her full attention. Up until now, Sasha thought Miles was just a bad cop using his badge as leverage, but as she looks into his beady blue eyes, she can finally see the evil that lies in the depth of his soul. Miles rocks back and forth with his fist clutched as if he wants to knock Sasha out of her heels.

"Sit down."

Sasha picks up her purse and does as she is told. Miles looks them each in the eye. "I am not your fucking friend, you work for me. It's either this or jail. Do I make myself clear?"

Sasha lifts up her head and already forming is a large, purple bruise around her left eye. "Yes," she mumbles.

On the surface, Miles looks under control, but behind those beady blue eyes is a man scared for his life.

# CHAPTER III

Kendrick sits in the last row of class near the door. Like most of the students who attend Mrs. Belvedere's class, he can't wait for it to be over. Kendrick has never been a troublemaker, but now that he is popular, his attention and focus has changed. Since losing his virginity, he has slept with multiple girls and is building a reputation for being hung-low. He is becoming the weed selling, well-dressed, bad boy that all the girls love and it is no secret that he is enjoying his newfound fame.

While Mrs. Belvedere writes on the chalkboard, Kendrick is trying to convince someone's daughter to let him in between her legs. Out the corner of his eye, he sees Carlos in the hallway signaling to get his attention. Kendrick gets a hall pass and meets Carlos in the bathroom.

"Wassup?"

Carlos has a weird smirk on his face, the same smirk that always gets them into trouble.

"I saw Sean put a bag in the bushes by the creek. I'ma take that shit."

"For what?"

"I think he got weed in there."

Kendrick leans up against the bathroom stall. "You about to do something stupid, ain't you?"

"You call it stupid, I call it getting money."

* * *

After school, Sean walks towards the creek and immediately notices his bag missing and calls Miles.

"I got robbed."

Miles bangs on the steering wheel. "What? Don't move, I'm on my way." Miles cuts on the police siren and speeds through traffic. "I can't believe this shit."

Miles pulls up abruptly and Sean is terrified. After watching how he brutally beat Sasha, Sean prepares for the worst.

Miles walks towards Sean and grabs him by his shirt. "What happened?"

"I put the bag right here and it's gone."

"You must think I'm stupid."

"I swear, I'm not try'na burn you. I would never –"

"Shut up."

Miles paces back and forth thinking of a way to recover twenty-pounds of weed. Losing this much product is a major setback and the clock is ticking.

"Who do you think took it? Does anybody else sell weed at school?"

Miles continues to interrogate Sean, but Sean isn't replying fast enough so Miles punches him in the face. Sean's nose pours blood, which only makes it harder for him to think.

"You better find out who took my shit," Miles demands before leaving.

With his shirt, Sean pinches his nose to stop the bleeding and it dawns on him. "I know who did that shit."

* * *

After school, Carlos drives in silence while Kendrick reads Carlos' little black book. With his index finger, he scrolls down looking for an 'X'. "Paul owes us one hundred dollars."

Carlos doesn't respond.

"Did you hear me? We need to pay Paul a visit. He's probably at the basketball court."

Carlos doesn't respond. He lights up a cigarette and continues to drive in silence. Normally, Carlos is eager to turn the 'X's in his little black book into check marks, but something is obviously bothering him. Instead of driving to find Paul, he pulls up to Motel 6 and parks.

Kendrick smiles. "You got some bitches?"

Carlos gets out of the car and pops the trunk. "I got something way better than that. C'mon."

Kendrick follows Carlos into room 58. He closes the blinds, and dumps the bag. A scale and twenty pounds of weed fall onto the bed. Carlos grins. "Do you have any idea how much money we're gonna make?" He turns up the television to muffle their voices and sits next to Kendrick. "What's done is done. Ain't no turning back now. You in or out?"

If Kendrick says he's out, not only does he risk not making money, but possibly losing Carlos as a friend. That could get his popular pass revoked and going back to being nobody. If Kendrick says he's in, he risks going to war with Sean, jail or even killed. In the pit of his stomach, Kendrick knows this is going to be a disaster, but being a nobody again simply isn't an option.

"Yeah, I'm in."

"Then let's get this money."

* * *

The next day at school, the bell rings dismissing everyone from class. Carlos and Kendrick walk outside and Sean is there to meet them. Kendrick cringes and tries to avoid eye contact, but Carlos loves to see Sean clueless and angry. Sean looks at Carlos and he can sense that he is hiding something. Sean knows that if anyone would have the balls to take his weed, it would be Carlos.

Sean pulls Carlos off to the side. "Did you hear anything?"

"Whatchu talking about?"

"Somebody took something from me."

"Oh really? Took what?"

Sean looks over at Kendrick. "You heard anything?"

Kendrick shakes his head. "Nobody told me anything."

"You know I'ma find out who did it, right?"

Carlos smirks. "I hope you do," he says sarcastically.

* * *

Four days after being approached by Sean, Kendrick lies on the bed staring at the ceiling. Every Saturday morning, he wakes up early in time for his mother's breakfast, but not anymore. He is not the same little boy who his mother raised him to be. Amy believes Kendrick is upstairs asleep, but he is waiting for the perfect time to sneak into the basement where he stashed his half of the weed. He springs up from the bed and places his feet onto the hardwood floor. He walks over to his closet, and gets dressed. Instead of wearing the clothes that his mother bought from the flea market, Kendrick decides to put on the clothes that he purchased. Kendrick knows this can be a huge mistake, but he is tired of being treated like child. He stands in the mirror and looks at himself from head to toe. "I'ma vampire," he says to his reflection. He walks downstairs into the kitchen and Amy notices immediately.

"Hey, ma."

"Who gave you those clothes?"

Kendrick thought he was prepared to tell the truth, but he isn't, so he lies. "Carlos gave them to me."

"I really like Carlos. He's such a sweet boy," she says mixing the pancake batter to the perfect consistency. She then plops a half stick of butter into one hot skillet, and turns down the flame on another. "You hungry?"

Kendrick walks towards the basement door. "Not really, I gotta –"

"You're not leaving this house without eating something, so sit down."

He sits down at the table and fifteen minutes later, Amy brings him a steaming hot plate with three perfectly browned pancakes, two sausage links, and scrambled eggs. Saturday mornings have always been time for Amy to play catch up with Kendrick, but he isn't as talkative as he usually is. Instead, he constantly checks his watch and picks over his food.

"Is everything ok?"

"Yeah," Kendrick replies stuffing his mouth with food as fast as he can. He pushes his chair back from the table. "Thanks, ma. That was good as always."

Kendrick excuses himself from the table, opens the basement door and closes it behind him. Kendrick hides his weed in the basement because his mother rarely goes down there. It is cluttered and filled with old furniture and almost impossible to navigate through. Ten pounds of weed is hard to hide, but Kendrick is very clever. Instead of keeping the weed in one place, he has it hidden in multiple locations. He walks to the back of the basement towards a broken dryer. He reaches behind it and grabs a bag containing fifteen hundred dollars worth of weed broken down into little baggies for sale. He places them into his pocket, runs upstairs and kisses his mother on the cheek.

"See you later, ma."

"Be good, Kendrick."

Kendrick sighs with relief. He did it, he managed to get out of the house without being interrogated by his mother. He opens the front door and the fresh Saturday air opens up his lungs. He looks up the street and sees Tamika surrounded by a group of people.

Tamika is a flat out 'weed head' with a bad attitude. Kendrick has always kept his distance from Tamika, but his world has become strictly about supply and demand.

He walks toward the crowd, pulls Tamika aside and shows her one of his bags.

Tamika rolls her eyes. "You know I get my weed from Sean. He got that good shit."

"Me and Carlos got that good shit now."

She sniffs the bag. "Hold up, this smell just like Sean's weed." Tamika cuts her eye. "I knew you and Carlos was up to something. Y'all the ones that took Sean weed. I knew it."

"We ain't take shit from that nigga. You want it or not?"

She reaches into her fake name brand purse that she got from the flea market and gives him ten dollars. Afterwards, she playfully steps back and spins around.

*I can't stand this bitch.* "What the hell are you doing?"

Tamika laughs. "I hope you like my dress, because this is what I'm going to wear at you and Carlos' funeral."

Kendrick lies, "The last thing I'm worried about is Sean."

For the rest of the day, Kendrick walks around the neighborhood selling weed until his feet hurt. He has been outside for six hours and only made fifty dollars. *I was better off getting a fucking job; this shit is less than minimum wage.* Kendrick knows that Tamika can't keep her mouth shut, so it's just a matter of time before the word gets back to Sean. Kendrick just wanted to fit in. He never intended to be a full-time hustler, but here he is standing alone, scared and in complete silence. *Where's everybody at?*

Three hours later and not one bag of weed sold, Kendrick sees a brown Honda Accord with dark tint slowly pulling up to him. His first thought is to run, but where? He is standing in open space with no way to escape. Kendrick has never been shot before and the thought of it is terrifying. The driver's window slowly rolls down, and he freezes. Kendrick can hear his heartbeat over his thoughts and a burst of bravery shoots up his spine. "Fuck this," Kendrick says before running in a zigzag pattern.

"Aye, Kendrick. What the hell are you doing?"

"Who's that?"

"It's Carlos."

Kendrick hasn't felt this embarrassed since his conversation with Melanie. His heart slows down and he walks towards Carlos. "I didn't know that was you," he says breathing heavily.

"What the hell were you doing?"

Kendrick thinks of a lie, but there's nothing he can say to cover up running zigzag in the street. Carlos waits for Kendrick to give him an explanation, but Kendrick just stares.

"Are you high?"

"Nah."

Carlos checks his watch. "Ain't it passed your curfew?"

"I'ma vampire, remember?"

Carlos laughs. "Vampires don't run zigzag. Tell the truth, you thought I was Sean, didn't you?"

"I don't giva damn about Sean." Kendrick pokes out his chest, and continues, "I'm out here making money."

Carlos looks around. "You're the only one outside. Nigga, get in the car, and I'ma show you where the real the money at. I know this girl that lives on Oliver Street."

"Whose car is this anyway?"

Carlos turns up the radio. "Don't worry about it."

Kendrick stares out the passenger window and the closer they get to Oliver Street, the area transforms from houses with yards and mailboxes to boarded properties, and liquor stores on almost every corner. He becomes uncomfortable. "You bring the gun?"

Carlos' head cocks back shocked. This is the first time that Kendrick has ever asked for it. "Of course, I did."

Surprisingly, Kendrick doesn't hesitate. He reaches under the seat, grabs the gun and places it inside of his back pocket. He looks Carlos in the eyes and mumbles, "Just in case."

Moments later, Carlos parks in front of a home on Oliver Street and honks the horn. An attractive plus-sized girl named Danyelle, comes outside. Kendrick instantly knows that Carlos is up to something.

"Whatchu doing round here?" Danyelle shouts from the porch.

"I came to see you."

Danyelle blushes. "Really? Hold on, I'll be back," she says running back into the house.

Carlos taps Kendrick on the shoulder. "C'mon."

Kendrick doesn't budge.

"What are you waiting for?"

Kendrick is clearly uncomfortable, afraid and clueless. He can't tell Carlos that being here is not the best idea, but he has a feeling that Carlos really doesn't have a plan and is just making it up as he goes along. Kendrick reluctantly opens the passenger door and places his foot onto the concrete. Kendrick can feel the hustle and immediately recognizes that he is out of his league. He lives in a different world that abides by different rules. Carlos walks onto Danyelle's porch and sits on the steps. Unable to relax, Kendrick stands with his hands behind his back like an army cadet.

Kendrick has heard many stories about the Eastside of Baltimore and so far, everything he has heard is true. While watching everything that moves, Kendrick hears a loud roaring sound. He turns around and sees a bunch of dirt bikes recklessly weaving through traffic. The dirt bike boys ride at high speeds popping wheelies and leaning back so far that they are just inches away from the ground. The slightest move could cause death and Kendrick is speechless at how careless they are.

"The Eastside is different," Kendrick says.

"It's a lot of money over here."

"I don't know whatchu got up your sleeve, Carlos, but these eastside niggas are not going to let us sell drugs on their block."

"We're not selling drugs on their block. We're selling drugs from Danyelle's porch."

Kendrick shakes his head. "Are you serious? We're still on their block."

"Trust me, I gotta plan."

"I ain't trynna hear that shit. This don't —"

87

Before Kendrick can finish, Danyelle walks out the front door clearly dressed up to impress Carlos.

"You look nice, Danyelle."

As he and Kendrick sit on Danyelle's steps, Carlos watches the blocks movements. Within an hour, Carlos sees how often the police ride by, what drugs are sold, and how the hustlers keep order on the block. He also questions Danyelle to find out the personalities of certain individuals, and she spills the beans on just about everything. In school, Carlos can't wrap his mind around basic math, but when it comes to the streets, Carlos' mind operates like a computer. He has this ability to spot a problem, find a solution and create results instantaneously. If given the opportunity, Carlos knows he could turn a neighborhood into a goldmine and that's his ultimate goal.

After watching the block for two hours, Carlos points at a guy leaning up against the mailbox wearing a black Baltimore Oriole's shirt. "Who's that?"

"They call him Twan. He's cool."

Carlos stands to his feet and stretches. "Aye, Kendrick, take a walk with me."

In Kendrick's mind, walking to a store in the middle of the hood is the worst idea that he has ever heard, but follows behind him. Kendrick remains quiet, with his eyes wide and his hands over the gun while Carlos fearlessly approaches Twan.

"Whatchu need?" Twan asks.

Carlos pulls out one of the dime bags. "I got weed for sale."

Twan signals and within seconds a group of men walk over. Carlos is afraid, but he remains calm. Kendrick doesn't want to make any sudden movements, and is remembering that his zigzag running might come in handy. Carlos knows that he could be risking their lives, but this is what it takes – balls and a whole lot of "fuck it".

Carlos doesn't blink or show weakness, "If y'all interested, I'll be at Danyelle's house."

Twan laughs. "You're talking about fat ass Danyelle?"

Carlos lies, "Yeah, that's my girlfriend."

The men laugh amongst each other because Danyelle is known for running men in and out of her mother's house, but Carlos doesn't care. All Carlos wants to do is show them the product and give them a location.

"Everybody sells weed out here, so what makes whatchu got so different?" Twan asks.

"Trust me, we got the best shit." Carlos reaches into his pocket and gives Twan a bag. "If you like it, we'll be at Danyelle's house."

Twan takes the bag, sniffs it. "I might come check you out later."

Kendrick and Carlos walk back to Danyelle's house and they can feel Twan and the rest of his friends staring at them. Carlos mumbles, "Don't turn around. Just be calm and keep your head straight."

"Yo, we need to get the fuck outta here. What the hell were you doing? We don't know these niggas."

Carlos lights up a cigarette while Kendrick continues to complain. "This is gonna work."

"We should just leave," Kendrick says while staring at two junkies pushing a shopping cart down the street.Kendrick hears voices in the distance. He squints his eyes, "Yo, you see that?"

Carlos turns around and sees a group of men walking towards them with Twan leading the pack. As they get closer, Carlos' undeniable confidence turns into fear. He stands up and places his hands in his pocket, forgetting that Kendrick has his gun. "Shit," Carlos says under his breath.

Twan looks at Danyelle. "Do you know these niggas?"

Danyelle smiles. "Yeah, they're cool."

Twan approaches them and grins. "Cool, let me get five bags."

Carlos sighs with relief. *This shit actually worked.* One by one, Twan's friends purchase multiple bags of weed and Kendrick can't believe that they are making money on unknown territory. The word quickly travels through the hood that some new niggas at Danyelle's house got good weed and the sales increase. At two fifteen in the morning, a twelve year old boy rides towards them on a bicycle.

"Y'all still got weed out?" The teenage boy asks.

Kendrick is stunned. "Shouldn't you be in bed?"

The twelve-year-old hustler pulls out a knot of money. "The money don't sleep, so why should I?" The young man licks his thumb, flicks through his money and hands Carlos sixty dollars. Still baffled, Kendrick watches the young man get onto his bike and ride away into the darkness.

Carlos looks at Kendrick with a huge smile on his face. "What I tell you? We landed on a fucking goldmine." Carlos spreads the money in his hands like a deck of cards and fans himself, "Sometimes you gotta take chances." He puts the money back into his pocket. "Now let's get outta here."

Danyelle places her hand on her roundish hip. "What about me, Carlos?"

Carlos walks over to her and kisses her on the cheek.

Danyelle opens her hand. "That was nice, but I want some money. If it wasn't for me you –"

"Ok, you're right."

Carlos gives Danyelle fifty dollars. He and Kendrick walk down the steps when a blue pickup truck with twenty-two inch rims pulls up. The passenger window rolls downs and a man screams, "What the fuck y'all doing?"

"What's his problem?" Kendrick asks.

"That's just Mack," Danyelle says. "He think he run shit around here, but don't worry about that nigga."

"I don't know who told y'all this shit is cool, but you better not be here when I get back," Mack threatens before speeding off.

Kendrick sighs. *I knew this shit was too good to be true.* "We need to get outta here. We made enough money."

Carlos walks back onto Danyelle's porch and sits down. "Nah, we ain't going nowhere."

"We've only been around here for one day and these niggas have been around here all their lives. It's not worth it."

Carlos lights up a cigarette. "I'm not leaving."

"What does staying prove?"

"It proves that we ain't bitches."

Ten minutes later, the same pickup truck drives down Danyelle's street.

"You niggas still here?" Mack yells. He gets out, reaches inside the back of his truck and grabs a bat. "I thought I told y'all this is my hood." Mack steps closer and stands face to face with Carlos.

"You can't run the hood with a bat. You're gonna need something more than that," Carlos says sarcastically.

Mack lifts his shirt and shows his gun. "Will this work?"

When Kendrick sees Mack's gun, his adrenaline rushes and the moment he's been dreading has arrived. Kendrick has been holding Carlos' gun all night and now he has to decide if he is going to use it.

Danyelle yells from her porch, "Stop it, Mack. It ain't even that serious."

"Shut up." Mack screams pointing his finger, "You shouldn't have let these niggas come round here."

"You need to chill out," Carlos suggests.

Mack steps in Carlos' face and their noses are inches away from touching. Carlos pushes Mack, Mack swings and punches Carlos in the face. The punch startles Carlos and before he can swing, he hears two gunshots. The impact pushes Mack back and he holds his chest in shock. Carlos stares at Kendrick as if he is seeing a ghost. Time freezes and all they can hear are the sounds of Mack moaning. Carlos looks over at Kendrick and Kendrick is so petrified that he doesn't realize he is still pointing the gun.

Kendrick panics. "I had to."

Carlos runs towards Kendrick. "Gimme the gun and go to the car. It's ok; you did what you had to do."

"Y'all gotta get outta here," Danyelle says.

Kendrick hands Carlos the gun and runs to the car. Carlos walks over to Mack and watches him roll around in pain. If Carlos doesn't finish Mack off, he'll be looking over his shoulder for the rest of his life. He cocks the gun, and grits his teeth. Police sirens are closing in, but all Carlos can hear is the beating of his own heart.

"Stop, Carlos," Danyelle screams. "Please don't, just go."

He takes one last look, tucks the gun into his jeans and runs to the car. Carlos may be many things, but a murderer he is not.

Breathing heavily, he opens the passenger door and jumps inside. "Drive."

Kendrick speeds down Oliver Street, swerves through the neighborhood and merges onto the highway. "Oh shit," Kendrick yells hysterically. "We shouldn't have been out there." Reality sets in. "What if I killed him? I'm going to fucking jail."

Carlos doesn't know what to say to ease his best friend. Even though Kendrick pulled the trigger, Carlos is the reason Mack is clinging on for his life. He fucked up royally, and by this time tomorrow – they might be in jail. Carlos lights a cigarette and inhales deeply to calm his nerves. Carlos thought it would be fun to take an innocent virgin and turn him into a hustler, but turning Kendrick into a killer is something that his conscience will not allow.

"Don't worry, I'll take the charge," Carlos mumbles.

"What is that going to fix?" Kendrick's mind is so shattered that he is running red lights. "I fucked up my life." He looks over at Carlos. "Did you prove your fucking point?"

"I know I messed up, but I can't change it. I'm sorry."

"Don't talk to me."

Kendrick pulls up to his home at three thirty in the morning. He opens the driver's side door, but Carlos stops him.

"This is all my fault, Kendrick, and if we get any heat from this shit, I'll take the charge. Everything's gonna be alright."

"Alright? I shot somebody. And for all we know, he might be dead." Kendrick sighs. "You think that bitch Danyelle won't rat you out? You barely know her."

"She won't."

"Can you promise me that?"

"Nah, I can't."

"Then don't say it."

Kendrick walks to his front door and pulls out his keys, but his hands are still shaking from the gun blast. He finally gets the door open, and sees his mother sitting in the living room.

"Kendrick, do you have any idea how worried I was about you? Listen, I –"

"Not tonight, ma, not tonight," he says slowly walking up the stairs and into his bedroom. Fully dressed, he collapses onto the bed and stares at the wall. He tries to close his eyes, but his mind replays the shooting. He has never felt this type of guilt before, and the only person that can forgive him is God. Kendrick falls to his knees and cries.

* * *

Days after the shooting, Carlos gets a phone call from Danyelle. He sees the number, but he is reluctant to answer. After three rings, he picks up, "Hello?"

"Mack is in stable condition."

Carlos holds the phone in silence. He is relieved that Kendrick doesn't have to deal with having murder on his conscience, but he isn't pleased that they will have to look over their shoulders for the rest of their lives.

Danyelle continues, "Everybody round here talking about what y'all did. Don't ever come to my house again."

"I'm sorry, Danyelle."

"Mack isn't going to cooperate with the police, but he has a big family and they're looking for y'all. You should've just left, Carlos."

Carlos hangs up the phone and calls Kendrick to relay the not so bad news.

"Hello?"

"I just spoke to Danyelle. Mack didn't die."

Kendrick places the phone over his chest and closes his eyes. "Thank you, Lord," he whispers.

"I'm glad that's over."

"This shit is far from over, Carlos. What would you do if somebody shot you?"

"I know you worried, but we can't let this slow us down. Forget the Eastside, we can set up shop in Heraldry Square."

"You just don't get it," Kendrick says before hanging up.

* * *

It's been a few days since Kendrick and Carlos have spoken, but that hasn't stopped Carlos from hustling. He drives house to house selling weed, and some nights he makes just enough to pay for gas. Carlos realizes he isn't using Kendrick just to help him conduct business, he also needs Kendrick's company. Carlos hates being alone; so until he and Kendrick mend their friendship, Carlos occupies that void with a girl.

One night, Carlos is staying at the Knights Inn motel laying on the bed smoking a blunt, when his freak of the week – Monica, walks out of the bathroom wearing powder blue panties and a bra.

Carlos blows a cloud of smoke. "You look good as shit."

"You want this, don't you?" she asks tapping her ass.

"Hell yeah. That's why we in this cheap ass motel, ain't it? Come here."

Carlos runs his fingertips down her curvy hips. He kisses her belly button slowly and squeezes her soft round butt with both hands until his fingers are between her ass cheeks. She pushes Carlos onto the bed, climbs on top of him, and bites his nipples. With her tongue, she works her way down. "Stop playing, Monica, and suck it."

She grips his dick, places it into her warm mouth and moves her jaw up and down.

"Spit on it," he says moaning.

Monica works up enough saliva in her mouth and does it. She pulls out his dick and a string of saliva is still attached to her bottom lip like melted cheese. He grabs her ponytail and pushes her head up and down as fast as he can until she gags. Carlos loves the sound of her choking and Monica loves the head of his dick hitting the back of her throat. She suddenly stops, slowly rolls her powder blue thongs over her knees until they hit the floor. She steps back so Carlos can see her beautiful naked body and shaved vagina.

"You ready?"

"I been ready, so stop playing wit' me."

She climbs on top of him placing her pussy close enough for him to smell her sweet scent.

Just before she feels his dick enter her wet pussy, his cell phone rings.

"You better not answer that," she says, playfully pushing him onto the bed.

"I gotta answer it."

"No you don't, Carlos."

"I'm serious, Monica. Get off me."

Monica playfully forces his wrist back onto the bed. "I'm your money right now."

"Unless you can magically turn into an old, dead, white man, you ain't money," he replies escaping her grip. He reaches for his phone on the nightstand. "M.O.E.I.U." he chuckles.

"What's that supposed to mean?"

Carlos grins. "Money over everything, including you."

Monica angrily snatches her thongs off the ground. "I knew I shouldn't have come to this dirty ass motel witchu. My friends were right, you ain't shit."

Carlos walks into the bathroom to get away from Monica's bitching, because if she says one more word, she's gonna be standing outside.

Carlos closes the bathroom door. "Wassup?"

"I heard you got some good shit," the voice says.

"Where'd you hear that from? Who's this?"

"Phil."

"Do I know you?"

"Nah, but –"

Carlos hangs up and the phone rings again. "Hello?"

"C'mon, man, you got the best shit out right now."

With Mack breathing down his neck, Carlos has no choice but to be careful. He only sells weed to a chosen few, but he didn't get into this business to turn down money.

"How much you want?"

"Two pounds."

Carlos stares at his reflection in the stained motel mirror. His sixth sense is telling him not to do it, but his ambition screams, *Get to the money.*

"Can you meet me at the Shell gas station on Rolling Road?"

"Yeah, I can do that," Carlos replies.

He walks out of the bathroom and into Monica's bitching. She yells at the top of her lungs, but Carlos can't hear a sound. All he can think about is the meeting with his new customer. He sits on the edge of the bed and begins to get dressed.

"Where you think you going? You can't leave me in here."

Carlos grabs his keys and walks to the door.

"I hate you, Carlos."

"I'll be back."

\*   \*   \*

Twenty-five minutes later, Carlos slowly pulls into the Shell gas station looking for anything suspicious, when he notices a familiar black van in the distance. He parks at pump six and a tall, light-skinned guy signals for his attention. He gets out of the car holding a bag containing two pounds of weed and walks towards him.

"How'd you get my number?"

"The streets talk, you feel me?"

Phil is dressed in all black wearing a black hat slightly cocked to the side. He is six-foot-three with broad shoulders and towers over Carlos. Everything about Phil screams this is a setup, from his jittery movements to that silly look on his face. Carlos knows he can't trade punches with him, so he keeps one hand on his gun.

"Where's the money?"

Phil points at a silver station wagon about forty yards from the gas station. "It's in my car."

"I'ma wait right here."

Phil grins showing his gold teeth. "C'mon, man, I ain't gonna do nothing to you. It's too many cameras around here anyway."

Carlos clutches his finger around the trigger and follows Phil when he feels a quick, thunderous blow to his head. The blow immediately distorts his vision and Carlos loses his balance. He aims his gun and squeezes the trigger, but it jams. Phil pulls Carlos' shirt over his bloody head and tosses his body around like a rag doll. Carlos' gun falls to the ground, just in time for him to hear people running in his direction who are obviously not coming to save him. He tries to fight them off, but only a prayer is going to stop this beating.

Carlos is being beaten so badly, he can't feel the torture, and he just wants to make it out alive. He can't see their faces, but he can hear different voices screaming, "Fuck this nigga. Kill 'em, take his money. Take his shoes. Get the weed." Carlos lies in pain holding his ribs while they snatch off his shoes.

Phil picks up Carlos' gun and presses it up against his head. "I should blow ya fucking head off."

"You got everything. Just let me go." Carlos pleads staring down the barrel of his own gun.

"Shut up," Phil yells, gun-butting him in the face.

Carlos lies face down in a puddle of his own blood. He tries to move, but he can barely breathe. Out of the corner of his eye, he watches Phil and the others run to a black van parked in the distance. After numerous attempts, he stands and drags his shoeless feet to his car. He adjusts his rear view mirror and notices a long bloody wound on the left side of his face. He pushes the key into the ignition, slams on the gas, and furiously speeds down Rolling Road until he is sitting outside of Kendrick's house. He repeatedly honks the horn until Kendrick opens the door.

Kendrick yells from his steps, "Do you know what time it is?"

Carlos is in too much pain to respond, so he continues to honk the horn until Kendrick walks to the car. Kendrick opens the passenger door, peeks in and sees Carlos' bloody gash.

"Yo, what happened?"

Carlos tries his best to speak, but first he has to swallow his own blood, "I got fucking robbed."

"You gotta go to the hospital."

"Fuck that. They took everything, my weed, my shoes and my money."

"Was it Mack?"

"I don't know," Carlos replies holding his stomach.

"Was it Sean?"

Carlos' light bulb goes off. If Mack was given the opportunity, he wouldn't rob Carlos; he would kill him. Carlos tries to light up a cigarette, but he can barely move. After numerous attempts, he flicks the lighter and inhales. "It was Sean, he set me up."

"You need to go to the hospital."

"I'm not going the damn hospital, Kendrick." Carlos flicks his cigarette out of the window, "Yo, I'll be back in ten minutes. Be ready."

"Ready for what?"

Carlos rolls his window up and speeds out of the complex.

Ever since the shooting, Kendrick has been looking for a way to tell Carlos that he is done. He realizes that as long as he and Carlos are friends, he will always be in the middle of some shit. Kendrick paces his bedroom floor. "I don't wanna do this anymore," he mumbles. Kendrick opens his closet door and looks at all of the clothes he bought, which suddenly have no value. After getting dressed, he falls to his knees and prays, "Lord, forgive me for my sins. I don't know what is about to happen, but please bring us home safe." In the middle of his prayer, he hears two soft knocks at the door. Kendrick runs downstairs, opens the front door and standing in front of him is evil ass Micky.

Micky is a freckled face 5-foot-6 bully. He is one hundred fifty pounds with a serious napoleon complex and has stories, scars, and a police record to prove it. Micky's presence alone signifies that something bad is going to happen tonight. Micky's eyes tell his story and through his pupils, you can see something is missing in his soul.

"Aye, nigga, you ready?" Micky asks.

In the back of his mind, Kendrick thinks, *I don't wanna do this,* but what comes out his mouth is, "Hell yeah."

He follows Micky to the car, and sees Carlos leaning over in the passenger seat. Carlos exhales a cloud of smoke. "You don't have to do this shit."

Kendrick watches Micky load bullets into his black nine millimeter, and he has to decide if he is man enough to go along for a ride that can change his life.

Kendrick reluctantly opens the back door. "I'm here, ain't I? Where we going?"

"Tamika's house. That bitch always know what's going on." Carlos faces Kendrick. "I need you to get some information."

Ten minutes later, they pull up in front of Tamika's house and Kendrick has never been this nervous in his life. He knocks on the door, Tamika opens it, and the smell of marijuana overwhelms him. Tamika's eyes are bloodshot red and she is obviously high.

Tamika steps outside. "Whatchu want, boy?"

"Did you tell Sean we took his shit?"

Tamika twirls her finger around her cheap matted weave. "I didn't have to. Everybody know y'all did it. If you stop following behind Carlos, you wouldn't be in this shit."

"When was the last time you talked to Sean?"

Tamika folds her arms. "Whatchu goin do for me?"

Kendrick reaches into his pocket and gives her five bags of weed, which isn't enough to last a chronic weed smoker. However, it's enough to make her talk.

"Sean hangs 'round Campfield, wit' this tall ugly nigga name Phil. He think he hard cause he big, but I heard –"

Kendrick doesn't stick around to hear another word. He walks back to the car and relays the news to the Carlos.

"I'ma kill that nigga."

Something about violence always arouses Micky. His gun is fully loaded and he's ready to put in work.

"Fuck all this talking," Micky demands. "Kendrick, you drive. We're going to Campfield to pay these niggas a visit, you feel me?"

Kendrick doesn't even want to be here, let alone drive, so he says the first excuse that comes to mind, "I don't have my license."

Micky shakes his head. "Are you serious? Take the damn keys and drive."

\* \* \*

Carlos and Micky pass the blunt back and forth until the car fills with so much smoke, they are too high to care about the consequences. No one is talking as the Couso II Cuzzo, "Live Strong" album blasts to set the mood. As they get closer to Campfield, they see a cloud of dark smoke from a grill. Kendrick circles the block and sees a group of people outside enjoying a late night neighborhood cookout. Carlos sits up and sees Phil standing on the corner with a group of people.

"That's that nigga right there," Carlos yells.

Micky takes a deep breath and pats Carlos on the shoulder. "We ain't come here for nothing, it's time to handle this business. Drive Kendrick, go."

"But it's other people out there. What if –"

Micky yells, "Shut up and step on the gas, nigga. I don't giva shit who outside."

Kendrick slams on the gas. Carlos and Micky roll down their windows and Micky doesn't hesitate. He squeezes the trigger and everyone standing on the corner runs for their lives. Carlos leans out of the passenger window and squeezes, but nothing happens. Micky continues to fire until his clip is empty.

"I think I got one," Micky brags.

While Micky tries to reload, Carlos sees Phil running in between two houses, so he hops out of the car, aims, and squeezes – but his gun jams again.

"Shit!" Carlos screams.

Kendrick has only seen shit like this in the movies. He cringes as innocent people fall to the ground from Micky's bullets. Time is not on their side and in a matter of seconds, they'll be cornered in by the police. Carlos is so determined to kill Phil that he doesn't care if he goes to jail. He re-cocks his gun, aims and shoots again, but nothing happens.

Kendrick screams, "Get in the fucking car."

Carlos jumps inside and Kendrick speeds through the neighborhood when they hear police sirens.

Kendrick panics. "Oh shit, we're gonna get locked up."

"Calm down, nigga. Go to 8th Avenue across from Corinthians. My boy lives round there," Micky says.

Minutes later, Kendrick turns onto 8th Avenue and a group of guys direct him into the garage. Kendrick parks, opens the car door, and vomits on the ground.

While Micky brags about how many people he thinks he shot, Carlos is pissed because he watched Phil escape death. Everyone is full of adrenaline except for Kendrick. He is the only one who wishes he were home.

Frustrated out of his mind, Carlos leans up against the car and mumbles, "I can't believe my fucking gun jammed. I had him."

"Maybe it wasn't meant for you to kill 'em."

"Whatchu say?" Carlos asks.

"Maybe it wasn't meant for you to kill him."

"You just don't get it, Kendrick. This ain't no fist fight, we at war."

Kendrick has had enough and finally snaps, "We at war because of your fucking greed."

Micky bursts out laughing. "I knew you was scared. Aye, Carlos, where you get this bitch-ass nigga from?"

"I ain't no bitch."

The minute he challenged Micky, Kendrick knew he fucked up. The last person he wants to piss off is a known killer.

Micky stands in Kendrick's face and stares him down. "Whatchu say?"

Before Kendrick gets the shit beat of him, Carlos steps in and pulls Kendrick away. "Are you trynna get killed?"

"I rather get killed then go to jail. Micky is a loose cannon."

"Don't worry about Micky. That's just how he is."

Kendrick grabs Carlos' arm. "I shot somebody because of you. And now, I might get shot because of you."

"You right, I did start it and I'd do it again. I'm tired of being broke. Do you gotta better plan? If not, leave me the fuck alone."

Kendrick steps back and looks at Carlos and he doesn't see his friend. Kendrick sees a man who is willing to risk everything to make a point, but even still, he can't let Carlos do this alone.

Carlos rests his arm around Kendrick's shoulders. "I know you mad, but if you down, then you down all the way. I'm finishing this shit with or without you."

Kendrick's eyes begin to water. "I don't have the guts to shoot again," he admits, "so how am I supposed to go to war?"

"All I'm asking is that you be by my side. We gotta do this."

"Alright."

"Don't worry, I got the perfect plan."

*　*　*

Micky walks to the back of the garage, returns with two different guns, and tosses one to Carlos. The gun has silver duct tape wrapped around the handle with scratch marks everywhere. This gun has been through many wars and if Micky was the owner, it definitely took a life or two. Carlos squeezes the handle, raises it and envisions putting a bullet through Sean's face.

An hour later, Kendrick knocks on Tamika's door and she quickly answers.

"Did y'all have anything to do with that shooting around Campfield? I heard four people got shot."

"I need you to call Sean and tell him you want to buy some weed."

"I'm not getting in the middle of this."

Kendrick grits his teeth. "Bitch, I ain't playing witchu. Tell him you want five pounds." He reaches into his pocket and gives Tamika enough money to pay for it. "Call him."

Tamika nervously dials Sean's number hoping he doesn't answer, but he does. She stutters from the pressure, "Hey, Sh…ah Sean, are you close by?"

"Whatchu want? I got some serious shit going on. Somebody tried to kill Phil, and I think I know who it was."

"Um, I just…I just wanna get something."

"Did you hear what I said? Not now, Tamika," Sean screams before hanging up.

Tamika looks like she wants to cry. "He hung up."

"Call again," Kendrick orders. "Tell him you want five pounds."

Tamika calls and Sean picks up. "You must've lost your mind, whatchu want?"

"Wait, don't hang up. I want five pounds."

There is an awkward silence on the phone because Tamika never spent more than twenty dollars at a time.

"Where you get that kind of money?"

"It's for my boyfriend, and he always buys a lot of weed."

Sean would rather tend to his friends who have been rushed to the hospital, but with Miles on his back, he can't afford to turn down money. "You better not be playing, Tamika."

"I swear."

"I'll be there in fifteen minutes."

Tamika hangs up and relays the news. Kendrick runs to the car and delivers the message. In exactly fifteen minutes, the same black van that Carlos saw at the gas station turns onto Tamika's block. Micky anxiously bounces in the backseat checking to make sure his gun is ready to do work. The van doors open and Sean, Donte, and Markus exit. Sean knocks on Tamika's door and she opens it clearly afraid.

"Where's the money? Hurry up."

Tamika looks around waiting for the unexpected to happen.

"By the way, when you get a boyfriend?"

Tamika is so afraid she doesn't even answer. She reaches into her jean shorts and pulls out the money. Sean takes it and counts it slowly. Every second that Sean, Markus and Donte stand on her steps, she fears being hit by gunfire.

"I gotta go, Sean."

"Hold up, Tamika. Have you seen Carlos and Kendrick?"

Tamika begins to sweat. "Only at school, why?"

"My cousin Phil told me they came round Campfield shooting."

Tamika bites her nails. "I haven't heard anything."

"The next time you see them, just give me a call. Can you do that for me?"

At this point, Tamika will say yes to anything. She just wants to get the hell out of the way and hide under her bed. Out the corner of her eye, she sees the passenger side door of Micky's car opening and she tries to rush the conversation.

"I really gotta go, Sean."

"Wait up; give me your boyfriend number. I wanna do business with him –"

While Tamika gives Sean a fake phone number, Micky yells, "Aye, Sean, is that you?"

Sean squints his eyes to get a better look. "Who dat?"

Micky is a great murderer for one reason, because he knows how to get close to his victims before they notice their life is on the line.

Micky smiles pretending to be Sean's friend. "Yooooo, where you been?"

"Do I know you?"

"You don't remember me?" Micky steps closer.

"Nah, but wassup?"

"Ain't shit up, bitch." Micky reaches under his shirt and pulls out his gun. "All of y'all get on the fucking ground."

Sean looks Tamika directly in the eyes. "Bitch, you set me up."

"No, I didn't. I swear," she screams before slamming the front door.

Moments later, Carlos and Kendrick stand by Micky's side. Carlos points his gun in Sean's face. The last time Carlos was in this situation, the power he had over someone's life was overwhelming, but this time he embraces it. Micky forces Donte and Markus to strip down to their underwear. Carlos' plan to cripple Sean's clientele wasn't flawless, but he couldn't have asked for a better ending.

"I've been planning to take your weed for weeks."

Sean shakes his head. "You shouldn't have took it. You don't understand, man. You're gonna have much bigger than problems than me."

"Shut up."

Carlos completely blacks out and repeatedly rams Sean face into the concrete. Sean begs him to stop, but that only makes Carlos ram it harder. Sean falls unconscious, but that still doesn't stop Carlos from bashing his head. All Donte and Markus can do is watch their friend being beat to death. Micky stares with a devilish grin, but Kendrick can't take anymore.

"That's enough." Kendrick yells pulling Carlos off of Sean's unconscious body. "Here, take the keys and check the van."

With bloody knuckles, Carlos rummages through the front seat of the van throwing any worthless items on the ground. He opens the side door and the potent smell of weed overwhelms him. He sees two large duffle bags stacked on top of each other. He opens it, and inside are large amounts of money, and more weed than he has ever seen. Sean regains consciousness, looks up and sees Carlos and Kendrick taking the bags out of the van.

"Don't take it, it ain't mine."

Micky laughs. "You're right, it's ours now." Micky presses the barrel of his gun onto Sean's temple.

Carlos throws the last duffel bag in the car. "C'mon, Micky, let's go."

This is the moment that Micky has been waiting for. "Turn around."

As they slowly turn around, Micky steps back, pulls the trigger and shoots Markus in the stomach, then shoots Donte in the ass. While they flop around in pain, Micky aims the gun at Sean.

"Just kill me. I'm already dead," Sean yells.

Micky stands shocked. Out of all the people he has robbed or killed, he has never heard someone beg to die. For Micky, hearing someone beg for their life is the fun part.

"You wanna die?"

Sean drops his head. "You don't understand."

Micky gives Sean one last look and runs back to the car.

* * *

Tamika watches the whole incident from her mother's bedroom window. Up until now, she used to think that being in the middle of drama was cute, but she feels regret because she is the reason that Donte and Markus are clinging on for their lives.

Moments later, cop cars and an ambulance arrive to the scene. They block off the apartment complex with yellow crime tape, and all the neighborhood residents are outside witnessing the chaos. The residents of this area are not strangers to violence, but they have never seen this many police cars and flashing lights. Sean sits on the curb with his head down being treated by one of the paramedics when he sees a pair of shiny black steel toe boots standing next to him. Sean looks up and Officer Miles is standing over him. The paramedic finishes wrapping a bandage around Sean's head and leaves.

Miles kneels down and whispers, "Please tell me this is a fucking dream."

Sean's mouth is swollen, but he tries to speak, "Carlos, Kendrick, and –"

"Who?"

"Carlos and Kendrick. They go to school with me."

"I can't believe you got robbed twice by the same people. All you had to do was drop the money off to Carter, so how could you fuck this up?"

"They set me up. I'ma get it back, I promise."

"It's too late for promises, you idiot."

\* \* \*

Miles was getting closer to paying off his debt, but now all of that was out the window because in less than an hour, Miles is expecting a call from Carter. While other police officers are on the scene performing actual police work, all Miles can think about is his body floating in the harbor. He sneaks away from the scene, jogs to his patrol car and leaves. While speeding through traffic, his cell phone rings and he knows who it is.

"Uh…Carter?"

"Where's your guy? He's late."

Miles lies, "His mother died and –"

Carter hangs up the phone.

"Shit," Miles screams while hysterically banging his fists on the steering wheel.

* * *

Twenty minutes after the robbery, Kendrick, Micky and Carlos walk into Micky's apartment. Micky dumps the bag onto his glass table, and out falls a few pounds of weed and the most money they've ever seen falls to floor.

"How we supposed to count all this?"

Micky walks into his bedroom and returns with a money counting machine. He grabs a stack of money, places it inside and waits for the 'ding' indicating that it has finishing counting. Carlos' eyes light up like they've hit the lottery. After counting the money, the total amounts to forty-thousand. They each stare at the money neatly stacked on the floor and something about seeing all this money quickly changes the mood in the room. Carlos gets so excited that he completely forgets that two people have been shot. Plus, if Tamika snitches, they could be in jail by the end of the night. From the very beginning of all this drama, Kendrick never wanted to be a part of Carlos' plan, but as he stares at the money, even he can't deny that this was the greatest robbery of all time.

Carlos yells at the top of his lungs, "We fucking did it. We need to split it three ways."

Carlos reaches for the money, but Micky stops him.

"Whatchu doing?"

Micky picks up his gun. "We ain't splitting shit."

Carlos laughs. "Stop playing." He reaches for the money again, but Micky cocks his weapon.

"This ain't personal, Carlos, but I can't split this wit y'all. I need all of it."

"You're serious?"

Micky raises the gun higher. "Whatchu think?"

Carlos fearlessly stares down the barrel of Micky's gun. "Fuck that. You wouldn't even have known about this if I didn't pull you in."

"I'm not going to say it again, and don't make me show you, Carlos. I've known you all my life, but if I have to, I will kill you."

Micky reaches down, grabs three thousand dollars and tosses it to Carlos. "Take it or leave it."

Carlos has seen Micky do many things to people, but he never thought he would be on the receiving end. His heart races and Carlos is actually contemplating dying just to prove a point. His gun is wedged behind his back, but he knows if he attempts to grab it, Micky will kill him and Kendrick. Carlos stands waiting for this sick joke to end, but it doesn't. Micky has always been a double crossing maggot, but this takes it to a new level.

"How we supposed to get home?"

Micky reaches in his pocket and tosses the keys to his old station wagon. "I don't need these anymore," he says arrogantly.

Micky aims his gun and walks them to the front door. "It's not personal, Carlos."

Carlos lunges for Micky, but Kendrick grabs him and forces him outside.

"Let's go. It's not worth it."

115

"Whatchu mean? That bitch ass nigga took everything."

Kendrick has never seen Carlos this angry. He has always been full of pride, but he's clearly broken by Micky's betrayal. Carlos continues to fight, but Kendrick holds him tighter until he finally stops.

"Why are you so mad about money that you didn't even know existed? We still got the weed that we took from Sean."

"That's not the point. We coulda had more."

Carlos gets inside the car and drives off. He watches Micky's apartment from the rear view mirror and the further he gets, the angrier he becomes.

"You think we can just go back to our normal lives? We got Mack, Sean, Markus and Donte on our backs and we ain't got shit to show for it." Carlos finally breaks down, "All I wanna do is be successful and stop living like a fucking bum. I'm taking care of myself and my mother. I'm just a child," Carlos cries. "I don't deserve this shit."

"Is forty-grand worth risking your life?"

Carlos stares Kendrick in the eyes. "Yeah, nigga, it is."

* * *

Afraid to go home, Miles turns off the dispatcher and parks in a secluded area. He reaches inside of a brown bag, pulls out a bottle of Vodka, leans his seat back and guzzles as much as he can. He grabs his gun and places it against his temple. "Do it." He mumbles.

116

"Just do it." He adjusts his finger around the trigger and closes his eyes, but he doesn't have the heart to take his own life. Miles isn't the type to face the consequences. If he is going to die, then he is going to make sure everyone feels the pain. At 6:44 am, the sounds of birds chirping wake him up. Miles opens the driver's door and stretches. He checks his phone and there are five missed calls from Carter. It's just a matter of time before they catch him, so he calls Sean.

Sean sits at home with a bandage around his face. When he sees Miles' number, he quickly answers, "I'm sorry, I –"

"Shut up, I know you're sorry. You're a sorry piece of shit. You cost me sixty grand, but do you know why you're still alive? Because I need to know everything about Carlos and Kendrick."

\* \* \*

Miles now knows that Carlos and Kendrick live in the Woodlawn area. Sean also gave him a detailed description of what they look like. The kids are out for summer vacation, so Miles hopes that Carlos and Kendrick are stupid enough to be outside. After hours of driving around the Woodlawn area, he calls in a favor.

"Aye, Tank, this is Miles."

"Wassup?"

"I need you to help me get some information out of these two kids who stole a lot of money from me. Can you meet me at the shopping center on Rolling Road in an hour?"

"Yeah."

Miles and Tank aren't friends, but they have an interesting relationship. Miles allows Tank to hustle without police interference and in return, Tank and his goons do Miles' dirty work when needed.

In exactly an hour, Miles sees a blue Crown Victoria pulling up beside him. Miles rolls down the passenger window and says, "Follow me."

Miles pulls out of the shopping center and Tank follows behind him. They patrol the area when Miles sees someone resembling Kendrick's description walking into the store. He slows down to get a better look. "I gotchu," Miles says. From inside the police car, Miles calls Tank.

"Yeah wassup?"

"The kid wearing a black shirt, shorts and a Baltimore Oriole's hat should be coming out in a second. That little bastard took a lot of money from me, but don't kill him. He can't help me if he's dead."

*   *   *

Kendrick walks out of the store, and notices a guy standing awkwardly in the distance. *Who the hell is that?* Kendrick tries to remain calm, but he can feel the stranger's eyes following him. Even though Kendrick vowed to himself to never touch or shoot a gun again, he wishes he were prepared.

From inside of the police car, Miles watches from a distance, "Get that muthafucker."

118

Tanks steps closer, "You Kendrick, right? I think you know why I'm here."

Kendrick's stomach turns in knots. He attempts to run in a zigzag pattern, but he doesn't get far. Tank grabs Kendrick's shirt and drags him to the back of a salon. He punches Kendrick repeatedly in the face.

"Where's the fucking money?" Tank yells.

Kendrick puts up a fight until he feels a sharp slash on his side. The slash startles him, but his adrenaline numbs the pain. He feels another sharp pain then again, and again, then again. He looks up and sees Tank holding a six-inch blade stained with his blood. A warm trickling sensation pours from his side, and his breaths begin to fade. Kendrick's life is leaving his body. He falls to the ground and Tank stomps him.

"Where's the money?"

Kendrick curls up on the ground. "I ain't got it! Please stop it."

Kendrick feels a thunderous blow across his back and the pain is so unbearable it takes his breath away. Tank picks up a piece of heavy plywood and raises it above Kendrick's head.

"Ok, ok. Please stop." Kendrick is in so much pain, he can barely speak, "M...Mic...ky got the money."

The back door of the salon swings open, the owner sees Kendrick on the ground bleeding and screams, "I'm calling the police."

Miles sits crouched in the patrol car, when he sees Tank running towards him.

"What happened?"

119

Tank breathes heavily with bloodstains on his shirt. "He said somebody name Micky gotcha money."

"Is that his blood on your shirt?"

"Yeah."

"Is he alive?"

"Barely, I cut him a few times."

"Just get outta here."

Tank runs to his car and leaves, but Miles stays to watch. He turns on the dispatcher and waits for the report. *"I need all units, in the Woodlawn area. A man has been brutally stabbed at Magnificent Hair Salon on Rolling Road."*

Within minutes, an ambulance and four police cars pull up to the salon. Miles hasn't smiled in weeks, but when he sees Kendrick being placed on stretcher he can't help but feel joy. He may not have his money, but he is getting closer to tracking it down. Miles slowly pulls off. Now, he needs to find out who the hell Micky is.

\* \* \*

Amy is working hard at her second job when she gets a call that her son has been critically injured. Still in her work uniform, she pushes open the hospital doors and runs frantically to the receptionist desk.

"Where is he?" she screams, "My son. He –"

"You have to calm down. Who are you looking for?"

"His name is Kendrick Rumsfeld. Please hurry."

The receptionist rummages through the logbook and gives her the room number. Amy rushes down the hall until she reaches the room where her son has been admitted. Kendrick's left wrist is in a cast, his eyes are swollen shut, and he lies motionless with tubes attached to his arm.

"It's me, mommy," she says crying.

"He's highly medicated and can't talk," the nurse says rolling Kendrick on his side. She lifts his hospital gown and peels off the bloody bandage exposing his stitched up scars.

"Can you please tell me something?"

"Your son was stabbed and lucky to be alive. I know this is hard for you, but I'm sure Dr. Douglas will be able to answer your questions. He'll be here shortly."

Soon after the nurse leaves, Dr. Douglas walks in. He lowers his glasses and flips the pages on the clipboard. "You must be Kendrick's mother. He has multiple stab wounds just inches away from a major blood vessel and we are experiencing problems with stopping the internal bleeding. We stitched him up pretty well, but he's losing a lot of blood."

"Is he going to –" Amy stops unable to fathom the question.

Dr. Douglas looks for the right words, "I promise you, we're going to do the best we can."

*  *  *

The morning sun beams through the hospital window awakening Amy. She falls to her knees praying for God's mercy when the hospital door opens. "What are you doing here?"

121

"I came to see my son."

"Your son? How'd you find out?"

"Word travels fast on the streets. I thought you were taking care of him. What happened?"

Amy clinches her fists in rage. "You no good son of a bitch. How dare you question how I raise my son?"

Gil steps closer. "I shouldn't have said that, so I'm sorry." He stands over Kendrick's body. "Where did we go wrong?"

"We? There is no 'we' Gil, it's been just me. And if you did your damn job, maybe Kendrick wouldn't be in this hospital fighting for his life."

She collapses on the couch clearly exhausted with grief. Gil sits down next to her and places his arm around her shoulder.

"Everything's gonna be alright."

Amy cries uncontrollably, "I don't know what to do. I can't work two jobs and watch him at all times."

"This isn't your fault. You're doing the best you can."

\* \* \*

Back in his day, Gil was a man's man, likable and full of promising hope and ambition. He was a hard worker and well respected in the community. Unfortunately, like most veterans, Gil got his first taste of heroin while fighting in the Vietnam War.

When Kendrick was born, Amy hoped that the birth of his first and only son would give Gil the strength to beat his addiction, but the pressure to provide only pushed him further into hopelessness. For years, Amy tried to help her husband get back to normalcy, but his addiction took complete control over his mind, body and soul.

Gil failed as a husband and a father, but today, he is doing something he hasn't done in over a decade, which is support his wife. Gil sits down next to Amy and places his arms around her shoulders. She may despise Gil for what he has become, but she still loves him. Amy, emotionally drained, falls asleep in Gil's arms while Gil admires her beauty. He remembers when they were just high school sweethearts planning their futures.

While holding his first true love, Gil begins to experience withdrawals. His skin crawls, his knees shake and beads of sweat roll down his back. He glances down and sees Amy's purse on the floor. With his left hand, he carefully pulls the zipper down and a twenty-dollar bill hangs from the side pocket. He snatches the money. Carefully, he slips out from under Amy's head. He walks over to Kendrick's ear and whispers, "Be better than me, Kendrick."

Hours later, Carlos pushes the hospital door open and taps Kendrick's mother on the shoulder awakening her. "How long have you been here?" she asks.

"I just got here."

Amy can tell someone touched her purse. "I can't believe it," she says, checking to make sure nothing else has been taken. "Once a thief, always a thief."

"Is everything alright?"

"Kendrick's father – never mind. Carlos, can you tell me what happened?"

Carlos still doesn't know what happened. He believes that Sean is responsible, but he won't tell Kendrick's mother. He stares at Kendrick's body and a great deal of grief comes over him.

Amy cries, "He's not moving or saying anything. Maybe you can get something out of him. I have to get some air."

Carlos watches Kendrick closely. He touches Kendrick's hand, bows his head, and begins to pray when he feels someone standing behind him. Carlos turns around."How you doing, sir?"

Officer Miles expected Carlos to be much bigger, but he's just a scrawny little kid.

"You're Carlos, right?"

"Yes, sir."

"Would this have anything to do with that shooting that occurred in Heraldry Square?"

"What shooting?"

"You don't know who I am, do you?"

Carlos glances at his badge. "You're Officer Miles."

Miles walks over to the bed and lifts up the blanket exposing Kendrick's bare feet. "This little piggy went to the market, this little piggy stayed at home, this little piggy had roast beef, and this little piggy had none." Miles squeezes Kendrick's toe. "And this little piggy went, 'wee wee wee' all the way home. He has the perfect foot for a toe tag. Another nigger bites the dust."

Before Carlos responds, Amy returns. Miles quickly plays the good cop, and Carlos despises every second of it. He takes off his hat and extends his hand.

124

"You must be Kendrick's mom. I am Officer Miles. I arrested the guys who did this to your son and I promise you, we're going to make sure they're prosecuted to the fullest extent of the law."

"Thank you so much, sir. It is good to know that there are still police officers out here that care. Please, make sure they pay for what they did to my son."

Officer Miles looks at Carlos and forges a smile. "It'll be my pleasure, Ms. Amy. Aye, Carlos, I'll see you around."

"I'm glad he's on the case," Amy says. "I hope he catch those bastards."

Completely dumbfounded, Carlos replies sarcastically, "Yeah, me too, Ms. Amy."

# CHAPTER IV

At 10:30 in the evening, Micky leaves McDonalds and walks to his black Range Rover. He's wearing a gold Invicta watch and a diamond bracelet. When people like Micky get money they spend it quickly, and clearly Micky is throwing money around. While Micky talks on the phone, a silver car with dark tinted windows pulls up and blocks him in. Micky places his cup on the hood of his car and reaches for his keys when Sean and two men jump out with guns. Micky stands stiff and braces himself.

"I knew I'd catch you."

"Fuck you. Go 'head. Whatchu waiting for?"

Sean raises his gun. "Where's the money?"

Micky grins showing his gold teeth and expensive jewelry. "You're looking at."

Sean cocks his weapon and Micky knows his next words will decide his fate. Micky is a strong believer in the term, *"Get it how you live."* So he does what he wants because he accepts his fate. While staring at Sean's gun, everything he has done flashes in his mind. Micky says a quick prayer to himself and looks them in their eyes just in case he survives.

Micky takes a deep breath, frowns and yells, "Y'all some bitches, you ain't got the heart to do –"

Sean squeezes the trigger, and empties his clip into Micky's body. He gets pleasure in watching Micky flop around like a fish out of water. He snatches off Micky's jewelry, reaches into Micky's pocket takes his car key and kicks his dead body in the face one last time. The two men run back to the car and Sean jumps inside of Micky's Range Rover and drives recklessly out of the McDonald's parking lot. While swerving through traffic, Sean calls Miles.

"You got a lot of fucking nerve calling me."

"I got Micky."

"Did you get the money?"

"Nah, but –"

"Meet me at Hurley Avenue near Gwynn's Falls."

Officer Miles leans up against his patrol car when a Range Rover parks next to him. Sean hops out and walks towards Miles with a huge smile on his face.

"I know I messed up, but look what I got."

Sean opens his palm and shows Miles the jewelry he took from Micky. Sean watches as Miles inspects the jewelry, and he can sense that he is not impressed. "You lost sixty grand and all you got is a watch and a bracelet."

Sean pleads, "What about his Range Rover? I know you can get at least seventeen grand for it."

"Do I look like a damn car salesman? Where's Micky?"

"He's dead, I killed him."

"You what?" Miles realizes that all the hard work he has done is in vain. Miles steps closer to Sean. "If Micky is dead, how am I supposed to get my money back? You cost me sixty-grand."

Miles hits Sean in the face as hard as he can and the more Sean screams, the angrier Miles becomes. With his steel toe boots, he kicks Sean's back. Sean knows if he puts up a fight, he'll die, so he deals with the torture.

"Open ya mouth."

"Just give me another –"

"I said 'open ya mouth'."

Sean closes his eyes and opens wide. With his right hand, Miles holds the back of Sean's head to keep him from moving. He grabs his mace, presses down on the nozzle and blasts pepper spray down Sean's throat. Sean feels like he is suffocating and he coughs so hard his chest hurts. Each time he gasps for air, it feels like his next breath may never come, but that doesn't stop Miles' torture.

"You dumb muthafucka."

Miles holds his baton like a baseball bat waiting for the right time to knock his head off. He swings and strikes Sean in the forehead. Not being able to breathe turns out to be the least of Sean's worries. His forehead leaks blood and everything is spinning.

Miles stands over top of him. "I told you if you ever fucked me over, you would spend the rest of your life in jail." Breathing heavily, Miles grabs his dispatcher and lies, "Officer in duress! This is Officer Miles. I'm at Hurley Avenue near Gwynn's Falls, and I need help. Suspect was resisting arrest, and he's armed and dangerous. Help." He screams and fires one shot in the air for the affect.

Miles doesn't have much time, so he puts two ounces of cocaine into Sean's pocket. Sean is so badly beaten that he doesn't realize that when he regains consciousness, he is going to be behind bars. Miles turns Sean's limp body on his stomach and cuffs him. Moments later, a barrage of police cars pull to the scene with their guns drawn. They secure Officer Miles and handle Sean with excessive force.

Officer Miles pretends to be a hero. "He tried to kill me. He got two ounces of cocaine in his right pocket. Run the tags on this Range Rover. I think it might be connected to a shooting."

The paramedic tries to tend to Miles' wounds, but he doesn't have that kind of time to waste. While the officers place Sean into the paddy wagon, Miles gets inside of his patrol car and leaves. He drives thirty minutes to Columbia, Maryland, and parks in Buckner's driveway. Buckner sees the headlights, walks over to his window and peeks through his shades. "What the hell is he doing at my house?" Buckner says. Since Miles' deal with Carter, Buckner distanced himself. Buckner is too close to retirement to deal with Miles' bullshit.

Miles rings the bell and Buckner cracks the door just enough to show half of his face. "What are you doing here?"

"I messed up, Buckner. Can I come in?"

Buckner reluctantly opens the door and looks around to make sure the coast is clear. He leads Miles downstairs to his basement and pours two shots of aged Whisky.

"You look like shit."

"I haven't been to sleep in days." Miles swallows the shot and signals for another. "I almost had Carter's money, but –"

Buckner can see it in Miles' eyes that he is about to ask for a favor, so he cuts to the chase. "I ain't giving you shit, Miles. You dug your own grave with this one. This is all part of the game."

Miles didn't expect Buckner to help but what irritates him is how Buckner casually talks about his death.

Buckner sits on the couch and lights up a cigarette. "You should've never promised Carter you could sell that much weight."

"Like I had a choice. If I said I couldn't, he was gonna kill me. And you sat there and watched."

"My hands were tied, but not anymore. I'm done with this shit. I got my money and I got my peace of mind. I'm retiring in three months."

Miles pulls out his gun and aims it at Buckner's chest. "I'm sorry, Buckner, but I ain't ready to die."

Buckner's cigarette falls out of his mouth and burns a hole into the carpet. "You fucking piece of shit. You bring this shit to my home?"

"It's all part of the game, remember? Now get up. I know it's here; I can smell it, and you're arrogant enough to keep it here."

Buckner stands up and Miles presses his gun against Buckner's back. He can see desperation in Miles' eyes, so all he can do is strike a deal to stay alive.

"Ok, how much do you owe Carter?"

"I'm eighty grand short."

Buckner leads Miles into the back of his basement. The lights are dim, the walkway is cluttered with worthless items and it looks like a trap. Buckner never told the truth about how much he made. He learned in the extortion business that you must always save enough money to pay your way out of danger.

Buckner stops. "Can you take your damn gun off my back?"

Buckner kneels down, and pushes a heavy box to the side. Inside of the floor is a custom-built safe. He punches in the code and the door pops open. Buckner reaches down and pulls out a black box. Buckner knew that one day, this black box would come in handy, but he never thought some rookie white cop would be the one to take it. Buckner flips opens the black box and Miles sees stacks of money lying perfectly side by side.

"That's a hundred grand which should cover your debt with Carter. Now get the fuck out my house."

"It's all part of the game."

"Carter is still gonna kill you, and when he does, we'll both be laughing at your funeral."

With his gun pointing in Buckner's face, Miles backs out through the cluttered basement and leaves. He doesn't feel one bit of guilt for taking Buckner's money. A huge weight has been lifted off his shoulders and he can finally get Carter off his back. Still afraid to go home, he drives to the liquor store and gets a room at a cheap motel across town. The motel room walls are dingy and the floor is surrounded with spots, but this is the most relaxed Miles has been in weeks. After taking a shower, Miles sits on the edge of the bed drinking a tall glass of Vodka. He isn't sure if Carter will kill him, but it's worth a try. He picks up his phone and calls Carter.

"I've been trying to reach you, Miles. I thought you left town."

Miles clears his throat. "Why would I do that?"

"You better be calling to tell me you have my money."

"That's exactly why I'm calling."

"Good, I'll see you tomorrow," Carter says before hanging up.

* * *

The next day, Miles meets with Carter at his downtown condominium. The last time he visited Carter's condominium, it was filled with people who wanted to kill him. He walks down the long hallway with a duffle bag over his shoulder. He knocks on the door and instead of some goon answering, Carter himself is there to greet him. Miles walks inside and throws the bag on the table. "It's all there.

Carter doesn't even look inside of the bag. He throws his arm around Miles' shoulders and escorts him to the patio.

"I spoke to Buckner."

"I'm sorry things didn't go the way I intended and –"

Carter bursts out laughing. "What are you apologizing for? In business, there's no such thing as friends. You do what you have to do." Carter continues to laugh. "If you were smart, you would've robbed him earlier."

"Were you really going to kill me?"

Carter smiles showing his perfectly straight white teeth. "Whatchu think?"

Miles looks at Carter from head to toe admiring his tailored suit and expensive shoes. Now that his debt is cleared, he can just walk away from the extortion business and become a legitimate cop, but giving out traffic tickets isn't going to give him the lavish life he wants.

Miles clears his throat. "I wanna start making some real money. Can you help me?"

Carter stares at the city skyline and laughs. "Why would I do business with someone that let two high school kids take 'em outta business?"

"You knew about that?"

Carter flicks his half-lit cigarette over the balcony. "I know everything, rookie."

# CHAPTER V

After his encounter with Officer Miles at the hospital, Carlos doesn't know what to believe. He sits in his room flicking through the television channels trying to put the pieces together, but nothing is making sense. After brainstorming for hours, he walks into the bathroom and splashes water on his face. "What the hell is going on?" He splashes his face with water again when he hears. *"Mikel Stafford, also known as Micky, was viciously shot down and killed at a McDonald's parking lot yesterday evening. The shooter, Sean Miller, was arrested and taken into custody."*

Carlos runs into his room and turns up the volume. He smiles, pointing at the television. "That's what you get." Carlos jumps up and down cheering like he won the lottery. He couldn't have asked for a better scenario; Sean is locked up and Micky is dead. Carlos still doesn't know why that cop came to visit Kendrick, but he doesn't care. He wishes he could call Kendrick and give him the news, but Kendrick is still recovering in the hospital.

The next day, Carlos wakes up feeling refreshed. He takes a shower, gets dressed and runs downstairs. The only thing on Carlos' mind is getting back to business and turning his neighborhood into a twenty-four hour weed strip. With his pockets filled with weed, he walks around the neighborhood looking for the perfect spot to setup shop. He walks towards the basketball court and it's filled with people. *Bingo.*

Carlos walks onto the basketball court and gives out free bags of weed. A crowd gathers around him and Carlos sees the potential. He spent most of his day at the basketball court and his plan is working to perfection.

Within a month, Carlos made a name for himself and customers come from different parts of Baltimore County to purchase his weed. For the rest of the summer, Carlos made thousands of dollars, purchased a red Lexus 400 and moved out of his mother's home and into a small one bedroom apartment. In the past, Carlos criticized Kendrick for trying to sell weed in their neighborhood, but now he sees that Kendrick's way is right.

Carlos hasn't visited Kendrick since his encounter with Miles, but he misses him greatly.

One hot afternoon, Carlos sits on the bench watching his friends play basketball when he receives a call.

"Hey, Ms. Amy, is everything ok?"

"Yes, Kendrick came home today and he wants to see you."

Carlos smiles because finally things are beginning to turn around. "I'm on my way."

\* \* \*

Carlos pulls up in front of Kendrick's home, runs up his steps and knocks on the door. Amy greets him with a huge hug. He walks upstairs and pushes Kendrick's bedroom door open.

He grunts in pain. "Wassup?"

Carlos pulls out two large knots of cash. "The money, that's wassup. I got the whole neighborhood buying from me. The basketball court is filled with people right now waiting for me to come back. Soon as you get back on your feet, it's on."

Carlos has so much to say that he can barely stand still. "You're not gonna believe what happened. Sean killed Micky, and his dumbass got locked up that same day. That's two birds with one stone."

Carlos thinks to tell Kendrick about Officer Miles' visit, but he doesn't want him to worry. He sits on the edge of the bed. "I'm glad you're home and soon as you get ready, we're gonna take this shit over."

Kendrick struggles to lift his head up. "Everything's fucked up."

"Did you hear anything I said? Sean ain't never getting out, and Micky's dead."

"My mother had to quit her second job to take care of me and the bills are backed up. I can't fool wit' this shit no more."

"That must be the pain killers talking. If your mother's bills are backed up, then you need to get out here with me."

Kendrick rolls over on his side. "I need you to change this bandage for me."

Carlos lifts up Kendrick's shirt revealing the puss filled scar. After putting on a fresh bandage, Carlos steps back and stares while Kendrick struggles to get comfortable. He hoped that Kendrick would be anxious to get back into the game, but he can see how that stabbing changed Kendrick's desire to hustle. Truthfully, Kendrick never had it.

For the first time, Carlos can see their lives going in different directions. Carlos knows if Kendrick doesn't possess the same passion, he'll just be in the way, so he makes a decision that he will never pull Kendrick back into the world of hustling.

After talking and playing catch up, Carlos stands to his feet and kisses Kendrick's forehead. "Yo, I gotta go, but call me if you need anything."

Before closing the bedroom door, Carlos looks at Kendrick for what might be the last moment they spend together. He runs downstairs and notices a pile of letters from bill collectors spread across the living room table.

Amy walks out of the kitchen and whispers, "Is he ok? He's been a little down."

"He'll be fine." Carlos looks into the kitchen and sees smoke. "I think you're burning something."

When Amy runs into the kitchen, Carlos snatches an empty envelope, stuffs cash inside and places it on the living room table.

"I gotta go, Ms. Amy."

"Ok, honey, don't be a stranger."

\* \* \*

After feeding and bathing Kendrick, Amy takes off her shoes and opens up her mail. After reading multiple late notices, she sees a strange unsealed envelope. She looks inside and almost loses her breath. "Oh my God." She screams dumping the money onto the table, "Keddy, you're not gonna believe it." She runs upstairs. "Look, this must be a mistake."

Kendrick grins. He knew Carlos put it in there because that's the kind of person Carlos is. He wants to give his mother a long hug, but all he can do is smile.

"You gotta keep it, mommy. Don't you need it?"

"Lord knows I do, honey. I can't believe this is happening." She counts the money. "Thank you Jesus. It's sixteen hundred dollars in here. I can do so much with this."

Kendrick loves seeing how happy she is, and he realizes that sitting around isn't going to help.

\* \* \*

A month later, Kendrick is fully rehabilitated, and the first thing he does is walk to the basketball court to see Carlos' weed strip. This area used to be as quiet as a library, but now it's the new hangout spot. Kendrick is impressed with what Carlos has done and decides he wants a piece.

Carlos sits on the bench watching his friends play basketball when he feels a tap on his shoulder.

"I'm back," Kendrick screams.

*Damn, I knew this was going to happen.* "It's good to see you, my nigga."

"I need to talk to you."

They walk away from the crowd and Kendrick looks him in the eyes. "Thanks, that money helped us out a lot. We almost got evicted."

"I owe you, and whatever you need just let me know."

Kendrick looks around in shock. "You really turned this old basketball court into a money making machine." Kendrick pats Carlos on the back. "I want in."

Carlos is glad to see Kendrick spirits are up, but he isn't convinced that Kendrick has the heart. In the beginning, it was part of Carlos' plan to have Kendrick by his side and now he has to find a way to talk Kendrick out of it.

"Say something, nigga. I'm ready to get this money. When do I start? I still got eight pounds in my mother's basement."

"You need to take it slow, Kendrick."

Kendrick steps back and stares. He always felt like Carlos didn't want him to be equal but now he knows it. "Take it slow? What's that supposed to mean?"

Carlos gets irritated. "This hustling shit ain't for you."

"It was my idea to hustle in our own neighborhood and now you telling me I can't get a piece? I knew you was a selfish ass nigga."

"I made you! Before me, you was nothing but a scared little virgin."

Kendrick steps in Carlos' face. "You made me? If it wasn't for me, Micky woulda killed ya ass."

Carlos pulls out his gun. "If you still that nigga, then take my gun and shoot it in the air."

Kendrick stares at Carlos' black nine millimeter and he doesn't even have the heart to touch it.

"That's what I thought. I'm dedicated to this shit." Carlos puts his gun into his pocket. "I built this neighborhood up and I worked too hard to let you mess it up."

Kendrick points his middle finger inches away from Carlos' face and yells, "Fuck you."

"Trust me; I'm doing you a favor," Carlos insists.

"Look around you, Carlos. You're surrounded by new faces, but as soon as you hit rock bottom, they're gonna disappear. And when they do, don't call me."

Carlos regretfully watches Kendrick walk away. He isn't happy with how their friendship ends, but he knows that he is doing what is best for Kendrick.

Later that evening, Carlos walks towards his Lexus, and he opens the door when a cop car pulls up abruptly. Officer Miles jumps out, grabs him by the shirt and forces him in the backseat.

"Whatchu want from me?"

"You know exactly what I want."

Miles drives into the police station and roughly escorts Carlos in to a cold room. "Strip," he orders.

Carlos takes off each piece of clothing until he is standing stark naked.

"Turn around and spread your butt cheeks."

Carlos has never been this humiliated and powerless in his life. He turns around and with both hands spreads his butt cheeks until he feels the cold air on his rectum.

"I'm tired of fucking around witchu. That money you took outta that van was mine." He removes his nightstick from his belt. "You got two options: work for me and pay me back or I'll make your life a living hell."

"I don't know whatchu talking 'bout."

"Sean was working for me."

"I didn't know. He robbed me, so I robbed him, that's how the game goes."

"Where's the money?"

"Micky took it, but he's dead."

"You must think I'm stupid. How else can you afford a Lexus at your age?"

Carlos lies. "It ain't mine."

Officer Miles places the tip of his nightstick against Carlos' anus. "I should ram my nightstick up your pretty little ass."

"Fuck you," Carlos yells, bracing for the excruciating pain.

"Fuck me? Nah, it looks like you about to get fucked."

Miles readjusts his fingers around the baton and begins to push his nightstick inside. Carlos clinches from pain until his fingernails bend from scrapping the walls.

"You're my little bitch," Miles whispers while pushing his baton further. "All you gotta do is work for me and all this will go away. You'll make more money than you ever have."

Carlos grunts. "I'd rather get fucked by a night stick than work for a dirty cop, you fucking pig."

Just before Miles shoves his nightstick, another officer bangs on the door. "Aye, Miles, I need this room. I gotta do a strip search, so hurry up."

"Ok, shit, gimme a second." Miles removes the tip of his nightstick from Carlos' anus and Carlos collapses to the ground. "Putcha clothes on, you faggot."

Carlos can barely move, but he gathers up enough strength to get dressed. Miles roughly escorts him into a waiting cell and for three hours, Carlos lies on the cold, hard floor.

On this same evening, Kendrick sits at the table eating dinner with his mother. Amy tries to have a conversation, but all he can think about is his argument with Carlos. Just around the corner from his home is a basketball court filled with customers and in his basement is enough weed to satisfy their needs. Kendrick never wasted Amy's food and she becomes worried.

"What's wrong, honey?"

"I'm just not hungry."

"I raised you, so I know when something is wrong. Do you wanna talk about it?"

Kendrick pushes his chair back. "No."

He leaves his plate on the table, walks upstairs to his room and locks the door. The last thing Kendrick wants to do is go to war with his best friend, but he has to think about himself. He's tired of seeing eviction notices on his door and seeing his mother stressing over the bills. He can help and he isn't going to allow Carlos to stop him. At 10:35 in the evening, Kendrick opens his bedroom door and quietly walks downstairs into the basement. He reaches behind the broken dryer, grabs the bag of weed and opens it. "I gotta do what I gotta do," Kendrick mumbles putting thirty bags of weed into his pocket. He puts the bag back behind the broken dryer and walks upstairs. He quietly opens the front door and leaves. Kendrick walks towards the basketball court when he sees his friend Jermaine.

"Yo, Jermaine, I got that weed," Kendrick shouts.

"I can't, man."

"Whatchumean you can't?"

"I don't know what's going on with you and Carlos, but Carlos told everyone not to buy weed from you."

"Stop playing, Jermaine. How many bags do you want?"

"I'm sorry, man."

Kendrick places his weed back into his pocket. *I can't believe this shit.* Kendrick can see all the people on the basketball court and his heart fills with hate. Before leaving, he faces Jermaine. "You're gonna let Carlos tell you what to do like he's your father now?"

"It's not personal, Kendrick, I just don't wanna get caught up in y'all shit. You feel me?"

All that he has been through to fit in, Kendrick has become an outcast in his own neighborhood. He glances at the basketball court one last time before leaving.

\* \* \*

Spending thirty-two hours in a small cell, gave Carlos time to put all the pieces together. All this time, Carlos thought Sean was his own man, but Sean's strings were being pulled by a corrupt cop.

After being released from jail, Carlos leans up against the wall waiting for a cab. A half hour later, the cab arrives and Carlos limps towards it. He sits down slowly and his ass is still sore from Miles' baton. Carlos knows that this isn't the last visit from Officer Miles, but next time he is going to be prepared.

While sitting in the back of the cab, Carlos stares out the window. As they drive through the city, Carlos' life flashes before his eyes and he feels guilty. For the mighty dollar, Carlos put people in harm's way, and lied and manipulated anyone who was weak enough to fall for it. Even though he is making money, he isn't proud of what he's become.

Twenty minutes later, the cab driver arrives at his destination. Carlos pays the fair, opens the door and walks towards his car. The basketball court is filled with people, but Carlos doesn't walk onto the court. Instead, he opens his car door and drives to Kendrick's home. Within minutes, Carlos is standing in front of the home. He doesn't know what to expect, but he knocks. The door swings open and Kendrick and Carlos stand face to face.

"Whatchuwant?"

Carlos shakes his head. "We got some serious problems."

"We? Oh it's 'we' now?"

"I know you mad, but I think you should know what's going on."

Normally, Kendrick would let Carlos into his home. Instead, he closes the front door and stands outside. "I'm listening."

Carlos tells Kendrick everything leaving Kendrick speechless. As Carlos continues to explain, Kendrick's hate begins to fade. They may not be as close as they once were, but Kendrick doesn't want to see Carlos get hurt.

"I don't know what to do anymore." Carlos sighs, "I can't do this without you."

"You were right about me, Carlos. I'm not built for this game, but you are. You'll figure it out, just like you always do. Wait right here." Kendrick goes back into the house and walks downstairs in the basement. He grabs his bag containing eight pounds of weed and walks back outside without his mother noticing. Kendrick hands Carlos the bag.

"You can use this more than me," Kendrick says.

Carlos is shocked. He can make a lot of money with eight pounds of weed, but this will never amount to the friendship that he had with Kendrick.

"I didn't come here for your weed, Kendrick."

"I gotta go, Carlos, but be careful."

Carlos wants to beg Kendrick to be by his side, but that time has come for them to part ways. Carlos throws the bag over his shoulder and extends his hand. "I'll see you around."

Kendrick watches as Carlos walks back to his car. He feels bad, but for the first time, Kendrick is thinking about himself.

# CHAPTER VI

Graduation from Woodlawn High school is no different from any other graduation ceremony. The year is 1996 and the future doctors, lawyers, scientists, killers, losers, and bums sit in boredom waiting to hear their name over the loud intercom.

The announcer calls Kendrick's name, and he grabs his high school diploma and poses for the picture. While standing on the stage staring at hundreds of people, Kendrick realizes that once he walks out of this building, he is no longer a teenager. He is a man and he has no plan.

Carlos, on the other hand, doesn't attend graduation; instead, he's shooting dice at the basketball court. While shaking the dice, someone calls his name.

Carlos looks up. "Do I know you?"

"Nah, I'm Antoine. We should talk."

"Whatchu need? I got dimes, twenties and Vicks."

Antoine chuckles. "I didn't come for that."

Carlos hates when people interrupt a dice game, but by the looks of Antoine's clothes and jewelry, a conversation might be worth it.

Carlos stands to his feet. "Follow me," he leads walking away from everyone.

"You gotta nice thing going on here," Antoine says. "You gotta connect?"

"You look like a cop."

"I ain't no fucking cop."

Antoine pulls out a tightly rolled blunt. He takes two longs drags and passes it to Carlos.

Carlos inhales and his eyes grow wide. The weed that Carlos has is just ok, but the weed that Antoine has is that real good shit.

Carlos coughs. "What the hell is this?"

"You should be asking me how much I got. I need somebody that can move this shit."

Carlos continues to cough. "You came to the right person."

"Take my number and gimme a call."

"Nah, we can talk right now."

\* \* \*

Carlos and Antoine discuss business and after a month of getting to know each other, Carlos and Antoine become partners. Within a short period of time, Carlos' clientele grows and he has the best weed on the Westside. Now that he is making thousands of dollars a week, he trades in his Lexus 400 and purchases a white 1996 Mercedes Benz 500. He's Antoine's number one dealer, but Carlos has no clue that he is doing business with a rat.

The summer has ended, and the leaves have fallen. It's winter season in Baltimore City. At 8:00 in the morning, Carlos gets a knock at his door. *Who's the hell*

147

*is that?* He frantically grabs his gun, tiptoes to the door and peeks through the peephole. Carlos sighs with relief and opens the door.

"I thought you were the fucking police. Whatchu want?"

"Ramon gotta large shipment coming, so I need to know how much you want."

Carlos rubs his eyes. "Who's Ramon?"

"My brother."

Even though Antoine is an informant for Officer Miles, he still works for his brother, which means he's making money on both sides of the spectrum and the only one who knows is him.

"You got the money?" Antoine asks.

"Just wait."

Wearing slippers, Carlos drags his feet to the bathroom. He places a hot rag on his face while Antoine sits on the couch nervously shaking his leg.

Carlos gets dressed. "I'm ready."

"Whoa, where you going?"

"I'm going with you."

"You got the money?"

"Stop asking me that shit. What the hell is goin' on?"

"My brother ain't giving you the weed unless he gets the money first. That's how he does business."

"Do I got 'Dumbo' written on my forehead? This shit don't feel right."

"Whatchu trynna say?"

Carlos stares into Antoine's eyes. He can't afford to miss an opportunity to get more weed, but he's putting himself at risk to be burned. He walks into the bedroom, returns with a bag and throws it on the table. Antoine reaches for it, but Carlos tightly grabs Antoine's wrist.

"I like you, but if you and your brother try some funny shit, we're gonna have some problems, you feel me?"

"Relax, I gotchu. I'll be back in an hour."

* * *

Carlos checks the clock on the wall and it's 9:52 am. Normally, he spends the earlier part of his day with a "wake 'n bake" blunt and watches television or plays video games, but today he's not in the mood for none of that shit. All he can envision is Antoine running off with his money. He paces throughout his apartment biting his nails, frequently looking out of the window. It's now 10:44 in the morning and Antoine has eight minutes until his hour is up. Carlos paces his apartment back and forth holding his gun. At 11:10, Carlos hears three soft knocks at his door. He opens it and Antoine is holding two large duffle bags, and all of Carlos' worries are gone. Carlos opens the bag and examines the quality.

"This is some good shit."

He grabs his cell phone and with five phone calls, he arranges to sell almost everything that he purchased. Antoine sits in shock because it would have taken him over a week to sell what Carlos sold in a matter of minutes. Antoine sits on the edge of Carlos' couch with his eyes filled with envy. While Carlos smiles, Antoine rocks back and forth chewing on a toothpick until it practically dissolves in his mouth.

149

For the next couple of weeks, Carlos' orders increase and he is selling close to one hundred pounds a week. Antoine can see that Carlos possesses that die-hard attitude that separates simple drug dealers from king-pins. He wants to introduce Carlos to Miles, but Antoine is afraid that Carlos will take his spot in Miles' operation – so he continues to keep his business with Carlos to himself.

\* \* \*

That evening, Antoine parks in front of his home when he notices a car parked in the distance flashing its lights. *What da hell does he want?*

Antoine walks into his home and unlocks the backdoor. Moments later, Miles steps inside.

Antoine closes his blinds. "Hurry up."

Miles places his gun on the kitchen counter and arrogantly opens the refrigerator. He spots a jug of Kool-aid and can't resist, "You niggers love that Kool-Aid. Pour me a glass."

"I'm not your nigger."

Miles pours himself of glass of red Kool-aid. "Stop being so sensitive, I'm just playing. You got something for me?"

Antoine reaches inside of a decoy cereal box and pulls out three large knots of money. Miles is surprised at how fast Antoine has been able to move the product.

"Do you gotta side hustle I should know about?"

Antoine nervously taps his fingers on the counter top. "Lately, I've been doing business wit a guy named Carlos and –"

"Who?"

"Carlos."

Miles stands to his feet. "Are you serious? That little muthafucka took forty grand from me."

While Miles continues to talk about how much he hates Carlos, Antoine thinks of way to use this to his advantage. He waits for the right time and blurts out, "You wanna make two-hundred and fifty thousand?"

"Who got that kind of money?"

"My brother. I know the combination to the safe and everything. If I set up Ramon and Carlos, I want us to be partners."

Miles grabs his gun off the counter and presses the barrel against Antoine's lips.

"Open your mouth." Miles pushes the barrel as far as he can. "You work for me, remember that shit." With his left hand, he squeezes Antoine's throat. "You hear me?"

Antoine tries his best to speak with a gun in his mouth, "Ugh…yeah."

Miles removes his gun. "Where's the rest of the money?"

Antoine gasps for air. "What money?"

"You must think I'm stupid. I know you getting product from your brother. So since you wanna be slick, I want it all or I'm taking you to jail."

"C'mon, Miles."

"Do I look like I'm playing?"

Miles follows Antoine into his room. Antoine reaches into his closet and grabs a laundry bag. Inside of the laundry bag are knots of money hidden inside of numerous pairs of socks.

Miles takes the laundry bag. "If what you're saying is true about your brother, we'll discuss your future. Oh, and don't you ever try to cut a deal with me," he says before leaving.

Out of frustration, Antoine kicks over his television, "I hate that muthafucka." Miles took over fifteen thousand from Antoine. The only way that Antoine is going to relieve himself of Miles' control is if he gives Miles a bigger fish to fry. After destroying his room, Antoine paces back and forth thinking of a plan. Now that Antoine knows that Miles wants to get even with Carlos, all he has to do is set up his brother, make Carlos his number one guy and use Miles' protection. If this works, he'll be one of Baltimore's top suppliers.

* * *

After leaving Antoine's apartment, Miles pulls into a vacant carwash and calls Sasha.

"I need to see you."

Sasha cringes at the sound of his voice. "Ok."

Miles patiently waits, when a blue Acura Integra pulls up next to him. He rolls down the passenger window. "Get in."

Sasha slides into the car and Miles can't help but gaze at her thick legs. "It's time for you to start earning your keep," he says putting his hands over her knee.

152

"Getcha hands off me."

Miles raises his hand and Sasha flinches. "Don't you ever yell at me again." He looks around to make sure the coast is clear, leans his seat back, and unfastens his belt buckle. "You know what to do."

Sasha's eyes fill up with tears. "I don't want to."

"Suck my dick! I'm not asking, I'm telling you to." He unzips his pants and pulls out his short, shriveled up white dick.

Sasha closes her eyes and pretends the dick in her mouth belongs to someone she loves. He grabs the back of her neck and pushes her head up and down until she gags. She tries to lift up for air, but he holds the back of her head. Miles' dick smells like he just came from the gym, so she holds her breath to keep from throwing up.

"I'm 'bout to cum," he moans.

Sasha cries.

"Shut up and taste it."

Miles' body jerks and he unloads filling Sasha's mouth. She chokes on his sperm and the taste is awful. She wipes his sticky, white cum off her chin.

Miles zips up his pants. "You and Antoine are all I got left. I gotta real special role for you, sweetheart. I'll call you."

Feeling abused, Sasha opens the passenger door, and slowly walks back to her car. She tries to be strong, but when Miles pulls off, she cries uncontrollably. She thinks about how she got into this mess and it seems as if the only way she is going to break free is suicide. She fixes her rear view mirror and is disgusted by the sight of Miles' cum mangled in her hair.

# CHAPTER VII

Kendrick finds a job to keep money in his pocket and to help his mother with the household bills. Kendrick becomes exactly what Carlos refuses to be, a slave to the workforce. Without Carlos by his side, Kendrick has surrounded himself around 'frienemies' who would rather watch him fail than reach his full potential. The main culprit of this lifeless cult is named Benny.

Every day after work, Kendrick visits his so-called friend Benny. Benny has always been a troubled child. At the tender age of seven, Benny's concept of love and compassion was destroyed. His mother was so strung out on drugs, that she took him to a department store and left him there. For most of Benny's life, he was bounced around from foster parent to foster parent, but no one could take his reckless attitude. Benny is now twenty-one years old and to this day, he has a hole in his heart.

Kendrick knocks on the door and Benny answers with blood shot eyes. Benny's home is always filled with people, and he makes sure everyone is accommodated. If you like to play video games, Benny ensures he has the latest. If you like to drink and smoke weed, he makes sure he has the best. Everyone thought Benny was being generous, but really, he's just afraid to be alone.

Kendrick watches television, while Benny is in the kitchen preparing a blunt. After breaking the weed into tiny pieces, he reaches into his pocket and pulls out a small plastic bag containing cocaine. He checks to make sure Kendrick isn't looking and sprinkles the cocaine on top. He rolls the blunt perfectly, lights it and inhales. He walks into the living room and passes it to Kendrick.

"Smoke this shit."

They pass the coke laced weed back and forth and Kendrick begins to feel something different. He looks around the room and his heart begins to pump faster. He searches for the wall, but instead he falls to the ground.

*Am I dying?* "I'm having a heart attack," he yells stumbling over his own feet. "I can't breathe. Call the fucking ambulance."

Benny laughs. "Chill out and enjoy the ride."

Kendrick crawls to the couch. "I need some water."

The high eventually mellows, and Benny watches with an evil grin as Kendrick sits in shock with his eyes wide open.

"That wasn't weed."

"I added a little special ingredient."

"What?"

"It's special."

\* \* \*

It doesn't take long before Kendrick becomes addicted to the combination of cocaine and weed and Benny has enough to go around. Kendrick is changing and the first person to notice is Amy. Just like his father,

Kendrick's urge to get high becomes simply too powerful. Whenever Kendrick goes home under the influence of drugs and alcohol, he locks himself in his bedroom for hours. His drug use eventually costs him his job, but instead of telling his mother, he continues to get dressed every morning and pretend to go to work.

Kendrick sits in his bedroom when he hears two soft knocks at the door.

"Keddy, we need to talk."

She sits next to him and kisses him on the cheek, which is the first sign that this is not going to be good.

"What's going on with you? You didn't pay me your rent in two months, and I need help."

Kendrick was never a good liar, so he comes clean. "I got fired."

"When?"

"Two months ago."

"Are you serious? Every morning, I watched you get dressed, so if you haven't been going to work, what the hell have you been doing?" She walks over to Kendrick's closet, pulls out a shirt, tie and pants and throws it at him. "Go look for a job, now."

"What I need to work for? I'm only gonna make minimum wage," he says with defiance as if that's a good enough reason to sit around the house.

"I don't care whatchu make. You're gonna help around this house." Amy pulls out the ironing board. "Get up, Kendrick. I watched your father do the same thing and I will not watch you."

"Nas didn't work for minimum wage."

Amy looks clueless. "Who?"

Kendrick points at a poster of the rapper, Nas, hanging on his wall.

Amy becomes so angry that she can barely speak. She takes a deep breath to calm her nerves, "Kendrick Rumsfeld, if you don't get out of that bed right now, I'm going to jail. The car keys will be on the kitchen counter and you better not come back without a job," she says slamming his bedroom door.

*   *   *

Kendrick gets dressed and goes on a job hunt. He walks inside of the Old Country Buffet and approaches who appears to be the manager. He glances at the man's nametag and tries his best to use proper English.

"Mr. Rolling, my name is Kendrick Rumsfeld. I'm here to inquire if you have any positions available."

Mr. Rolling is a fifty-two year old white guy who is clearly not in the mood. He looks Kendrick up and down. "Do you have any experience working in a restaurant?"

"No, sir, but I'm a quick learner."

Mr. Rolling sighs. "No experience, huh?" Mr. Rolling asks sarcastically, "You know how to use a broom?"

If Kendrick could smack the shit outta Mr. Rolling he would, but he can't go home without a job – so he deals with this snobby, arrogant attitude. "Yes, sir."

"Good, I need someone to clean up the eating area and the kitchen. You will also be responsible for the trash. This position starts at $4.25 an hour. You can start tomorrow."

Kendrick just stares. He would have never thought that he would be mopping floors at a restaurant.

Mr. Rolling grows impatient. "I need to know if you'll take this position. I have many people that will."

"Yeah, I'll take it."

* * *

Every day before work, Kendrick goes to Benny's house to smoke cocaine laced blunts, because this is the only way that he can cope with being a janitor. Some nights at work he sees his old friends from high school and it's difficult hearing them laughing at him. He has never felt more embarrassed in his life. While Carlos rides around in a brand new car, he is picking up trash and cleaning up after his old classmates.

One evening, Kendrick – unable to find Benny, shows up at work sober. While mopping the filthy kitchen floor, his skin begins to crawl. Kendrick has never felt this feeling before. He can't think straight and becomes extremely anxious. Kendrick assumes he is just having a bad day, but actually he is going through withdrawals. He reaches for his phone and calls Benny.

"Where are you? I need some of that shit."

Benny laughs. "I don't have a lot left, so if you want it, come get it now."

Kendrick knows if he leaves, he will be fired, but he can't do the job without getting high. He peeks into the dining area and sees Mr. Rolling at the cash register. He grabs his jacket, and sneaks out the back door.

Twenty minutes later, he pulls up to Benny's home and knocks on the door. The house is crowded as usual, and Kendrick gets excited to be closer to satisfying his urge.

Benny leads him upstairs into one of the rooms. "That shit had you itching, didn't it?"

"How'd you know?"

"Everybody goes through that. Don't worry, it's normal."

Benny prepares the blunt and sprinkles cocaine on top. Kendrick licks his lips as if he is about to eat a steak dinner. He reaches for the blunt, but Benny stops him.

"Whatchu doing? This shit ain't free, you got the money?"

Kendrick reaches into his pocket and pulls out the money he was supposed to give his mother.

Benny grins. "Enjoy."

Kendrick walks around looking for a private place, but that'll be impossible. The hallway is filled with clouds of smoke and beer bottles all over the floor. The base rattles the walls while drunk girls dance seductively with each other. Everywhere Kendrick goes, there is someone getting high. Kendrick doesn't know anyone in Benny's home, but they all have one thing in common – drugs. Kendrick sees a door in the distance and works his way through a crowd of people. He pushes the door open, peeks inside and it's empty. He quickly walks in and slams the door behind him. The room is dark, so he flicks the light switch, but nothing happens. The moon shines through the window and Kendrick sees a crate in the middle of the floor. He sits on top of the crate, lights up the cocaine laced blunt and inhales.

This combination of drugs takes him on such an emotional roller coaster that he can't control himself. He cries, laughs, and feels unstoppable and insecure all at the same time. His mind is so open, he can feel the presence of death around him and hears voices. In this dark room, he hallucinates, talks to himself and stares at the changing streetlights from the bedroom window.

Whenever his high mellows, he lights it up again and prepares for another ride. He eventually learns how to control the high and it becomes even more enjoyable. His body has a mind of its own and he goes in and out of consciousness until he falls asleep on the dirty wood floor.

The morning sun beams through the window and Kendrick awakens. When he realizes that he is not at home, he panics.

"Oh shit, my mother gonna kill me."

He runs downstairs and the house is still filled with people getting high.

"Where you going?" Benny asks.

"I gotta go."

"You'll be back."

Kendrick drives at top speed. He pulls in front of his house and sees his mother standing outside clearly pissed. Kendrick knows he fucked up. He walks towards her, but stays far enough to avoid being smacked.

"I'm sorry, ma, I –"

"Where have you been, Kendrick? You know I gotta go to work." She snatches the keys. "You better be here when I get back because we need to talk."

After work, Amy pulls up to the house with one thing on her mind and that is to slap the shit out of Kendrick. She opens the door and throws her keys on the ground.

"Kendrick. Get down here."

She runs upstairs and pushes his bedroom door open, but he isn't there. She continues to look around and there is a sudden feeling of emptiness in his room. She opens his closet and all of his clothes are gone.

"Oh my God," she says clutching her chest.

Kendrick has never been on his own, but he'd rather live on the street than deal with his mother's wrath.

Misery loves company and nothing pleases Benny more than Kendrick showing up on his doorstep with two large duffel bags. Benny always knew how to capitalize off someone's misfortune and he gladly takes Kendrick in like a lost puppy.

Kendrick looks around his new room and it's nothing like he is used to. Everywhere he looks, he sees water stains, exposed drywall and holes in the ceiling, *You gotta be fucking kidding me,* he steps over mice droppings, soda cans, and take out boxes. His twin bed's thin mattress is covered with stains, but beggars can't be choosey. He looks through the broken window and has a view of the dirtiest alley he has ever seen. Kendrick tosses his bags on the floor and owns up to his decision to leave home. He finds the cleanest spot on the bed and sits down when Benny walks in.

"You alright?" Benny asks.

"Yeah, I guess so."

"This ain't no shelter, so you gotta earn ya keep."

"Just tell me what I gotta do."

Benny grins. "Since you don't have a job, you can help me with my business. I'm into merchandising. I take things and I sell it for profit."

Kendrick laughs. "That ain't nothing but a cool way of saying you a thief."

"And now, so are you. Now c'mon, it's time to earn your keep."

If Kendrick says no, he'll have to face his mother, so agrees to help Benny with his so-called merchandising business.

* * *

For the next couple of months, they break into sheds stealing expensive gardening supplies, tools, and bikes. They steal clothes, electronics, and perfume from the shopping mall. All merchandise was sold on the streets or to a pawnshop, but the profit wasn't always worth the risk. Running the streets and getting high is beginning to take a toll on Kendrick and he looks ill.

Stealing items and selling them at the pawnshop isn't enough to the pay the bills and feed their addiction, so every Friday evening, they lurk around Downtown Baltimore. To Kendrick and Benny, the Downtown Baltimore area is a gold mine because it attracts thousands of tourists. Kendrick and Benny sit by the bridge just a few feet away from the Harbor looking for the perfect victim. They pass the cocaine laced blunt back and forth until their sense of reality fades.

"I think I see somebody."

"Where?"

Kendrick points. "Her."

"C'mon."

The sixty-something year old white woman is driving a champagne colored convertible Jaguar. The woman is probably not a tourist, but she definitely looks rich. She pulls into the parking garage and Kendrick and Benny follow behind her and wait until she exits. Kendrick signals and Benny walks slowly behind her.

"Excuse me, Miss, but do you know what time it is?"

She smiles. "I sure do. It's five –"

Benny punches the old woman in the face knocking her out cold. He snatches her purse, removes her jewelry and they run towards South Calvert Street. In the alley, Benny rummages through her purse tossing unwanted items to the ground.

"Why'd you hit her?"

"Because, I felt like it," he yells. "Fuck that bitch." Benny continues to search her purse, "She ain't got no money. We just ran three blocks for nothing."

Kendrick always knew that Benny was twisted, but the way he hit the innocent woman was pure evil. She is probably somebody's grandmother and Benny hit her like she's a man. While Kendrick drives, Benny unravels a small plastic bag filled with cocaine. He places his pinky finger in the bag and stuffs his nose.

"Did you just sniff that shit?"

"It's time you stepped up to the big league." Benny passes Kendrick the bag. "Try it."

Kendrick dips his finger into the powder, raises it to his nose, and sniffs. The impact hits him like nothing he's ever felt before and he swerves almost hitting a parked car.

"That's some good shit, ain't it?"

Kendrick screams, "I feel like I can fucking fly."

An unexplainable focus overcomes him. He feels sharper, intelligent and unstoppable. Kendrick wants to feel this way for the rest of his life, but cocaine is an expensive habit and he doesn't have a dime in his pocket.

Unable to sleep, Kendrick waits for the morning sun to rise. He walks into Benny's room and grabs his car keys off the dresser. His skin crawls and the need to get high increases with every second. To avoid waking Benny, he creeps down the steps and quietly opens the front door. It is only 7:15 in the morning and Kendrick can't live another second sober. He slowly drives into his mother's complex and doesn't see her car. Before ransacking his mother's home for valuable items, reality sets in and he just stares at the front door. All of his childhood memories are behind that door along with the one person who has loved him unconditionally. Unfortunately, childhood memories and his mother's love aren't enough to stop him from doing what he knows is wrong.

Kendrick nervously looks from left to right, pushes his key inside the lock and turns, *"Yes."* he whispers. The door opens and he looks around. He runs upstairs, opens her bedroom door, and grabs her jewelry box located on the dresser. Amy always keeps a stash of emergency money somewhere, so he tears through the closet throwing shoeboxes and clothes to the ground. He lifts up her mattress and finds two hundred dollars. His eyes grow wide from excitement. He stuffs the cash in his pocket, looks to the left and sees his high school graduation picture sitting on the nightstand. In the picture, Amy holds him tight with the biggest smile he has ever seen. Kendrick stares at the picture, but he doesn't recognize his own face. Back then his pupils were clear and full of hope, but now he is just a lowlife stealing from the woman who brought him into this world. Kendrick places the picture back on the nightstand runs downstairs, when the front door suddenly opens.

"Kendrick? What are you doing?"

"I just came to grab a few things and –"

Amy looks down and sees Kendrick holding a black trash bag. She snatches the bag and dumps everything onto the floor.

"Oh my God."

Amy has been down this road before with Kendrick's father. She doesn't even have the energy to argue, so she hysterically paces back and forth with her hands over her face.

"What did I do wrong, Lord? Where did I go wrong?"

"I just needed a few dollars, ma. I was gonna give it back."

With all her might, she pushes Kendrick and he stumbles over the coffee table. "How dare you steal from me? What else did you take?" She reaches into his pocket, and pulls out two one hundred dollar bills that she purposely marked up. "I can't believe you."

"I'm sorry, ma. I —"

"You were gonna take my last?" She grabs the glass vase from on top of the television and raises it high. "I should break this over your damn face."

Kendrick continues to beg for her forgiveness, but he knows that he crossed the line. Amy is so hurt with grief that she begins to hyperventilate until she loses her balance. She stumbles into the wall.

Kendrick tries to help her, but she screams. "Get the hell off me. I'm not the one that needs help, you are." She regains her balance, and locks the front and back door with the key. "Don't you move." She walks into the kitchen, picks up the phone and dials 911. "Someone broke into my house."

"Are you ok?" The 911 operator asks.

"No, it's my son Kendrick Rumsfeld, and I want him out of my house. He doesn't belong here."

Kendrick hysterically runs to the front door, but without his keys, he can't unlock it. He begs, "Please, ma, let me out. I can't go to jail."

Amy cries, "You need help, Kendrick."

"Fuck you. You don't care about me. I hate you," he screams knocking her television off the stand. Breathing hard, he steps in front of his mother with his fist clinched.

"I wish you would," Amy says gritting her teeth. "You ain't that high!"

Within minutes, two police officers bang on the door. Amy opens it and the officers quickly surround Kendrick.

"Sir, you need to come with us."

As they place him under arrest, Kendrick looks at his mother. "I thought you loved me."

"This is love."

"This ain't love. You never loved me."

Kendrick doesn't know what he is saying; he is going through withdrawals and losing his mind. All Amy can do is watch her son slowly turn into his father. Kendrick continues to kick and scream as the officers aggressively try to get Kendrick into their police car, but Amy can't stand to watch, so she closes the door.

When the officers pull out of the complex, Amy runs to her car and leaves. She isn't sure how this is going to turn out, but she is going on a manhunt for Kendrick's father. She drives to North Avenue and Payson and sees Gil staggering up the street. Amy stares with disgust as he approaches a group of hustlers on the corner. Gil makes the transaction, cuts down the alley and she follows him to an abandoned house.

"Gil."

"What the hell are you doing here, Amy? Look, I'll pay you back the damn twenty-dollars."

"I gotta talk to you. It's about your son."

"Whatchu want, Amy?"

Her eyes fill up with tears. "I never asked you for anything, but I'm begging you to help him before it's too late."

"Do I look like I can help anybody?"

"I took care of OUR child while you shot that poison in your veins. Please, Gil. Can you at least try?"

"I gotta go, Amy, I'm sorry. Now get outta here, cause this ain't the place for you," he says leaving her standing in the middle of the alley.

"Please, Gil."

"Get outta here, Amy."

\* \* \*

After spending ninety days in jail for trespassing at his mother's house and the string of robberies, Kendrick sits in his cell when the light turns on and his name is yelled over the intercom, *"Rumsfeld."* He eagerly hops up and waits for the steel door to slide open.

After being released, Kendrick walks to the nearest pay phone and calls Benny. Forty-five minutes later, Benny pulls up blasting NWA's song "Fuck the Police."

Benny playfully chants, "Free Kendrick, free Kendrick."

"It's good to be out, man."

While Benny drives, Kendrick notices a weird smirk on his face.

"You got out just in time. I got the perfect plan to get us back on our feet." Benny smiles. "If you look in the glove compartment, I got something for you."

Kendrick opens the glove compartment and sees a brown bag. He reaches inside and pulls out a small bag of cocaine. Kendrick hasn't touched a drug in ninety days, so he frantically rips open the bag, places his pinky finger inside and takes a sniff. The impact hits him like an electric shock.

Kendrick closes his eyes and enjoys the ride. "I miss you," he says wiping any residue off his nose. "What's the plan? I'm down for whatever."

"I had a feeling you would say that. This guy named Harvey gotta recording studio in Essex. On any given night, it's thousands of dollars in there."

"Whatchu want me to do?"

Benny smiles. "Just watch my back."

"When is this supposed to happen?"

"Tonight."

"Tonight? I just came home."

"I don't giva shit, I've been planning this for weeks."

Kendrick hasn't even taken a shower and he is already in danger of risking his freedom. Benny pulls up in front of Harvey's studio and parks.

"You ready?"

"Yeah."

Benny reaches under his seat, grabs a gun and hands it to Kendrick.

"I don't want it."

"Whatchu mean? This is a robbery, nigga."

"I told you I don't want it."

Benny places the gun under his seat. "Suit ya' self."

170

Kendrick nervously stands in front of Harvey's studio taking deep breaths. He has done many things, but robbery is a first. They don't know if Harvey's studio is filled with people, but based on the look in Benny's eyes, it doesn't matter; this is happening and it's gonna happen right now. Benny knocks, the door opens and they rush in wearing black masks.

"Get the fuck down," Benny screams.

Harvey drops to the floor and pleads, "Please don't kill me."

"Where's the shit at?"

"I don't know what –"

With his gun, Benny strikes Harvey in the face as hard he can. He raises the gun again, but Harvey can't take another hit like that.

"Wait. Please don't, I'll show you where it's at. Just don't kill me."

Benny grabs Harvey by the shirt and pulls him up to his feet, "Let's go."

Harvey walks down the hallway and leads them to a brown colored door. Before opening the door he mumbles, "Benny, is that you?"

Benny snatches off his mask.

"What the hell are you doing?" Kendrick screams.

Benny looks Harvey in the face. "Yeah it's me, now what?"

"We been friends for ten years. Why are you –"

"Open the fucking door, before I put a bullet in ya' back."

The door opens and Benny hits Harvey across the back of the head knocking him out. Kendrick searches the room and notices a bag hidden behind old studio equipment. He opens the bag and inside are multiple knots of money. Benny watches the door with his gun raised while Kendrick continues to look around.

"Hurry up, Kendrick."

"I am."

Kendrick searches the room and spots a set of speakers. He can feel that there is something hidden in this room, but he doesn't know where. In frustration, he kicks one of the speakers over and a brick of cocaine falls out.

"Oh shit."

Kendrick reaches inside of the speaker and pulls out nine more bricks of cocaine. Benny looks at Kendrick like they've hit the lottery and in the hood, they have. Kendrick places the cash and bricks in the bag.

"We need to go."

Benny doesn't budge. Instead, he cocks his gun and empties his clip into Harvey's body. The shots startle Kendrick and he jumps back.

"What the fuck," Kendrick yells.

Benny breathes heavily. "I had to, he know me."

"Are you crazy?"

Kendrick is numb. Just a few moments ago he was sitting in a cell and now he is watching a pool of blood form under Harvey's chest.

Benny taps Kendrick. "Yo, let's go."

Inside of the car, Benny celebrates stealing ten bricks of cocaine as if he didn't just commit murder. All Benny can think about is flooding the city with cocaine, and ten bricks is enough to make a name for himself. At this moment, Kendrick realizes that if Benny can kill his friend of ten years without blinking, then it's just a matter of time before he becomes Benny's next victim.

Moments later, they arrive at Benny's home. Kendrick expected Benny's home to be filled with drug abusers, but for some reason, it is very quiet. Benny places the bag on the bathroom counter.

"I told you this shit was gonna work," Benny says, rubbing his hands together in excitement, "We did it, I can't believe we fucking did it."

Benny pulls out his knife and cuts a slit into one of the bricks of cocaine. He raises the knife to his nose and sniffs. His nose begins to burn, his face tingles and he can feel the "white" moving through his system almost immediately.

"Gotdamn. Kendrick, come get some of this shit. We're gonna make some serious money."

Normally, Kendrick would have been eagerly standing next to Benny to get his hit, but not this time and Benny becomes suspicious.

"What's wrong witchu?"

"You knew Harvey for ten years and you killed him?"

Benny chuckles. "We got all this money in here and you still talking 'bout that? So what if I knew him for ten years, he wasn't my nigga. He woulda did me the same way."

The last time Kendrick was in a room filled with money and drugs, he watched how it turned Micky into a selfish snake and he now knows that Benny is no different. Ever since Kendrick met Benny, there has been

173

nothing but pure destruction. He has helped Benny orchestrate many robberies on innocent people, but murder takes it to a new level.

While Benny sits in the chair paralyzed by the best cocaine his nose has ever sniffed, Kendrick is plotting on a way to remove himself from Benny's karma.

"I can't do this no more."

Benny sits up. "There's nothing to do about it now. We got ten bricks of cocaine, and we're rich," he yells stuffing his nose with more cocaine. "You being real emotional right now, so I'ma give you some time to –"

"I don't need time, I'm done."

"You'd be fucking crazy to turn all this money down."

"All money ain't good money."

Benny picks up his gun and approaches Kendrick. "All money is good money, nigga. This is our way out. No more living in that shitty house eating Ramen noodles five days a week. We can finally afford the life that we've been chasing, and you want out?"

Benny paces back and forth waving his gun wildly and the more animated he becomes, the more Kendrick can feel his life is in danger.

"Why'd you kill him? What if he had cameras and –"

"I don't giva fuck about that, Kendrick!" Benny yells, "This is the dope game. Hustlers, cops, stickup boys and fiends…which one are you?"

Kendrick looks up. "I'm just me."

"That ain't good enough."

"We'll see."

Kendrick walks towards the door and reaches for the doorknob when he hears the sound of Benny's gun cocking. *He*'s *not stupid enough to shoot me in a house full of bricks.*

Kendrick turns around and looks down the barrel of Benny's gun. "You got the coke and the cash. Just let me go." Kendrick turns around and opens the door, "If you're gonna shoot, then shoot, but I'm done with this shit."

Kendrick closes his eyes and waits for a bullet from Benny's forty-five caliber to blow his head off, but nothing happens.

"All money ain't good money."

Benny lowers his gun. "Get da fuck outta here."

Kendrick closes the  door and vows to distance himself from people like Benny, but that's almost impossible in Bmore City. He has no car and nowhere to go, but anything is better than sitting in a room with Benny's sick ass. After hours of searching for a safe place to sleep, he stops at Memorial Park and sits on the bench. He hasn't had this much time to himself since he got locked up. His whole life flashes before his eyes from his days at Woodlawn High School, to robbing tourists to get high. The one thing that hurts him the most is the pain that he has caused his mother. No words can fix it, but his heart will never heal if he doesn't at least try. He takes a deep breath and dials.

"Hello?"

Kendrick grips the phone; just the sound of her voice makes him whimper. "Ma. Don't hang up."

"Whatchu want, boy?"

"I know I messed up."

Kendrick finally breaks down and cries to the point where he can barely get his words together. Even though Amy is disappointed, she hasn't heard him cry like this since he was a child, but she continues to stay firm.

"Kendrick, I have to go."

"Please, ma. I don't have anywhere to go."

Amy knows if she doesn't help, her son will become another statistic. Her gut screams, "don't do it," but her love is simply too strong. She holds the phone in silence.

"Ma, please say something."

"I'm gonna give you a chance, but I'm going to be very hard on you."

Kendrick closes his eyes and tears of joy roll down his face. "Thank you. I'm sorry, and I promise I'm going to show you that I –"

"Where are you?"

"At Memorial Park."

"I'm coming to get you."

"Don't worry about me, ma. I need this time alone, so I'll see you tomorrow."

Amy is confused by Kendrick's response, but she doesn't push the issue. "Okay."

"I'll see you tomorrow?"

"Okay, Keddy."

Kendrick places his jacket over his head, lies down on the cement bench and gets the best sleep he has had in months.

# CHAPTER VIII

At 11:47 in the evening, Sasha sits in the passenger side of Officer Miles' tinted Ford Mustang on Baltimore Street. After being forced to taste Miles' cum, she realizes that Miles will never let up – so she gives in. Sasha's role in Miles' operation is to set up major drug dealers throughout the city. Miles realizes that he will never get close enough to propose a deal himself, so he uses Sasha's beauty to nab what he calls a 'big fish.'

Tonight's big fish is Todd, who is not just a dope boy – but a businessman who owns numerous pieces of property. He's a compulsive gambler, known for spending tens of thousands without blinking an eye.

Miles leans his seat back and points. "That's him right there. I need you to get close to him." Miles puts his hand on Sasha's knee. "Do whatever you gotta do."

From a distance, they watch Todd and his crew stand in front of Norma Jean's strip club. Todd leans up against his white Bentley coupe wearing a white V-neck t-shirt and dark shades. Todd has always had a weakness for a fine piece of pussy, and all the strippers know when Todd visits the club-it's going to be a big payday.

Inside of the car, Sasha nervously fixes her hair and makeup. "What if this doesn't work?"

"It'll work. Just make sure you go home with him."

"Ok."

Wearing a snow-white Prada shirt, low rider jeans and red three-inch heels, she struts towards the entrance of Norma Jean's and immediately catches Todd's eye. He scans her from head to toe and there is no way he is going to allow her to walk by him and his one hundred and seventy thousand dollar car.

"Aye, shorty, come here."

*Just like taking candy from a baby,* Sasha says to herself, pretending not to hear him.

Todd excuses himself from the crowd and steps closer. He gently grabs her arm. "Where you going?"

"Do you know me?"

"Are you a dancer?"

"No, sweetie, I just like watching sexy women."

Todd smiles. "We got something in common. Are you alone?"

"You ask too many questions. Whatchu want?"

"I can show you better than I can tell you." Todd follows Sasha to the entrance of the strip club. She reaches into her purse, but Todd stops her. "When I'm with a woman, she ain't gotta pay for nothing."

Sasha bats her eyes. "Who said we were together? I can pay for myself."

"But I insist."

"I'm not one of these hoes, soooo you can't buy my time."

Todd smiles, *We'll see about that.*

Norma Jean's is your typical strip club filled with shady characters, alcohol, and voluptuous women. Sasha heads to the bar where women with black sequin bra

179

tops, panties, and fishnet stockings serve drinks and stacks of one-dollar bills.

The barmaid yells over the loud music, "What can I get for you, hon?"

Sasha hands the bartender a fifty-dollar bill. "Fifty ones."

Todd is used to getting whatever he wants, but Sasha's independence is a turn on. The lights in the club flash while the DJ introduces the next dancer, *"Alright, alright. Coming to the stage is Jazzy Jazmin."*

Jazzy Jazmin commands everyone's attention. She seductively walks onto the stage wearing nothing but a pair of heels. Her coke bottle figure and picture perfect shaven pussy makes her undeniably the baddest bitch in the club. Jazzy Jazmin's hair is short. She has a colorful tattoo from her neck to her lower back that highlights her golden skin. Her sexiest attribute is how her tan line cuffs her ass and wraps around her inner thighs perfectly. Sasha always felt confident about her looks, until tonight. Sasha isn't into women, but if she were to ever experiment, Jazzy Jazmin would be the prototype.

The crowd rushes to the stage and the energy in the strip club increases. The DJ plays R. Kelly's song "Twelve Play" to set the mood while the barmaids walk around exchanging large bills for change.

"She's beautiful."

"Yeah, she is," Todd replies.

Jazmin walks around the pole a few times and begins her routine. Men throw dollars onto the stage to get her attention and Jazmin melodically teases them. She turns around, spreads her butt cheeks and shows her pink pussy lips. While Sasha wishes she could move like Jazzy Jazmin, the barmaid approaches Todd. Todd whispers something into the barmaid's ear and she leaves. Less than five minutes later, the barmaid returns with stacks of money. Todd pops the band wrapped around the stack of bills and throws the money in the air. Seconds later, he pops another and Todd's money falls slowly to ground like confetti. Todd knows that Sasha is impressed, so he grabs another stack and gives it to her.

"Here, you try it."

"How much is it?"

"It don't matter, just throw it."

Sasha's eyes widen. "Are you sure you want me to just throw it?"

"Yeah. If you don't, I will."

Sasha rips off the band and tosses it in the air. She never thought throwing money in air could make her feel this alive. There is so much of Todd's money on the stage that the barmaids had to bring out a broom to sweep it all into a pile. After a few drinks, Sasha begins to loosen up. She takes a twenty-dollar bill and places it into her mouth. Jazmin seductively crawls and spins Sasha's chair around. Jazmin reaches under Sasha's arms and pulls her onto the stage. She lays Sasha on her back and tenderly runs her fingers down to Sasha's low rider jeans. She pulls down Sasha's pants exposing her round ass and forest green thong. Jazmin kisses Sasha's lower back tattoo and everyone watches with excitement at the girl on girl action. Todd continues to throw money in the air and Sasha loves the feeling of cash falling all over her body.

The music stops and Jazmin's set comes to an end. With her hair mangled, Sasha stands to her feet, pulls up her pants and climbs off the stage.

Todd stands to his feet and claps. "I can't believe you just did that. If I didn't know any better, I'd say you enjoyed it."

Sasha blushes. "I did."

After her erotic performance, Jazmin walks along the bar for more tips. She approaches each customer until she reaches Sasha and Todd. Todd picks up one of his stacks and places it in her garter belt. Jazmin stands in front of Sasha and pushes her perky breast together. Sasha licks her lips clearly intrigued by Jazmin's seduction.

Todd whispers into Jazmin's ear, "I wanna take you home."

"I'm expensive."

"Do I look like I can't afford it?"

"I'll talk to you when I'm finished."

Sasha has dealt with many hustlers, but Todd is probably by far the richest. He moves closer to Sasha and whispers, "I know you like her."

"Like who?"

"Don't play shy. You wanna fuck Jazmin just as bad as I do." Todd swallows his shot of Vodka, "I can make that happen."

"What are you talking about?"

"Me, you, and Jazmin."

Just before Sasha can respond, she receives a text. She reaches into her purse, pulls out her phone and it reads, *"Don't fuck this up."* Sasha looks at the time on her cell phone and realizes that the club is closing soon; she has to seal the deal.

"Was that your boyfriend?"

"Don't worry about it," Sasha replies placing her hand on Todd's knee. "You're right, I do wanna fuck her, and I wanna fuck you too."

Todd smiles. "Say no more."

* * *

Jazmin exits the back room fully dressed and surprisingly, she looks even better wearing clothes. She places her arm around Todd's shoulder. "You ready?"

"Hell yeah. But first, I want you to meet Sasha."

With her eyes full of lust, Jazmin looks at Sasha and extends her hand, "Have you ever been with a woman?"

Sasha is used to using her extraordinary seductive ways to get what she wants, but she is clearly no match for Jazmin. Sasha suddenly becomes bashful. "No, but —"

Jazmin leans towards the left side of her face and whispers, "After me, no man will ever eat your pussy the same." Jazmin faces Sasha and their lips are just inches apart. "Can I kiss you?"

Sasha nods her head, closes her eyes and anticipates her first kiss with a woman. Jazmin romantically pecks her on the lips and Sasha can taste her strawberry lipstick. Sasha didn't expect to enjoy it as much as she does and she's curious to know how Jazmin's soft full lips would feel on her pussy.

The doors of the strip club open and Miles watches the crowd. His adrenaline pumps when he sees Todd and Sasha get into Todd's Bentley coupe. He smashes his cigarette into the ashtray, and turns on the ignition.

"That's my girl," Miles says before driving out of sight.

Todd pulls in front of his home and leads the girls to the front door. He pushes the door open and Sasha admires the décor. While Sasha and Jazmin stand in the foyer, Todd runs upstairs to set the mood.

"Make yourself comfortable. The liquor is in the cabinet by the fridge and the glasses are above the sink."

Jazmin isn't new to selling her pussy to rich perverts like Todd. She walks into the kitchen, reaches into the cabinet and grabs a bottle of Moscato. "You want something to drink, sweetie?"

"Sure."

Jazmin sits with her legs crossed seducing Sasha with her eyes. "Let's toast."

"To what?"

Jazmin smiles. "To the greatest orgasm ever."

"I'll drink to that."

Sasha wants to know so much about Jazmin. After a few sips she blurts out, "Why do you dance?"

"Because men will do anything for bitches like me and you." Jazmin lowers her voice. "Take Todd for example, he is probably upstairs jumping around like a child. I can do whatever I want to Todd, like I can get him robbed or even killed. He has completely exposed himself for a piece of pussy. The sad part is ninety-nine point nine percent of all men would do the same."

"How much did you make tonight?"

"About twenty-five hundred."

"In one night?"

"That's nothing sweetie. I have a few clients that will fly me first class to wherever they are." Jazmin brags, "My pussy has literally taken me around the world."

"How much is Todd paying you?"

"I hate to say this sweetheart, but you're playing this game all wrong. Even though we're both fucking the same guy, only one of us is getting paid."

Sasha has been dealing with hustlers since the ninth grade. She's spent countless nights on her back only to receive a pair of expensive shoes or a handbag, but Jazmin has turned the game of seduction into a profit. Sasha knows she will never free herself from Miles' grasp but tonight, she decides that if Miles is going to use her body, she might as well make a profit.

Jazmin fills up their glasses. "Stand up."

Sasha stands to her feet and Jazmin twirls her around inspecting her body. "You're a bad bitch. I know plenty of men that will pay big money to spend a night with you."

Jazmin walks over to Todd's stereo system and scrolls through his selection of music. When she finds the perfect song, she presses play. Sade's "Sweetest Taboo" plays and Jazmin dances melodically to the rhythm. Sasha stares at Jazmin's hips and she has never been this turned on before.

"Come dance with me."

Sasha walks over and Jazmin places her hands on Sasha hips and moves her to the baseline. She turns Sasha around, holds her from behind and kisses her neck. Sasha closes her eyes while Jazmin's petite hands reach under her shirt and gently squeeze her breasts. Sasha never thought a woman's hands could feel so good. From behind, Jazmin pulls Sasha's shirt over her head and runs her fingertips down to her belt buckle.

"Let me show you why people pay for my time."

"Okay."

Jazmin kisses her stomach and Sasha feels goose bumps the closer she gets to her pussy. "You smell so good. I can't wait to taste you."

Sasha gets on all fours, faces the window, and arches her back. Jazmin runs the tip of her tongue down Sasha lower back until it grazes her ass. Sasha jumps from pleasure.

"You like that?"

"Yes," Sasha moans.

Jazmin licks Sasha's pussy and sucks gently on her clit. With her left hand, Jazmin pushes two fingers inside of her and rotates them in a circular motion. Jazmin increases the speed and the faster she goes, the more Sasha's body shakes. Sasha's toes curl and she digs into the carpet.

"Cum baby, cum."

"Ah fuck. Don't stop."

"Let me taste you, baby."

Just before Sasha can reach her orgasm, Todd jogs downstairs wearing nothing but a towel. "What the fuck? Y'all couldn't wait?"

186

"I was just getting her warmed up for you. She is definitely ready for some dick, ain't that right, Sasha?"

Sasha breaths heavily and says, "Yes."

Todd drops his towel and he has the biggest dick Sasha has ever seen.

"Oh my God. That's not going to fit."

"Don't worry, baby. I won't hurt you."

Todd climbs in-between Sasha's legs and rubs his dick against her clit. He pushes himself inside of her and Sasha can feel every vein in Todd's dick. She digs her nails into the carpet and bites her lip from the wonderful pain. Jazmin rubs Sasha's leg to relax her while Todd goes in and out of Sasha's dripping pussy. The pain fades and pleasure takes over. Sasha asks for more, so Todd obliges and turns Sasha her over. After a few more long strokes, he pulls out and Jazmin sucks off Sasha's juices.

It is now Jazmin's turn to feel Todd's massive dick and she can't wait. Todd lies down and Jazmin straddles him. Sasha watches as his dick falls into her pussy with ease. Jazmin's soft ass bounces up until her cum covers his dick. Sasha is so turned on that she plays with herself to the soundtrack of Jazmin's moans. Todd stands to his feet and Jazmin opens her mouth wide ready to receive his load.

Todd yells, "Ahhh shit."

Jazmin takes control, grabs his dick and jerks him until his knees buckle. With her face full of cum, Jazmin crawls over to Sasha and kisses her. This isn't the first time Todd paid for sex, but this will be the most memorable. Sasha can't believe she just had a threesome, but she promises herself that the next time she'll be the one getting paid for it.

The next day, Sasha sits Indian style on her bed wearing a t-shirt and panties. In complete silence, she holds a bottle of wine while staring at the walls in her small one bedroom apartment. All she can think about is watching Todd pay Jazzy Jazmin fifteen hundred dollars for thirty minutes of pleasure when all she got was a cab ride home. She places the empty bottle on the floor and stumbles over to the mirror. She turns around and admires her apple bottom ass. Sasha wants to be Jazzy Jazmin, but better. After taking a shower, she reaches into her closet and picks out her favorite red Gucci dress, Gucci belt, and heels. While dolling up, she puckers up and blows herself a kiss, "You gotta use what you got, to get want you want." She reaches into her jewelry box, grabbing her gold bracelet and necklace.

Her apartment is a complete wreck, but she is stunning and undeniably ready to get what she deserves. Before leaving, she swallows an ecstasy pill, opens up another bottle of champagne and pours herself a glass. This combination puts Sasha exactly where she needs to be. She flips open her cell phone, takes a deep breath and dials.

"Hello?"

"This is Sasha. I need to speak to you."

"About what?"

Sasha voice slurs, "I don't wanna talk over the phone."

"I'm at the Marriott."

Sasha pulls up to the front of the Marriott hotel and walks to the clerk at the front desk.

"Welcome to the Marriott. How can I help you?"

"I don't know the room number, but the name should be under Miles."

The clerk looks Sasha up and down and a judgmental smirk appears on her face. "He seems to be a popular guy."

"Whatchu mean?"

The clerk whispers, "Well, let's just say he's had a lot of female visitors."

Sasha rolls her eyes and walks away. She steps onto the elevator and the closer she gets to Miles' suite her confidence begins to wither. She stands in front of Miles' door and gathers her thoughts. The reason Sasha is standing in front of Miles' suite is because she no longer wants to work for free, and she wants a piece of the pie. Sasha knows she is taking a huge risk, so before she knocks on the door, she takes a deep breath and fixes her hair.

"You can do it," she repeats to herself. "Just like taking candy from a baby."

Sasha knocks and Miles opens the door wearing nothing but a towel wrapped around his waist, "Come in, but make this quick. I'm expecting someone. Whatchu want?"

Sasha hoped that Miles would be enticed by her expensive Gucci outfit, but he is clearly not amused.

While he impatiently waits for Sasha to speak, she struggles to utter a word.

"Don't just stand there. You obviously want something, now spit it out."

"Ah…I wanted to talk you about Todd, I –"

"I'm glad you brought that up. I knew he couldn't resist. I wantchu to go out with him again so I can rob his ass for everything he got."

Sasha sits down and crosses her legs. "Seeing as how I'm the only one that can get close to the "big fish", I think it's time that we discuss my take."

"Your take? What makes you think you deserve anything from me?"

Sasha knew getting Miles to give her a cut of the robberies would be like pulling teeth, so she tries to seduce him. She does her best Jazzy Jazmin impersonation, and seductively walks over to the bed and turns around.

"Can you unzip me?"

Miles looks her up and down and the blood begins to rush to his dick. He slowly unzips her dress and it falls to the floor exposing her soft pink bra and thong.

Miles runs his fingers down her spine. "Now what?"

"Now, you fuck the shit outta me." Sasha pulls down her thong and twirls it around her fingers. "What are you waiting for?"

Miles gently places his left hand on her hip and with his right hand, he grips her neck and squeezes. "You must think I'm fucking stupid."

Sasha struggles to breathe. "You're hurting me."

"Shut up," he yells and pushes her into the wall.

"What are you doing?"

Miles drops his towel to the floor, grabs Sasha's ponytail and drags her to the bed. He presses his weight onto her back and attempts to ram himself into Sasha's ass. She puts up a fight, but she's not strong enough to stop Miles' attempt to sodomize her.

"Please don't."

Sasha clinches her butt cheeks, but the more she fights, the more he tries. Miles places the head of dick against her ass and thrusts himself inside. Sasha screams from the unbearable pain.

"Say my name, bitch."

"Stop!"

"Say it."

Miles pulls out and forces his dick inside of her pussy. The closer he gets to cumming, the more his pumps increasing the pain. He wraps his fingers in her hair and pulls until her chin is up in the air.

A large vein bulges through his forehead. "I'm gonna cum all in your pretty little black pussy."

"No!"

Miles cums and he makes sure his dick is inside her as far he can push it. "Take it."

He collapses on top of her, and the feeling of his cum oozing down her vagina makes Sasha sick. Miles has no remorse, grabbing Sasha's dress, thong and heels and throwing them at the front door.

"Don't you ever try to use your pussy to bargain with me. If I want it, I'll take it. You hear me?"

Sasha mumbles, "Yes."

Exhausted, humiliated, and in pain, she slowly stands to her feet and walks towards the door. While she gets dressed, Miles crumbles two twenty-dollar bills and throws them at her feet. "Getcha hair done, you look like shit."

Holding her expensive purse and heels, she opens the door and limps down the hallway into a crowded elevator. The elevator doors close, and her reflection bounces off the gold plated interior. Her hair is mangled and her left eye is swollen.

"Are you ok?" a concerned man asks.

Sasha nods.

"Are you sure?"

"I said 'yes.'"

The elevator doors open and Sasha limps through the lobby. She walks passed the front desk and the receptionist can't resist. "That was fast," the receptionist says, with that same silly judgmental smirk on her face.

If Sasha had the energy, she would slap that nosey bitch's head off, but she is in too much pain. Everyone in the lobby is staring at her, but all she can do is pretend like she wasn't brutally raped. As she limps through the never-ending lobby clutching her purse, Sasha refuses to be Miles' punching bag any longer. "I'ma get his ass," she vows.

Sasha gets inside of her car, reaches inside of her glove compartment and pulls out a small black book. She opens the book and frantically writes the time, her location and Miles' hotel room number. "You're gonna pay for this you fucking pig."

# CHAPTER IX

Ever since Antoine started selling drugs for Officer Miles, his brother Ramon has noticed that something is different. Antoine has been purchasing more product than usual and Ramon has been in the game long enough to know when someone is cutting side deals. Since they were kids, Antoine has always admired his brother's ability to make money, but as he got older, his admiration turned into jealousy. Antoine wants a more important role in his brother's operation, but he will never escape the title as Ramon's little brother.

Even though he can afford it, Ramon doesn't drive the latest car or live in a big home. Instead, he lives in a neighborhood zoned for section eight and drives an old truck. Ramon didn't get in the drug game to look flashy and fuck neighborhood freaks. His low-key demeanor is what kept him in the game for over ten years, and he plans to keep it that way. Ramon never wanted to stop his brother from becoming his own man, but he knows that Antoine's selfish nature will destroy everything that he has built.

Antoine is making good money, but he knows if he stays under his brother's wing he will never rise above the corner-boy level. It's time that Ramon gets to the bottom of this feeling in the pit of his stomach. He would hate to choose money over blood, but if Antoine gives the slightest idea that he is undercutting him, Ramon will treat Antoine like anyone else.

The night is young, and Ramon paces back and forth until he hears knocks at the door. Antoine walks in and looks around. Ramon doesn't say much, but walks out onto his patio and sits down. Antoine takes a seat and flicks the ashes from his cigarette. Antoine can feel that his brother has something serious on his mind.

"Something you wanna tell me?"

Antoine finishes one cigarette and lights up another.

"I spoke to Mommy the other day and –"

"Don't play with me, Antoine. I'm not one of these little niggas you play with. I'm your brother, and I know you. Wassup?"

Antoine's voice cracks, "Everything's alright."

"I'ma cut straight to it. You buying weed from somebody else?"

Antoine would never admit that he is working with a dirty cop, but he has convinced himself that he is a victim of circumstances. Cloaked in this denial, tonight is the first time that Antoine feels like a traitor. While Ramon waits for an answer, Antoine feels like his chest is caving in.

Ramon places his arm around Antoine's shoulder. "We're family, and we don't keep secrets from each other – right?"

Antoine has always fallen for Ramon's family talk, but not tonight. He may be wrong, but he's tired of bottling up his feelings. He shrugs Ramon's arm from around his shoulder and stands up.

"I'm not your child."

"I know you."

Antoine yells, "Stop saying that shit. You don't know what I'm going through."

"Talk to me then."

Here is the moment for Antoine to come clean, but he is too selfish and in too deep to speak the truth. Besides, if his plan comes together, Ramon will be behind bars. Antoine lights his cigarette and stares at the full moon. While he has Ramon's attention, Antoine uses this time to put his plan into effect.

"I met this nigga named Carlos, and with my own eyes, I saw him sell thirty pounds just by making a few phone calls."

Ramon looks Antoine directly in the eyes. "I need to meet him."

Antoine knew that once Ramon found out how much weed Carlos was selling, Ramon would try to undercut him.

"Sure, I'll set it up."

Ramon smiles. "It's always business little brother."

"Never personal, right?"

"Exactly." Ramon rubs his hands together. "So when do I get to meet this Carlos?"

Antoine pulls out his phone and dials.

\* \* \*

Carlos is enjoying dinner at Moe's Seafood Restaurant with his bed buddy, Maria, when he receives a call. He excuses himself from the table and steps outside.

"Hello?"

"My brother wants to meet you. Will you be ready tomorrow?"

Carlos is excited, but he keeps his composure. Carlos clears his throat, "Sounds good."

"I'll call you later with the details."

Antoine has completed his goal, which is to get Ramon and Carlos in the same spot at the same time. Antoine grins and says to himself, "Checkmate."

"So, is it done?" Ramon asks.

"Yup."

Ramon jumps up. "This calls for a drink." He walks into the house, grabs two glasses and a bottle of Hennessey. He fills their shot glasses to the top and shouts, "Let's toast to family and money."

Antoine raises his glass. *Your days are numbered, Ramon, and you don't even know it.*

After speaking with Antoine, Carlos looks up to the sky and smiles. He knows with Antoine out of the picture he will have a direct connect, which means he is finally going to start making some real money. He walks back to the table and Maria notices that his attitude is completely different. He grins from ear to ear and signals for the waiter to come over.

"Yes, sir," the waiter addresses.

"Can you bring over a bottle of champagne, please?"

Maria bounces up and down in her seat. "What's the celebration, Carlos? Tell me."

"We're celebrating life."

Maria sighs. "I thought you were gonna ask me to marry you."

Carlos cuts his eye. "I'm married to the money."

After dinner, Carlos and Maria enter his apartment and all he can think about is tomorrow. He lies on the bed in deep thought when Maria enters wearing a purple sheer chemise. She lights a candle and seductively crawls onto the bed, but Carlos isn't interested. She kisses him on his head and works her way down to his belly button. Maria runs her hand over his zipper and grabs his dick. She drops to her knees and positions herself in-between Carlos' legs. She lifts his shirt, unbuckles his belt and kisses his navel. She is waiting for Carlos to react, but he just stares.

"What's wrong witchu? One minute you're happy and popping bottles and the next minute you're not in the mood to do anything. I'm tired of this bipolar shit."

"You know what, blow out the candle, get dressed, and leave." Carlos grabs his car key off the nightstand and tosses it towards her. "Take yourself home, I'll call you tomorrow."

Embarrassed beyond words, Maria snatches the key, gets dressed and leaves.

* * *

The next morning, Carlos wakes up around 11:00 and quickly gets dressed and waits for Antoine to arrive. The meeting was scheduled for 12:00 noon and Antoine is already fifteen minutes late. He finally arrives, and Carlos swings open the door clearly frustrated.

"You're late, I –"

"Calm down, we'll make it. I gotta use the bathroom."

"Hurry up."

Antoine enters the bathroom, calls Miles and turns on the faucet to muffle his voice.

"Carlos and my brother are meeting today. Do we have a deal, or what?"

While Antoine is waiting for a response from Miles, Carlos is banging on the bathroom door.

Antoine screams, "Wait. I'll be out in a sec."

"Yeah, we gotta deal," Miles says.

This is all Antoine needs to hear. They arrive at Ramon's townhome and Carlos is unpleasantly surprised. He expected Ramon to live in a five-bedroom, single-family home with a long driveway and a two-car garage. Antoine knocks on the door and a thick, curvy, beautiful, dark-skinned woman greets them. Carlos steps inside and the living room is crowded with goons who look like killing is their hobby. He looks into the kitchen and notices a guy leaning against the wall with a huge bulge on the left side of his hip. Ramon may not live in a five-bedroom home like a major drug dealer, but he is certainly heavily guarded like one.

Carlos follows Antoine upstairs and they stand in front of a small bedroom door. Ramon opens the door and extends his hand.

"You Carlos? Antoine told me that you built up a weed strip in Heraldry Square. I'm impressed."

"Yeah, I'm doing ok."

"Come on in and have a seat. You think you can handle moving large quantities?"

"That's why I'm here, right?" Carlos pulls his chair closer to Ramon. "I'll do anything for the people I do business with, and I ain't no snitch."

Ramon takes a long drag from the blunt and grins. "That's why I keep my brother around; he's the only one I can trust." Ramon glances over at Antoine. "Ain't that right, bro?"

Antoine looks them both in the eyes and lies, "Death before dishonor."

Ramon pats Carlos on the back. "I like you. We just met so I'm not gonna call you family, but I think we can get there. If Antoine says I should do business with you, then we'll do business."

*　*　*

Later that day, Antoine calls Miles to let him know that he has done his part. Within weeks, Carlos' hustle expands as he ends up supplying forty percent of the weed on the Westside. He no longer walks around Heraldry Square for hours selling dime bags. Instead, he only visits to pick up money and show off his latest luxury toys. Carlos didn't get in the drug game to stay in the hood and live a modest life like Ramon. Carlos got in the drug game to become a legend. Ramon knows that Carlos is just a young hustler enjoying his new wealth, but some of his flashy ways are concerning.

At 12:30 in the morning, Carlos pulls up in front of Ramon's house honking the horn. Ramon hats when people draw attention to his home, and Carlos' loud music and brand new Mercedes Benz are definitely making a scene.

Carlos screams, "C'mon, we're going out. It's my birthday."

Ramon doesn't like going to the club, but he and Carlos are making so much money that he doesn't want to disappoint his top earner.

Ramon opens the passenger door and gets inside. "I didn't know it was your birthday. How old are you?"

"I'm twenty, but I feel like an old man." Carlos drives out of the complex.

"Where we going?"

Carlos turns down the radio. "I'm going to pick up your brother."

Ramon and Antoine haven't spoken much lately, and Ramon knows that the lack of communication may come from Antoine's jealousy. Ramon isn't proud of the way he treated Antoine, but being a nice guy isn't how Ramon makes his money. Ramon isn't sure how Antoine will react, but it's too late to stop the inevitable. Now that Carlos is buying directly from Ramon, Antoine isn't making the same money.

While he suffers financially, Antoine remains patient. While waiting for Carlos to arrive, Antoine calls Miles to give him the news. After getting off the phone, Miles calls Sasha.

\* \* \*

Sasha sits at home alone sipping wine and jotting in her little black book when her cell phone rings. She picks up the phone, looks at it and just the sight of Miles' number makes her sick. After the fourth ring, she answers.

"Hello?"

"I need you to go to Club Reign. Antoine is going to be there, so he'll tell you the rest. Make sure you look nice," he says before hanging up.

Sasha closes her book and walks into her closet. She grabs her red dress and lays it across her bed. She walks into the bathroom and stares at herself. While putting on her makeup she mumbles, "I'm gonna make all you muthafuckas pay." She gets dressed and pours herself another glass of wine. Afterwards, she grabs her keys and drives to the club.

Antoine peeks out of the window and sees fluorescent lights pulling into his complex. He pulls his shade to the left, and sees the prettiest white Mercedes Benz he has ever seen and his heart is immediately filled with envy. *Greedy ass niggas.* Before opening the door, he gets control over his emotions and forces a smile on his face.

"Happy birthday." Antoine shouts. He doesn't want to say a word to Ramon, but he has to play it cool. "Hey, Ramon, long time no see. Where you been?"

"It's good to see you. Just taking care of business. You know how it is, little brother."

"Business must be going well because I haven't heard from y'all," Antoine says.

"Things are going very well." Carlos lifts up his wrists and shows Antoine his diamond bracelet. "I got it today. Whatchu think?"

*I should take that shit.* Antoine forces a smile, "Damn, how much you pay for that?"

"Seven grand."

Antoine replies sarcastically, "I wish I was making money like y'all."

Carlos is having such a good time, he doesn't realize that he is rubbing his wealth in Antoine's face. "Let's celebrate."

Ramon doesn't say much on the ride to the club and Carlos can sense that there is tension between them, but he minds his own business.

They pull up to the front of Club Reign and everyone outside admires Carlos' car. Once inside, they head to the V.I.P section and order bottles. The club is packed, the drinks are flowing and Carlos is having a memorable twentieth birthday. Antoine watches with envy as Carlos and Ramon celebrate. All Antoine ever wanted was to be respected by his older brother, but he realizes that Ramon's 'family talk' is all bullshit. Money is truly all that matters.

Ramon taps Antoine. "You alright?"

"Yeah, I'm cool."

Ramon yells over the loud music, "You know I love you, right?"

Before Antoine can respond, he sees Sasha and excuses himself. Antoine walks through the crowd and pulls Sasha aside. Sasha's dress screams for attention, but her face says, 'Leave me the hell alone.'

"You look nice," Antoine says.

"Miles told me to meet you here. What do you want, Antoine?"

"I need you to get to Carlos and –"

"I'm sick of you and Miles treating me like a prostitute."

Antoine tightly grabs her by the arm and escorts her outside. "Look, you're not the only one being controlled by Miles. I have a plan that will free us both. All you gotta do is get close to Carlos."

Sasha folds her arms. "What's in it for me?"

"Carlos is making a lot of money and I'm sure you know how to empty a man's pockets. Whatever money you swindle from his ass is yours to keep; I just need you to keep tabs on him." Antoine releases his tight grip from her arm. "Can you do that for me?"

Sasha mumbles under her breath, "Ok."

He walks back inside the club and Sasha follows. Antoine escorts Sasha to Carlos' V.I.P section. "Aye, Carlos, I gotchu a birthday present. This is Sasha."

Carlos is floored by Sasha's beauty. He extends his hand. "Would you like to dance?"

"Sure."

Carlos leads Sasha to the dance floor and they dance through multiple songs. Carlos is mesmerized by Sasha's coke bottle shape and the sexual energy between them is undeniable.

For the rest of the night, Antoine watches Sasha and Carlos and there is an obvious attraction. Antoine couldn't have asked for a better situation. While Carlos dances with Sasha, Ramon takes this time to settle their differences.

"You haven't said much to me all night. Everything alright?"

Antoine looks Ramon in the eyes and says, "Every dog has his day."

"What's that supposed to mean?"

Before Antoine can respond, Sasha and Carlos return to the table. Carlos orders more bottles and Ramon pretends to enjoy the night, but Antoine's statement bothers him.

Carlos is so drunk that he doesn't recognize the turmoil at his table. He stumbles over to Antoine and yells, "How do you know Sasha?"

Antoine lies, "I don't. I thought she was beautiful and I wanted y'all to meet." Antoine smirks. "My gift to you."

In the middle of the celebration, Sasha feels her purse vibrating. She reaches inside and reads the text message. *Meeting at my house, tonight.* Seconds later, Antoine receives the same text. Antoine and Sasha look at each other.

Sasha puts her phone into her purse, and stands up. "I have to go."

"Go where? We're just getting started," Carlos says.

"I'm sorry, but I gotta go."

"What's your number?"

Sasha writes her number down on a piece of paper and frantically cuts through the crowded dance floor. Now, it's Antoine's turn, but the only way he is going to be able to cut Carlos' birthday celebration short is to lie.

Antoine yells over the loud music, "I gotta go too."

Carlos can barely keep his eyes open. "You ain't going nowhere, man. It's my birthday."

"I just got an important text about some business. I gotta take care of it."

They swallow their last glass and leave. Inside the car, Ramon drives while Carlos brags about how he's going to fuck the shit out of Sasha. Ramon adjusts the rear view mirror so he can see Antoine's face. Carlos eventually falls asleep. Ramon turns down the radio, "What did you mean by 'every dog has his day?'"

Antoine grins. "I didn't mean anything by it. You're thinking too much."

"Yo, if you gotta problem with me, just be a man and say it."

"I don't have a problem with you, Ramon. We're family."

Ramon pulls up to Antoine's house. Antoine opens the back door and gets out. His conversation with his brother is far from over, but it will have to wait for another time. Antoine watches Ramon drive off, and when he is out of sight, Antoine runs to his car and drives to Miles' house. A half hour later, Antoine rings the bell.

"You're late."

Antoine walks inside and sits next to Sasha.

Miles paces back and forth, "I'm going to take care of Ramon this weekend, but that money better be there."

Antoine smiles. "Don't worry, my brother always keeps his money in the house. What about Carlos?"

"I'll let you and Sasha deal with him."

Miles continues to talk as Sasha reaches into her purse, wraps her fingers around her six inch blade and daydreams about slitting Miles' neck. Sasha feels like she is in the presence of the devil and she wants nothing more than to pay him back for all the evil he has done. While sitting in the meeting, she receives a text message. She discretely looks at her phone and the text reads, *"Hey its Carlos, where are you?"* Sasha grins, *I'm going to milk this nigga for everything he got.* Sasha knows that Miles and Antoine are going to look out for themselves, so she promises to do the same.

# CHAPTER X

Kendrick has severed all ties with the underworld and he is a different man with a different attitude. In order to stay with his mom, he had to enroll in college, and Kendrick keeps his word. He goes from line to line for hours, and when he finishes the enrollment and registration process, he owes Morgan State University and the State of Maryland thousands of dollars in student loans. Confused and exhausted, he sits in front of the library and people watches.

Until today, Kendrick had a narrow perception of college. He thought only the uppity people attended, but as he looks around, he sees people of all different races and colors. He walks inside of the crowded cafeteria and it's completely segregated. Football players eat with football players, pretty girls hang with pretty girls and the outcasts sit by themselves. Kendrick scans the cafeteria looking for his place within this segregated society, when a guy standing at the doorway signals for him.

Kendrick walks over. "Do I know you?"

"Nah, but you can get to know me." He opens the palm of his hands.

"What's that?"

"Ecstasy."

Kendrick has heard stories about ecstasy, but he's never seen it. He remembers his vow to his mom. "Nah, I'm cool."

"Aye look, if you ever need anything, grass, pills whatever, just holla at me. My name Redz."

Kendrick just stares. Redz's ambitious attitude reminds him of Carlos. *I thought I got away from this shit.*

Kendrick watches Redz approach other people on campus and he can't believe his eyes. Still in shock, he calls home to give his mom the good news. Even though Amy is giving Kendrick a chance to redeem himself, she keeps a close eye on him and applies even stricter rules.

"Hey, ma."

"Did you handle everything?"

"I think so, but I'm nervous."

"You'll do fine. Just stay away from the wrong people."

Kendrick can sense that something is bothering her. "What's wrong, ma?"

"I'm two months behind with my rent and if I don't do something, they're going to put me out – but don't worry, God has always found a way. I love you and I'm proud of you, Kendrick."

It's moments like this where he wishes he stayed with Benny so his mother wouldn't have to worry. But he also knows that his mother would rather sleep on the curb than accept drug money. Kendrick knows he is doing the right thing, but these books in his book bag can't help his mother pay the bills. While reading his syllabus, he sees a beautiful, young woman with long

208

black hair and smooth dark skin. Trying his best not to look lame, he makes his move.

"Excuse me, uh…hi. What's your name?"

"You're the first guy to say 'hi' to me. Usually I hear, 'hey shorty' or they'll just whistle. My name is Donna."

"It's nice to meet you, Donna."

Kendrick has been chasing the street life for so long, that he never found time for a relationship. Kendrick isn't in love, but the feeling he has in the pit of his stomach is new and worth exploring. He admires her beauty and hopes his next words don't ruin his chances. "I'm new to this whole college thing."

"This is my second year."

"Well maybe you can show me around."

Donna smiles. "Sounds good."

For the next few weeks, Kendrick and Donna study together. One Tuesday afternoon, Kendrick walks into the library to meet Donna. He looks around and he has never seen so many young people focused on their future. At Woodlawn High School, whenever Kendrick went to the library, he fooled around, but the college library is a very serious place. It is awkwardly quiet and all he can hear is the sounds of pages turning.

"PSST. Kendrick," Donna whispers.

Kendrick walks over and sits down next to her. "Is it always this quiet in here?"

Donna smiles. "It's a library." Donna reaches into her purse, pulls out a pair of thick coke bottle glasses and puts them on her face. "Don't laugh," she says slightly embarrassed.

"Those are the thickest glasses I've ever seen."

"Don't make fun of me."

Kendrick covers his mouth to muffle his laughter. "I'm sorry, but it's actually kinda cute."

"Let's get serious. We have a lot of work to do."

Kendrick hates the library, but if going to the library will allow him to spend time with Donna he'll be here every day. While Donna turns the pages in her three hundred page physics book, Kendrick just stares. In high school, Kendrick wouldn't be seen with a girl with thick glasses and now he can't stay away from one. Every Tuesday afternoon, Kendrick meets Donna at the library and it is no secret that they are attracted to each other. During most studying sessions, neither of them can interact without giving off sexual energy.

One evening, Kendrick softly knocks on her dorm room door and Donna opens it wearing only a long t-shirt and slippers. With lustful eyes, he admires her legs, her pretty toes and nipples poking through her t-shirt.

"Can I come in?"

"I don't know, Kendrick. I –"

"C'mon, Donna. I won't stay long. I just wanna see you."

She looks down the hall to make sure no one is watching and playfully pulls him in. As they stand face to face the room becomes awkwardly silent. "I really like you, Donna."

"I like you too, Kendrick, but I'm not a one man type of girl."

"Whatchu mean?"

"I like to have fun," she says seductively licking her lips.

"Nerds don't know how to have fun."

"Oh really?" She walks into the bathroom and returns with a pink bag the size of a stamp.

"What's that?"

"Shhhh." She reaches inside the bag, swallows a pill and puts another pill in-between her teeth. She puckers her lips inches away from his. "Kiss me."

Ever since Kendrick stopped smoking cocaine laced blunts, he promised himself and his mother that he would never travel back down that road, but one little pill can't hurt. He opens his mouth and with her tongue, Donna pushes the ecstasy pill into his. She uses her left hand to unbuckle his belt and grab his dick. Kendrick thought Donna was the 'take to see mommy' type, but she is clearly the 'fuck tonight' type. Kendrick would like to credit his looks, charm, and humor for Donna's actions, but what he doesn't know is, Donna is a pill popping sex addict.

Kendrick closes his eyes while Donna pecks his neck. She escorts him to her gold brass bed and he lies down. She pulls off each shoe, and rubs his feet. Kendrick has never been pampered, especially by someone as beautiful as Donna. She pulls down his pants and Kendrick quickly unbuttons his shirt.

"Eat my pussy."

"Lay down."

"No, I wanna stand."

Kendrick falls to his knees and pushes his tongue into her bush. Donna grabs the back of his head and moves it in a circular motion. She loves looking down at men when they taste her; it gives her a feeling of power, "Look at me," she demands.

Kendrick can barely breathe, but he'd rather pass out from suffocation than stop. Donna turns around, places her ass in Kendrick's face and spreads her butt as wide as she can. "Lick my ass."

If Kendrick was sober, this request would have killed the vibe, but his ecstasy pill has kicked in and he'll do just about anything to please her. Kendrick closes his eyes, sticks his tongue out as far as he can until the tip of his tongue touches Donna's asshole. The sound that she makes encourages Kendrick to go further. Donna turns around to face Kendrick and pushes him onto the bed. She straddles Kendrick backwards, grabs his dick and pushes him inside. While Donna rides Kendrick's dick like a pogo stick, Kendrick places his thumb on her ass.

"Push it in."

Kendrick pushes his thumb further inside of her ass giving Donna enough pain and pleasure to ask for more.

"I'm 'bout to cum," she moans holding onto the brass rails. "I'm cumming."

Donna shakes and her pussy contracts squeezing Kendrick's dick. Her pussy juices drip down Kendrick's thighs and soak his pubic hairs. Kendrick is clearly not packing enough inches to hang with Donna, but he does the best he can.

"Get on ya back," he orders pushing her legs back as far as he can.

"Go slow."

"No, you need to get fucked."

"Yes, fuck me."

Their chests touch and they look into each other's eyes. Kendrick doesn't know if it's the drug, or the sex, but he's definitely falling for her.

"You feel so good, baby."

Soaked in sweat, Kendrick tries every position he knows. He doesn't want this "sexcapade" to end, but when the human body is ready to explode, you can't stop it. "I'm 'bout to cum," he moans pumping harder. Kendrick pulls out, squirts cum all over Donna's chocolate skin and collapses onto the sex stained sheets. He can't believe this is the same girl he met a few weeks ago. He stares at her with a confused look on his face.

"Why you looking at me like that?"

"You said that you wasn't a one man type of girl, but what does that mean?"

Donna rests her head on Kendrick's chest. "I'm too young to be in a relationship, that's all."

Kendrick laughs. "Never judge a book by its cover."

"Nerds know how to have fun too."

"I see."

Donna may be passionate when she's having sex, but she's not the type to cuddle. Using her bed sheets, she wipes off Kendrick's cum, springs up outta bed and grabs her robe. "Have you ever been to a rave party?"

"No."

Donna smiles. "It's tomorrow, and don't worry, they'll be tons for us to do." She walks into the bathroom, grabs two more ecstasy pills and swallows them. "You ready for round two?" She asks dropping her robe to the ground.

Kendrick is all too familiar with gateway drugs and he didn't come to college to go back to his old ways, but he is simply not strong enough to withstand his other addiction – pussy. Sasha pushes him onto the bed and climbs on top of him. "You ain't seen shit yet."

\* \* \*

The next day, Kendrick and Donna stand outside of Donna's dorm room when Redz pulls up in a baby blue Chevy Impala with chrome wheels. His music is ridiculously loud and he has leaned as far back as he can in his seat. At first, Kendrick thought Redz was just some struggling student selling drugs to get by, but Redz's car is a clear indicator that he's getting money.

Donna walks over to the driver's side window. "Can my friend, Kendrick, come with us?"

"Yeah, that's cool."

Kendrick sits in the backseat. "So where we going?"

"To my friend Trish's house. She lives in Towson." Donna looks at Redz. "Kendrick has never been to a rave party."

"Are you serious? We gotta pop his cherry."

Redz reaches into his pocket and pulls out six ecstasy pills. Donna swallows hers, but Kendrick hesitates. Redz adjust his rearview mirror so he can see Kendrick's eyes.

"Whatchu waiting for?"

*I shouldn't do this,* Kendrick doesn't want to look lame, so he takes the pills and swallows them. Kendrick can hear his mother's voice and feel her disappointment, but it's too late now. He is unsure of how his body will react to two ecstasy pills, so he takes deep breaths in an attempt to control the high. Moments later, Redz drives into a gated community and parks in front of a beautiful seven thousand square foot home. Cars are parked everywhere and from the outside, they can feel the base rattling the ground. Kendrick doesn't know what to expect, but it doesn't matter; his ecstasy pills have kicked in and he is already having the best time of his life.

Donna knocks on the door and Samantha opens it, wearing a lime green fluorescent glow stick around her neck. Samantha is a rich white girl who goes to Towson State University. She is in her third year and has yet to choose a major, and probably never will. Samantha's parents are celebrating their twentieth anniversary in Hawaii and they left Samantha in charge. Kendrick steps inside looking around, admiring the expensive furniture, and marbled floors.

Samantha gives Redz a hug. "I'm so glad you're here. Everybody was starting to panic." She sees Kendrick and introduces herself, "Hi." She walks over to Kendrick and playfully presses her body up against his. "I like him, Donna."

Kendrick has only seen a white woman fucking a black man in porn. He never thought that he would be getting sexually harassed by one, but he likes it.

Redz pulls out a bag containing over a hundred ecstasy pills and Samantha jumps up and down like a child. If Redz didn't provide the pills for Samantha's parties, he would've never been invited. But, being the supplier for Samantha's party gives him a V.I.P pass. Instead of serving each person, Samantha collects the money from her guests and pays Redz upfront.

"Where's the money?"

Samantha reaches into her purse, pulls out a large knot of money and counts it. "I got two grand," she says.

Redz takes the money and gives Donna a zip lock plastic bag with two hundred ecstasy pills inside. Kendrick keeps his cool, but in the back of his mind, he's thinking, *Did this nigga just make two grand?* Kendrick can't believe how easy it was for Samantha to give Redz two thousand dollars, but to a bunch of kids with rich parents, two grand is nothing.

Donna leads them to the basement. Kendrick walks downstairs and is shocked. He watches almost one hundred people jumping around like maniacs wearing glow sticks all over their bodies. Samantha walks to the middle of the crowd and holds the bag in the air.

Redz whispers in Kendrick's ear, "Watch this."

Everyone flocks towards her as if she was giving out free money. Kendrick may have promised that he would never touch drugs again, but there's no way he can deny what his eyes are seeing. Whenever Kendrick thought of the word "fiend", he envisioned a black homeless person, but not a white college kid. He stares in awe as the future doctors, lawyers, scientists and teachers, get high like fiends.

216

Before going to college, Kendrick was conditioned to believe that school is for suckers and nerds, but it's the exact opposite. Maybe it's the drugs, but Kendrick feels like he may have found the final piece to the puzzle that will not only make his mother happy, but also put money in his pocket.

Redz taps Kendrick on the shoulder. "You look like you need some air."

"Yeah, it's crazy in here."

They step outside and the brisk air wakes Kendrick up. Redz pulls out a knot of money, counts it and Kendrick can't help but stare. As Redz flicks through twenty-dollar bills, Kendrick thinks about how his mother is facing eviction.

Redz brags, "I ain't never leaving college."

"You don't wanna graduate?"

Redz laughs. "For what? Every year a pill popper, weed smoker, or coke sniffer enrolls with nothing but their parent's money to spend."

In the middle of their conversation, Donna opens the front door. "Kendrick, I've been looking for you. I wanna show you something."

Donna leads Kendrick upstairs, pushes open the bedroom door and Samantha is lying under the sheets. Kendrick stands stiff. *Oh my God, this isn't really happening.*

What are you waiting for?" Samantha asks.

High and confused, Kendrick slowly walks over to the bed. He gently grabs the sheet and pulls it down exposing Samantha's naked body. With both hands,

Samantha grabs her breasts and pushes them together. *Got damn she got some big ass nipples.*

"Have you ever fucked a white girl before?" Donna asks.

Kendrick looks like a fish out of water. The last time he was this nervous, was when he was with Ebony. Kendrick says softly, "No."

Samantha positions herself on the bed, spreads her legs and shows Kendrick her blonde trim bush. Kendrick tries to convince himself that pussy is pussy no matter the ethnic background, but something about seeing it up close is very intimidating. Samantha can sense that Kendrick is out of his league so she sits up, grabs his belt buckle and pulls him closer. Samantha is so high that she can barely keep her eyes open. She unfastens his belt, wraps her small petite fingers around his dick and swallows him.

*I can't believe this white bitch is sucking my dick.* Kendrick runs his fingers through Samantha's hair as her head moves up and down.

"I love black dick," she says while slapping Kendrick's manhood against her face.

Samantha stops, stretches out across the bed and opens her legs. Curious to know what a white woman tastes like, Kendrick crawls on top of her and kisses her neck.

"Bite me," she orders.

Kendrick sinks his teeth into her neck and Samantha's toes curl from the pain. Kendrick kisses his way down to her belly button and he can smell Samantha's pussy. He runs the tip of his nose into her

218

bush and she flinches. Kendrick opens his mouth wide enough to suck her clit like a vacuum.

"Oh my God." She yells at the top of her lungs, "Don't stop."

With his fingers, Kendrick spreads her pussy and pushes his tongue further inside until her juices form a wet spot on the sheets.

"Put it in."

"You want me to fuck you?"

"Yes, fuck this white pussy."

Kendrick doesn't have a lot of experience, but something about hearing a white bitch beg for some dick turns him on. Kendrick grabs his dick and runs it against Samantha's dripping clit. "Oh shit, I don't have any condoms," he says, but neither of them really cares. Kendrick knows that Samantha and Donna are two freaks who probably do this sort of thing often, but his urge to please his flesh won't allow him to stop. He convinces himself that Samantha is disease free because she is white and pushes himself inside of her. Samantha's squeaky voice gives Kendrick a sense of power and he pumps her as hard as he can. Samantha's eyes roll into the back of her head and she screams. Completely turned on, Donna walks over to the bed and stares. Donna enjoys watching Kendrick's dick move in and out.

Donna stands at the edge of the bed, unbuttons her pants and puts her hand inside of her panties. Redz has had enough of listening to Samantha yell, so he opens the door and peeks inside. "Oh shit," Redz mumbles. Seconds later, he walks inside and signals for Donna to come over. Redz has had numerous threesomes with Donna and Samantha, so he doesn't waste time getting down to business.

"You know what to do," Redz says unbuckling his belt.

Donna faces the wall and pulls her sky blue thong over her ass.

"I'ma fuck the shit out you," Redz says while reaching into his back pocket. He pulls out a condom and rips it open, but before he can start, the bedroom door swings open and a chubby white guy named Timothy bursts in.

Redz quickly pulls up his pants and screams, "What da fuck, fat boy?"

"I'm sorry, I was looking for Samantha."

Donna looks over and yells, "Get the fuck outta here, Tim."

Tim pleads holding a fist full of money, "We need more pills. I got eight hundred dollars."

Donna tries to push Tim out, but Redz stops her. "Hold up," Redz says buckling his belt, "I gotchu, fat boy."

"My name is Tim."

Redz snatches the money. "Whatever."

Samantha and Kendrick are so engulfed in their fuck-fest that they don't even realize Tim is in the room. Kendrick is determined to bust a nut all over this white girl's face.

Donna grabs Redz wrists. "C'mon. Tim can wait."

Redz snatches his arm away. "Get the fuck off me, Donna. Aye, Kendrick."

Kendrick can hear his name being called, but he can't stop. Frustrated and horny, Donna folds her arms and pouts. Redz cuts on the lights, walks over to the bed and hits the headboard.

Kendrick stops and looks around. "What, nigga? I'm 'bout to cum."

"Fuck that, take a ride with me."

Kendrick sighs. *Cock blocking muthafucka.*

Kendrick lifts up, but Samantha pulls him back down on top of her. "C'mon, Redz, he'll be out in a second," she says breathing heavily.

"Shut up." Redz looks at Kendrick. "Take a ride with me," he says as if he isn't taking no for an answer.

Kendrick pulls his dick out of Samantha's pussy and every inch that Samantha loses the angrier she becomes. While Kendrick gets dressed, Samantha covers herself with the sheets. She's afraid to check Redz, so she turns to face Tim.

"Why are you still standing there? Get out."

Tim stutters, "I…I'm sorry. I –"

"Just leave," Donna shouts pushing Tim into the hallway.

While tying his shoes, all Kendrick can think about was how close he was to cumming, but he knows if he chooses pussy over money, Redz will never do business with him.

"We'll be right back," Redz says before turning the door knob.

Samantha mumbles under her breath, "You could have at least let us finish."

"Whatchu say?"

"Nothing."

"I didn't come here to fuck, pop pills and dance to that crazy ass music like the rest of you muthafuckas. I came here to get money," he yells opening the door. "I said we'll be back."

Kendrick follows Redz to his car. "Damn, nigga, I was about to bust."

"Fuck them bitches. Trust me, they already found our replacements." Redz opens the car door, and he asks, "Did you go raw?"

Kendrick lies. "Hell no."

"Good, that bitch burnt me twice. Ain't nothing worse than rich white trash, you feel me?"

Inside the car, Redz plays his music loud bobbing his head to the music. Kendrick looks at him, *Damn this nigga remind me of Carlos.* Kendrick has been waiting all night for the right time to ask about Redz's hustle and there is no better time than right now.

"I know we don't know a lot about each other, but I'm trynna get down with you."

Redz exhales a cloud of smoke. "When I first saw you, I knew you was a hustler. You don't look like the college type." Redz turns down the radio, "What really brought you to Morgan State?"

"You right, I'm not the college type, but I made a promise to leave that street shit alone and get my degree."

"So why you asking me about my business?"

Kendrick grins. "I just saw you make two grand in one fucking night. That's why."

222

"Yeah, I hear you. But you still haven't answered my question about why are you in college?"

"I wanna degree, I guess."

"A degree in what?"

Kendrick never thought that far. He hoped that if he just enrolled into college that his problems would fade away, but everything that he has tried to get away from, found him. He stares out the window looking for an answer and he realizes that he is still very lost.

Redz shakes his head. "By the time you graduate, I'll be making enough money to hire you. I don't care what kinda degree you get, they ain't gonna pay you this kinda money." Redz pulls up to a red light and points at a group of drug dealers standing on the corner. "Look at them niggas all hustling backwards," Redz says, rolling down his window.

"Whatchu mean?"

Redz chuckles, but he is dead serious. "The hood trained me to think that niggas in college were stupid. So while they shoot each other up and compete over broke junkies, all I do is walk around a college campus and I'm making twice as much than all dem niggas." Redz brags. "Their customers get food stamps, my customers got student loans." Redz looks at the hustlers on the corner like they're beneath him. "I used to be just like them, stuck to the block and caught up in bullshit. I had no idea that the world was larger than my neighborhood."

"Where'd you grow up?"

Redz grins. "I'm from the eastside, and I used to hustle with this nigga named Mack. I heard he got popped by some niggas from Westside."

Kendrick almost swallows his tongue. *Bmore is too fucking small,* he thinks while Redz continues to share stories of his days hustling on the block. For the rest of the night, Kendrick keeps his cool, but he knows it is just a matter of time.

* * *

The next morning, Kendrick sits in Professor Wynfield's Biology class wearing dark shades. Normally, Kendrick always participates in Professor Wynfield's lecture, but his head is hurting so bad from last night that he can barely keep his eyes open. After listening to Professor Wynfield's monotone voice for an hour, he falls asleep.

Professor Wynfield yells, "Wake up, Kendrick. Class is over."

Kendrick jumps up, looks around and notices that he is the only one in class.

"Yeah, wassup?"

"Take off your shades when you talk to me."

"I can't, it's too bright in here."

"What's going on with you, Kendrick? I used to look forward to seeing you participate in my lessons and now, you're just a disruption. Is everything alright?"

Kendrick grunts. "Yeah."

"I used to be just like you. I wanted the success, but I didn't want to work for it. But I made a choice to stop

224

living a destructive lifestyle and now look. I have my doctorate, and I'm a college professor molding the minds of the future."

Kendrick bursts out laughing. "Are you serious? You sound like one of those corny ass commercials." Kendrick claps his hands. "Good for you. You're a teacher." He cheers sarcastically.

Professor Wynfield picks up his briefcase. "In order to be successful in society, you gotta come through college. You don't play sports, you don't sing, and you don't rap, so how are you going to secure your financial future? I wonder how your mother would feel if she saw how you're conducting yourself."

That plucked a nerve. Kendrick takes off his shades and looks Professor Wynfield in the eyes. "You wake up every morning, put on your cheap ass suit and drive around in your little ass car, and you think you can tell me about being successful?"

"Why are you here, Kendrick? Why bother?"

Kendrick glances at the clock hanging on the wall. "I would answer that, but you stopped being my professor when class ended."

"What a waste," Professor Wynfield mumbles before closing the door behind him.

Kendrick simply doesn't give a fuck, so he puts on his sunglass and leaves. With his head feeling like it was hit with a sledge hammer, he walks outside and sees Redz sitting on the library steps. Kendrick sits down next to him and covers his face with his hands.

"Whatchu doing out here?"

Redz anxiously looks around. "I'm waiting for somebody."

Kendrick sits down next to Redz. "Last night was crazy. My head is killing me."

"You better be careful with Donna and Samantha. Them bitches need help; all they do is pop pills and fuck," Redz replies.

"I thought Donna was a good girl and then outta nowhere, she switched it up."

"That bitch always been like that. She will sell her soul for a bag of ecstasy pills."

Kendrick rubs his temples trying to ease the migraine that has now moved to the left side of his head. "Oh yeah, Professor Wynfield tried to give me a lecture today."

Redz bursts out laughing. "Oh shit, I can't stand his Uncle Tom ass. I had him last semester, and that nigga really think an education is all you need," Redz jokes. "I know he ain't gettin bitches driving that old ass hatchback. That nigga look like he driving a turtle."

Kendrick doesn't want to laugh because it'll make his head hurt, but he can't front; that shit was funny. "You right, that shit don't even sound right."

Redz pats Kendrick on the shoulder. "That's what I've been trying to tell you." Redz reaches into his pocket and pulls out the largest knot of money that Kendrick has ever seen. "I got enough money in my pocket to buy Professor Wynfield's car and the clothes off his back, you feel me? What he got?"

"A turtle."

Redz laughs, but his playful attitude quickly fades. "All jokes aside, you ready to get this money or what?"

"Yeah."

Kendrick stares off into space. *College is a fucking hoax.* Kendrick thinks back to when he walked across stage at his high school graduation and looked out to the thousands of faces. Each person from his graduating class was sold a dream that he is no longer buying. He realizes that no matter where you are in life, everyone is trying to find themselves and that there is no one path to success. He hated how Professor Wynfield treated him and he was even more motivated to prove that he can be successful without a college degree.

Thirty minutes later, the hardest black Range Rover that Kendrick has ever seen pulls up across the street. Redz looks at Kendrick and winks his eye. "Today is your lucky day. That nigga in the Range Rover is who I get my shit from. Follow me."

Kendrick fixes his clothes, while admiring the twenty-two inch chrome rims. *I'm bout to get this money.* They walk over to the luxury vehicle and the tinted passenger window rolls down.

"Kendrick?"

*This nigga know me?* Kendrick steps closer and peeks inside. "Benny?"

"Small world, huh?" Benny unlocks the doors. "Get in, we got some catching up to do."

Kendrick is speechless. *Is this really happening?*

Benny grins showing his gold teeth. "I knew you was gonna come back."

"How do y'all know each other?" Redz asks.

"We used to be partners, and we did everything together." Benny chuckles, "Then he all of a sudden had a change of heart. I told this nigga to stick wit me." Benny shares the story of how Kendrick walked away from thousands of dollars as if Kendrick isn't sitting there. The more Benny brags, the angrier Kendrick becomes – but he keeps his composure.

Benny looks at Kendrick and notices that he has a book bag in his lap. "Yo, please don't tell me you actually go to Morgan State. You a fucking student?" Benny laughs, "So, you wanna work for me?"

Kendrick grits his teeth. "I guess so."

"You guess so? Nah, nigga, you better know so. You gotta start at the bottom just like the rest of these niggas and work ya way up. Ain't that right, Redz?"

Redz nods his head from the backseat. Benny could've said anything and Redz would have agreed. Redz is nothing but an ambitious follower and will do anything to get to the top of the hustlers ladder. Since Kendrick and Benny have a past, Kendrick may be a clear threat to his plans to become Benny's right hand man.

Benny pulls into the gas station and parks. "Aye, Redz, I need to speak with Kendrick in private."

*I should've never brought this nigga around.* Redz reluctantly opens the back door. He stands outside and stares at Kendrick with envy, but all Redz can see is his reflection from the dark tint.

"Redz reminds me of you," Benny says lighting a cigarette. "He was just a dirty ass eastside nigga. But I took him off the block, enrolled him into Morgan State with one purpose, to move my product. He trusted me and now he's making a lot of fucking money. You should have listened to me, Kendrick, but you didn't."

"You killed your friend. How was I supposed to trust you? You shot that nigga like he was a piece of meat."

Benny yells, "He was a piece of meat. Look, I didn't get in this game to make friends, and I don't need friends." Benny lifts his shirt and shows his gun. "This is my fucking friend right here. He do what I say and he'll never get scared like you."

"I ain't no killer, so I'm not going to pretend to be," Kendrick turns to face Benny, "and I'm not gonna apologize for wanting to change my life. But you're right, I shoulda never left."

Benny takes off his shades. "That's why I didn't kill you, Kendrick. No matter what, you say whatchu feel, but why should I trust you now?"

"Because I'm still the same nigga," Kendrick declares trying to convince himself that he still possesses the heart to hustle.

Benny cuts his eye at Kendrick. "We'll see." He rolls down the window. "Aye, Redz, get back in."

Benny drives into the inner city slums of Baltimore City. He parks in front of a row home and rolls down the driver's window. A group of kids run to his car and drop bundles of cash into his lap. Kendrick looks on with amazement at how disciplined Benny's workers are. Everyone is involved in his operation, including the owners of the local liquor stores and laundry mats. In a matter of minutes, Benny collects close to fifteen thousand dollars.

Benny can feel Kendrick staring at the knots of money on his lap. He drives around the block and gives Kendrick a tour of his drug operation. Benny pulls up in front of another home and parks. As soon as he places his foot onto the concrete, people of all ages swarm him. Kendrick thought that Karma would have placed Benny in a casket by now, but instead, Benny is a certified kingpin.

Kendrick and Redz follow Benny into the row home. Kendrick looks around and this doesn't look like the home of a kingpin. He notices a twenty-seven inch outdated television, pictures neatly placed on the wall, flower patterned curtains, antique fixtures on the coffee table and plastic covering on an aqua blue couch. Benny leads Kendrick and Redz into the kitchen and standing over the stove wearing a colorful nightgown and slippers is a woman named Silvia. For whatever reason, Benny is clearly using Silvia for his own personal gain.

"Hey, Silvia, this is Kendrick. He's the one that left me in the motel with ten bricks, and now he's in college."

Silvia grins showing her toothless smile. "College? You a damn fool."

Kendrick feels like an idiot. He expected someone of her age to be happy to see a young man get an education, but instead Silvia makes him feel like the dumbest nigga alive. He wants to cuss her old ass out, but holds his tongue. Benny leads them to the basement and Kendrick can't believe his eyes. Two men are cutting coke on a glass table, while another man stands over a portable burner, turning coke into crack cocaine. Benny walks around like a true boss and his workers acknowledge him with respect. Kendrick can't help but think that if he stayed with Benny, he would be overseeing this operation.

"Follow me," Benny says.

Kendrick and Redz follow him to the back of the basement. Benny reaches into a cabinet, pulls out his personal stash of cocaine and pushes it towards Kendrick.

"I don't do that shit anymore."

"Yeah you do."

"I'm serious, Benny. I ain't touching that shit."

Benny lifts up his shirt showing his gun. "Yeah you are."

"Are you serious?"

"This time you can't walk away, and you gotta earn my trust."

Kendrick dips his pinky finger into the powder and all he can think about is his mother. He places it near his nose, but Benny stops him.

"Nah, nigga, that's for amateurs," Benny says rolling up his sleeve. "This how the big boys get high."

Benny places pieces of the cocaine on a rusty spoon, grabs the lighter and watches the narcotic bubble. He grabs a long rubber band and wraps it multiple times around his arm. Benny's heart races with excitement and his veins pulsate as if they are screaming for the drug. He grabs the needle filling it with the narcotic, and pushes it into his vein. Kendrick watches the drug flow into his blood and Benny stumbles into the wall.

Kendrick can remember his father leaving used needles and rubber bands in the living room after he got high. Kendrick always hated needles, but if he doesn't do it, it could cost him his life. He struggles to wrap the rubber band around his arm, so Redz uses this opportunity to let Kendrick know where he stands. Redz forcefully grabs Kendrick wrists and wraps the rubber band around his arm as tightly as he can. Kendrick's hands shake the closer the eye of the needle gets to his skin.

"This nigga scared. Let me do it," Redz suggests.

Kendrick thinks to pass Redz the needle, but the way Redz is staring makes Kendrick uncomfortable. "Don't fucking touch me, I got it." If Redz would have taken the needle, he would have filled Kendrick up with so much shit, he would have overdosed. Kendrick takes a deep breath and slowly pushes the needle inside. *I'm sorry, ma.* He drops the needle and stumbles into the wall.

Benny watches Kendrick slowly fall to the floor. "Let our new customer enjoy the ride. C'mon, I gotta handle some business."

"What about Kendrick?"

"He ain't going nowhere."

Kendrick's eyelids become heavy and he stares off into space. Benny walks out, but Redz stays behind. While Kendrick goes in and out of consciousness, Redz leans towards and whispers into Kendrick's right ear, "I don't giva fuck about you, nigga. Have fun."

Hours later, Kendrick wakes up and realizes that he is still in Benny's basement. He stands up, steps over the needle and looks around. He walks towards the steps expecting to see Benny's workers cooking and bagging up coke, but it is completely empty. When Benny brought him down into the basement, he saw piles of cocaine all over the old wood table and he could smell the money brewing from the portable stove, but everything is gone as if what he saw never existed.

The basement is spotless and Kendrick can't seem to figure out where the time has gone. He walks up the squeaky steps, unlocks the basement door and softly pushes it open. He walks into the kitchen expecting to see Silvia's mean ass, but she isn't there either. Kendrick repeatedly calls Benny's name, but no one responds so he walks toward the front door and steps outside. The streets are quiet and it seems like the only thing moving is him. Afraid to step off the porch, Kendrick sits on the step. An hour later, a white Toyota 4 Runner pulls up in front of the house. Benny gets out, walks towards the house and sits next to Kendrick.

*I never thought I'd be happy to see this nigga,* "Where's everybody at? I thought I was in the fucking twilight zone." Kendrick says.

Benny checks his watch. "Shop closed. It's three o'clock in the morning." Benny pulls out a small plastic bag containing coke. He dips his long pinky finger nail into the powder then stuffs his nose, "You wanna take a hit?"

Kendrick's conscious screams, *No,* but his body says, "Yes." He stuffs his nose and his nervousness and fear goes away almost instantly. He is so high that he forgets that he is sitting in the middle of the hood with someone who once wished he were dead.

Benny wipes any remaining residue off his nose. "Look, if you selling my shit, you gotta do it my way. It's very simple, you go where I tell you go and you do what I tell you to. I promise you, if you follow my rules, you'll make a lot of money."

"Just tell me whatchu want me to do."

Benny smiles. "Good answer. I want you to handle the weed and Redz will handle the ecstasy."

"But it's more money in ecstasy."

"You haven't even started yet and you're breaking the fucking rules already. Besides, Redz earned that, and you gotta work your way up, you feel me?"

\* \* \*

It takes Kendrick a few weeks to build up his clientele and within a few months, he's supplying half of the students on campus. He isn't making as much as Redz, but Kendrick is making enough to help his mother with the bills. Whenever Kendrick speaks to his mother, he creates such a web of lies that he often forgets. To keep his mother from asking a thousand questions, Kendrick tells her that he's working a part-timejob on campus and that his classmate allows him to stay overnight in the dorms, but he is actually usually too high to leave Benny's couch. Kendrick is making money, but he spends hundreds a week – sometimes a day – on cocaine, which is exactly where Benny wants him.

At 12:00 in the afternoon, Redz is walking across the campus when he sees Donna running towards him. She gives him a long hug and seductively licks her lips.

"Hey, I've been looking for you," she says, pulling Redz into the empty auditorium.

"What are you doing?"

"I wanna suck ya dick."

She loosens his buckle and his pants fall to the ground. She grabs his dick and swallows it until she gags. This isn't the first time Donna wanted a dick in her mouth, but this time she has a trick up her sleeve. While Redz's eyes are closed, Donna reaches into his pants pocket, grabs his bag of ecstasy pills and slips them inside of her purse. Redz breathes heavily until he fills her mouth with cum. Donna stands to her feet, wipes her mouth and walks away.

"C'mon, let's go back to your room and finish," he says placing his hand up her blue skirt.

"I just wanted to suck ya dick."

"I'm tryna fuck." Redz shakes his head. "You need to slow down, Donna. Them pills gotchu going crazy."

Donna bats her eyes. "You wasn't saying that when I was sucking ya dick," she says before leaving.

Redz pulls up his pants. "That bitch got problems," he mumbles under his breath.

Later that day, Redz meets with Kendrick in the school cafeteria, but Redz looks frustrated. He talks to himself and constantly pats himself down checking his pockets.

"I can't find my shit and I gotta pay Benny today." Redz stops talking and tries to recall what he did and it hits him. "Fuck. I knew that bitch was up to something. Donna took it."

"You sure?"

235

"Yeah, I'm sure."

Redz takes off running towards Donna's dorm room and Kendrick follows. He bangs on the door. "Open up."

Donna runs to the bathroom and hides the bag inside of her tampon box. She knew Redz was coming, but she doesn't care; she grabbed enough pills to last her a few weeks. In Donna's world, ruining her friendship with Redz is worth one hundred pills of ecstasy. She takes a deep breath and opens the door. Redz rushes in, grabs her throat, and forces her onto the bed.

"Bitch, you must be crazy."

Donna struggles to breathe. "I didn't do anything."

Redz grabs Donna by the hair and throws her frail body over the bed. He kicks her repeatedly until she begs him to stop. While Donna cries, Redz searches the room destroying everything he sees. The longer it takes him to find his pills, the angrier he becomes. With his eyes full of rage, Redz hits Donna in the face breaking her nose. Donna is tougher than Redz thought. He hoped by now that she would confess, but she doesn't and he is exhausted.

"Bitch, I know you got it."

With her hair mangled and her nose dripping blood onto the floor, Donna balls up her body into the fetal position.

"She's not gonna talk," Kendrick says.

As hard as he can, Redz kicks her again and Donna loses her breath. She violently coughs and struggles to find her next gasp of air. Kendrick has seen enough. He walks over and grabs Redz by the arm.

"People are standing outside of the door. We gotta go."

Redz snatches away from Kendrick's grip and balls up his fist. "You better getcha fucking hands off me, nigga." Breathing hard, Redz stares Kendrick into the eyes. He's been waiting for the moment to lay Kendrick on his ass.

Kendrick steps in Redz face. "I ain't no bitch nigga, so you better watch who you talkin to. She's not going to tell you shit."

Two hundred ecstasy pills are worth at least two thousand dollars on the street, and now Redz has to explain this loss to Benny. Kendrick is right, Redz can beat Donna until she's blue in the face, but she isn't going to utter a word. Redz trashes her room breaking anything of value before pushing his way through the crowd and leaving.

\* \* \*

Days later, Kendrick sits on the bench in the middle of the campus surrounded by people when his cell phone rings. He pulls out his phone and looks at the number. "Shit." He excuses himself from the crowd and answers, "Hey, ma. Did you get the money I sent you?"

"I got it, and thank you, but when are you coming to see me?"

"Um…I've been having a lot of tests and I've been studying real hard, ma."

"You can't find no time in your day to come see me? I still worry about you," she replies.

"Don't worry about me, I gotta three point seven grade point average." Amy doesn't respond. "Did you hear me?"

"Kendrick, you don't have to impress me. I know you are a smart boy. I just wanted you to give it a try and put up a real effort." Amy cries, "I'm so proud of you."

"I love you, ma, I'll come see you soon. Ok?"

Amy is tired of him making excuses, so instead of responding, she hangs up the phone.

To hear his mother cry touched Kendrick's heart in ways unimaginable. He has become so comfortable with lying that he forgot how much his mother means to him. From the beginning of his life, his mother has been his safety net and all she wants is for him to try. Kendrick hasn't been to class in weeks and the only things in his book bag are a knife, a scale and bags of weed. Instead of walking back over to the crowd, he checks his watch and remembers that Professor Wynfield's class starts in three minutes. *If you want me to try, then I'ma try.*

Kendrick opens the classroomdoor and tries to make a quiet entrance, but the professor won't let him get off that easy.

"Mr. Kendrick Rumsfeld. It's nice to see you."

Kendrick finds a seat in the last row. "Nice to see you too." He mumbles under his breath, "Punk muthafucka."

During Professor Wynfield's class, Kendrick's skin begins to crawl from withdrawals. He takes deep breaths and constantly readjusts in his seat, but nothing works. The Professor's class is scheduled an hour and a half long and Kendrick has an hour to go. The more

Professor Wynfield talks, the more confused Kendrick becomes. He doesn't want to disappoint his mother, but as he watches his classmates jotting down notes and raising their hands to answer questions, Kendrick becomes certain that college is not for him. He looks around the room and an arrogant grin appears on his face, *Why the fuck am I here? I got more money than everybody in this damn room. How is any of this shit gonna make me rich? Fuck this.* In the middle of the lecture, Kendrick excuses himself through the rows of students.

"Kendrick, where are you going? We have an exam tomorrow."

"I'm done wit' this shit."

Professor Wynfield uses this opportunity to make an example out of Kendrick's decision. "I want you all to get a good look at what happens when you let this wonderful experience called 'college' pass you by."

All of the students burst into laughter as Kendrick crosses the room. The professor continues to mock Kendrick until he makes it to the door.

Professor Wynfield sits down and crosses his legs. "Kendrick, before you leave, can you please tell the class your plans for the future?"

Normally, Kendrick would have a sharp, funny, sarcastic reply but nothing comes out of his mouth, because the truth is, he has no plan. His classmates wait with anticipation for him to put the professor in his place, but Kendrick just stares.

"That's what I thought." Professor yells, "Now, get out of my class so I can teach the future doctors, lawyers, and professors of this generation."

Kendrick reaches into his pocket and pulls out a wad of cash. "How much money do you got in your pocket, professor?"

Professor Wynfield empties his pockets and places his items on the desk. "Money comes and goes, but an education lasts forever."

"Fuck you and this school."

Kendrick spits on the floor and never steps foot into a classroom again.

# CHAPTER XI

Carlos is making too much money to be faithful, but one particular girl manages to grab his attention. Rhonda, who is seven years older than Carlos, is nothing like the other chicken heads who he spent his money on. Rhonda is a single mother who runs a successful hair salon on Reisterstown Road. After her baby father's incarceration, she vowed to stay away from hustlers, but she sees a level of maturity in Carlos that is promising. Rhonda has been trying to get Carlos to move in with her, but Carlos is too much of a playboy and he isn't ready to live with her bad ass eight-year-old son, Malik.

One night, Carlos and Rhonda are sitting on the couch watching television. Normally, Malik is trying his best to stop Carlos from trying to get inside his mother panties, but tonight, Malik is gone. Between running her salon and being a mother, free time doesn't come often – so when it does, all Rhonda wants to do is be under her man. While watching television with Rhonda's head buried into his chest, Carlos receives a phone call from a number that he doesn't recognize.

"Where you going?" she asks.

"I gotta take this call." Carlos walks into the bathroom. "Yeah, who's dis?"

"Hey, Carlos. How are you? It's Sasha. Remember me?"

Just the sound of her voice makes him smile. The last time he saw Sasha, she was rushing out of the club. He closes the bathroom door and whispers, "I thought you forgot about me."

"Can you meet me at Red Lobster on Security Boulevard?"

"When?"

"Now."

Carlos knows how much quality time means to Rhonda, but there is no way he's going to miss out on a chance to see Sasha. He walks into the bedroom and Rhonda is waiting for him to lie down so she can finish cuddling. Every time Carlos lies, he has this nervous twitch that causes him to scratch his head and Rhonda knows it.

Scratching his head, Carlos walks to the edge of the bed and lies, "Aye, babe, I gotta…um…I gotta meet with Ramon to get some –"

Rhonda sits up and looks him up and down. "How long are you gonna be?"

"I'm just gonna run out for a second and –"

"How long?"

"I hate it when you do that, Rhonda."

"And I hate it when you do this. We barely get to see each other." Rhonda slowly unbuttons her blouse. "Can whatever you gotta do wait?"

"I can't, but when I come back, we can do whatever you want."

Fifteen minutes later, Carlos pulls into Red Lobster's parking lot. He walks inside, and Sasha is sitting in the back looking gorgeous. They talk for hours and the alcohol begins to take its toll. Carlos stares into her eyes and he cannot deny his physical attraction.

Sasha is here for one reason, to take Carlos for everything he's got and he has no clue. She doesn't have time to play the innocent little girl, so she moves her chair closer.

"Can I say something without you looking at me crazy?"

"Yeah."

"The first time I saw you, I knew I wanted to give you some."

"Some what?"

"You know," Sasha says running her fingertips up her inner thigh, "so don't play hard to get when you know you want to."

"When?"

"Tonight."

"Hold on, I gotta make a call."

Sasha teases, "You gotta girlfriend?"

"Not really, I mean… it's kinda complicated. Just wait right here." Carlos walks away and calls Rhonda. "Hey, Rhonda, is everything ok?"

"I'm sorry I had an attitude with you. Can I make it up to you?"

"Uh sure."

"I'm gonna make our favorite dinner tonight, so on your way home grab some Moscato."

While Carlos is on the phone with Rhonda, Sasha walks up behind him, wraps her arms around his shoulders and kisses his neck. Carlos tries to keep his cool, but Sasha's soft lips are clearly a distraction.

"Oh...ah...ok, what you say, Rhonda?"

"I hate it when you don't listen to me. Before you get home, buy some Moscato."

Sasha moves her hand under Carlos' shirt and rubs his chest.

"Baby, I'm not going to make it tonight. I –"

"Carlos."

"Ok, ok, but I gotta make another stop first."

"Alright, I love you and don't forget the –"

Carlos hangs up the phone.

Sasha grins. "I thought you said she wasn't your girlfriend."

"It's complicated."

Carlos has never felt guilty for dealing with multiple women, but for some reason, this voice in the back of his mind whispers, *Don't do it.* Unfortunately, that voice can't compete with the urge he has in his pants. He follows Sasha to her car and watches her soft ass move from left to right.

"Are we going back to your place?"

"You need to get home, dontchu?"

Carlos steps closer. "I'm with you right now."

Sasha opens her back door, turns around and lifts up her skirt exposing her white thong, "Whatchu waiting for?" she asks arching her back.

Carlos looks around. "Right here?"

"Whatchu scared?"

Carlos unzips his pants, pulls her panties to the side and pushes his unprotected dick inside of her moist pussy. He pumps Sasha as hard as he can until white foam covers his dick staining his boxers. He spreads her butt cheeks more so he can see her pretty pink and brown pussy. He pulls out, kneels down and sucks her pussy. Sasha screams and the sound of her high pitch voice turns Carlos on.

"Put it back in." she moans, "I wanna feel it."

Sasha's pussy is so wet that Carlos slides back in with ease. She thrusts her hips back to prove that she can take all the dick that Carlos can give.

"I'm 'bout to cum."

Carlos pulls out and Sasha kneels down before him, stroking his manhood up and down until he shoots his load into her craving mouth. Out the corner of his eye, Carlos notices a couple walking towards them but he doesn't care. He watches Sasha lick her mouth clean of his cum and just like that, he is hooked. Carlos hasn't felt this sneaky since high school, and this sexual, spontaneous excitement is exactly what he needed. Rhonda would never have sex in a public parking lot; she is too much of woman to stoop to such a level. At this moment, Carlos realizes that he doesn't need a woman, he needs a freak bitch and Sasha is his number one candidate. Sasha stands up and fixes her clothes.

"Shouldn't you be leaving?" she asks.

Carlos checks his watch. "I don't want to."

"Tell your girlfriend I said 'hello.'"

"She ain't my girl."

Carlos races out of the parking lot hoping to make it in time for Rhonda's dinner. While he fights traffic, the smell of Sasha's pussy stains his upper lip. He checks the rear view mirror for any evidence of another woman, but he forgets that all the evidence is tangled in his pubic hairs. He parks in front of Rhonda's home, takes a deep breath, opens the door, and Rhonda is there to greet him. She motions for a kiss, but Carlos manages to twist and turn himself out of it. The last thing he needs is Rhonda smelling Sasha.

"Why you avoiding me?" Rhonda wraps her arms around his waist and tries for a hug, but Carlos fakes a disgusting cough.

"Awww, baby, are you sick?"

"I think so. I gotta get outta these clothes. I just wanna eat and relax."

"Where's the wine?"

"Damn, I knew I forgot something."

Carlos rushes upstairs into the bathroom. He strips down and from the mirror's reflection, he sees Sasha's cum stains. He cleans up and tightly wraps his sex-scented boxer-briefs into a plastic bag.

"Everything's ready," Rhonda screams.

Carlos walks downstairs and even though he is clean, his conscience is drowning in filth. Rhonda grabs his hand and leads him into the dining room. She set the table with candles and Carlos' favorite meal is steaming from his plate.

"Have a seat, my king," she says playfully.

Carlos pretends to deserve this royal treatment, but he is far from royalty.

Rhonda closes her eyes. "Say the grace."

Carlos is too embarrassed to talk to God, so he lies, "My throat hurts. Can you bless it for me?" He closes his eyes and tries to stay focused, but while Rhonda blesses the food, all Carlos can envision is Sasha's soft ass bouncing up and down.

Just before he slices the medium rare steak that Rhonda prepared, his cell phone rings. After all the thought she's put into making this dinner, she gives Carlos a look that says, "You better not answer that phone."

Carlos looks at his phone and sees Sasha's number. "That's Jamal. Something must be wrong, but I won't talk long – I promise," he lies.

"Who's Jamal?"

"This guy I met." Carlos gets agitated. "Look, I ain't gotta tell you who I'm on the phone with."

Carlos excuses himself from the table and Rhonda slams her fork onto the table. She would have appreciated it if he at least tasted it.

Carlos walks into the living room. "Wassup, Sasha, I really can't talk."

"You wanna know what I'm doing?"

Carlos checks over his shoulder and whispers, "What?"

Sasha places the phone over her vagina, fingers herself and it sounds like she is playing in a puddle of water. "Spend the night with me."

"I can't."

"C'mon, Carlos. Earlier was just a tease. I'll be up all night. I don't care what time it is, just come. The door will be unlocked."

"I gotta go. What's your address?"

Carlos returns to the table, but his appetite is gone. His plate is cold and so is Rhonda. He forces himself to eat a few bites. "I'm sorry, I didn't mean to snap at you," he says pretending to be distraught. "One of my partners got robbed."

"Is everything ok?"

Rhonda's motherly instincts always causes her to place Carlos' feelings over hers. Carlos feeds off of her unselfish nature and when he realizes that she has fallen for this lie, he goes a step further.

"All I wanted to do was come home and have dinner, and now I gotta deal with this shit." Carlos scratches his head. "One day, I'm going to leave all this hustling shit behind and become a legitimate businessman."

Rhonda is so concerned with easing Carlos' mind that she missed Carlos' tell all sign that he is lying. She walks over and gives him a hug. "Everything's gonna be ok, Carlos."

"I really appreciate dinner, but I gotta drive all the way out to Towson, and I could be gone all night."

Rhonda places her head on his chest. "Don't worry about me; just go handle your business."

Twenty minutes later, Carlos is standing in front of Sasha's unlocked door with a bottle of Moscato. He turns the knob and enters. He walks into the kitchen and the first thing he sees is Sasha naked on all fours.

She whispers seductively, "I just want you inside me."

Fully dressed, he drops to his knees, and pulls down his pants. While Sasha is in the perfect position to be fucked, Carlos tears open the condom wrapper.

"Hurry up," Sasha demands.

He struggles with the condom and his failed attempts are killing the mood.

"Why'd you bring a condom?"

"I just wanna be safe."

Sasha laughs. "You shoulda thought of that the first time. Trust me, this pussy is disease free."

Carlos brushes the head of dick against her clit. The more he rubs, the wetter she becomes and the wetter she becomes the harder he grows. Sasha holds onto whatever she can as her knees rub against the tiled floors. Carlos pulls her hair from behind, and Sasha loves the pain. While Carlos watches himself go in and out of Sasha, he has thoughts of Rhonda sitting home alone. Unfortunately, those thoughts don't stop the sounds of Sasha's butt slapping against his thighs.

"Fuck me harder."

"You want this dick, don't you?"

"Yes. Harder."

"Harder?"

"Yes, harder!"

"I'm about to cum." He pulls out of Sasha's wet pussy and covers her cinnamon colored ass with cum. He collapses onto the kitchen floor and shakes his head.

"What's wrong?"

Carlos examines her naked body. "Nothing's wrong, except you're addictive."

Sasha crawls over to him. "I am?"

"Hell yeah."

"One day, I'm going to spend the night, but …"

"You don't have to explain anything to me, I understand. I just wanted some dick. What me and you got is simple and that's how I wanna keep it."

Sasha's plan is working to perfection; she knows that in order to gain Carlos' trust and get his money, she needs to draw a wedge between him and Rhonda.

"Something tells me your girlfriend doesn't please you sexually because if she did, you wouldn't be here, right?"

Carlos doesn't answer her question. He pulls up his pants and walks to the door when all of a sudden, Sasha's attitude changes.

"What's wrong?"

"Don't worry about it. It's not your problem," she says.

"If I can help you I will, just tell me."

"My mother is dying from cancer and she doesn't have insurance. Her church helps with some of her bills." Sasha fakes a few tears. "I'm sorry I –"

"How much?"

Sasha covers her face and sobs, "Ten thousand."

Carlos isn't the only one who knows how to act. Ten thousand dollars is a lot of money to give someone he just met, but Carlos has it, and this would be a great way to get closer to Sasha. If Rhonda ever asked Carlos for ten thousand dollars, he would decline her without blinking. The same potential that Rhonda sees in him, he sees in Sasha and he doesn't plan on letting Sasha go anytime soon.

Carlos holds her tight. "Don't worry, I'll make sure your mother is ok."

"No, this is my problem. Besides, I can't pay you back, I don't –"

"I told you not to worry."

Sasha wipes away her fraudulent tears. "Your girlfriend is a lucky woman."

"I told you, she's not my girlfriend."

On the ride home, Carlos finds himself in the same predicament as before; the smell of sex is all over him, but this time he is prepared. Before walking inside of his home, he sits in the driveway, adjusts the rear view mirror, and inspects his face. He sniffs his fingertips and the smell of Sasha's pussy takes him back to his guilty pleasure. He engulfs himself in Versace cologne, opens the door, and there to greet him is Rhonda.

"Did you straighten everything out?"

Carlos has completely forgotten about his lie, but he gets back into character. "Oh, yeah everything's cool," he replies scratching his head.

Rhonda shoots him a strange look. "Why do you smell like you spilled a whole bottle of cologne on you? When did you find time to put cologne on?"

"What are you saying? Damn, I can't put on cologne without you asking me a thousand questions."

"I'm sorry, it just seems a little suspicious."

251

"Suspicious? Look, you ain't my fucking girlfriend. I'm sick of you acting like you own me, when I ain't gotta answer to you."

"Why are you so angry?"

"Because you getting on my fucking nerves. If you don't trust me, why are you here?"

Rhonda steps closer. "Baby, I'm sorry. It just seemed a little weird, that's all, but please don't take your frustration out on me. I'm here for you, I've always been here for you."

"I don't have time for this shit." Carlos brushes passed her, walks to his bedroom, slams the door and locks it.

"Open the door, Carlos."

"Just leave me alone."

"Tell me what I did wrong?"

"Just leave me alone. Got damn. Gimme some space to breath."

While Rhonda stares at the closed door confused, Carlos uses this time to remove his sex scented clothes. Afterwards, he sighs with relief and flops on the bed. Rhonda has learned to accept Carlos' bipolar ways, but even she has a breaking point.

\* \* \*

Before Rhonda can get to the bottom of his new attitude, Carlos distances himself to spend more time with Sasha. Before Sasha, Carlos and Rhonda would see each other often. Carlos would bring Rhonda lunch from her favorite restaurant and pop up at the salon, but not

252

anymore. These days, the only time Rhonda sees Carlos is if she visits him. Rhonda can sense that another woman is pulling him away and she's determined to find out who this bitch is.

One night, Carlos sits on the couch watching television when Rhonda slides her hands down into his sweatpants and massages his dick.

"Whatchu doing?"

"I'm horny," she says licking her lips.

"Stop," Carlos says flicking through the television channels.

"What the hell is wrong with you?"

"Whatchu talking about, Rhonda? Don't start no bullshit."

Rhonda stands to her feet. "You must think I'm stupid. You would fuck a tree if it looked good enough. Something's going on, Carlos, I can feel it," she yells. "I can't keep lying to myself about you. If you don't love me anymore, just say it."

"I don't love you. Now what?"

Rhonda wasn't prepared for his response to roll off his tongue so easily. She tries to keep her composure, but she can't fight back her tears.

"Why? What did I do?"

"That's the problem, you ain't doing shit."

"Whatchu mean? I cook and clean after you and –"

"I already got a mother. I need you to be my freak." With a cold stare he mumbles under his breath, "You just too fucking old."

Rhonda steps back, unable to believe what Carlos has just said to her. "I'm too old?"

253

Rhonda is so hurt that she can barely think. She pulls herself together, grabs her keys and walks towards the front door. Carlos knows he was wrong, but in his immature mind, this was the only way that he could end the relationship. Before leaving, Rhonda stands at the door waiting for Carlos to say something to make her stay. Instead, he continues to flick through the channels as if she is invisible.

"I hope whoever this bitch is take you for everything you got."

"I guess we'll have to see, huh?"

"Fuck you, Carlos."

Phase one of Sasha's plan has been completed, as she has managed to replace and position herself as Carlos' next adventure. Carlos continues to pay her fake mother's hospital bills and fill her closet with Gucci, Prada, Louis Vuitton shoes, dresses and jewelry.

One afternoon, Carlos knocks on Sasha's door and she greets him with a long warm hug. She takes off Carlos' jacket, grabs his hand, leads him into the living room, and gives him the remote control.

"Are you hungry?"

Carlos laughs. "Girls like you don't cook."

"Girls like me? Whatchu mean by that?"

"You're not the housewife type," Carlos jokes, "so just seeing you in the kitchen is hilarious."

Sasha winks her eye. "My pussy ain't the only reason why niggas can't keep their hands off me. You sit right there."

An hour later, Sasha walks in with a steaming hot plate of salmon, homemade mashed potatoes and greens.

Carlos cuts his fork through the steaming hot salmon, takes a bite and is pleasantly surprised.

"Good food and good pussy? Whatchu trynna get me to marry you?" he asks jokingly.

*By time I get done with you, you won't have enough money to throw rice.* She wraps her arms around his shoulders and kisses him on the cheek. "I'ma good woman, Carlos, just a little misunderstood. I'll be right back."

From her bedroom, Sasha stares at Carlos and something unexpected happens, she feels guilt. Because of Miles, Sasha is on a warpath to get whatever she can, and Carlos just happens to be caught in the crossfire. Sasha manages to get twenty-five thousand dollars worth of fake hospital bills paid for her "mother" and he's never questioned her. She knows that Carlos is a good person and if it wasn't her job to destroy him, she could fall in love. While contemplating if what she is feeling is real, her cell phone rings.

"Hello?"

"I haven't heard from you. How are things going with Carlos?"

Sasha peeks out into the living room and sees Carlos' innocence. The more Antoine talks, the more she realizes that what she has become is beyond disgusting. If it wasn't for Antoine, she wouldn't be in this mess, but she is and the wrong answer could cost her life.

"Where does he keep his money?" Antoine asks.

"I don't know."

"What the hell have you been doing?"

"I'm sorry I –"

"Bitch, don't play with me. How much you got?"

Sasha lies, "I don't have anything, but give me some more time."

"You got until tomorrow to find out." Antoine breaths heavily. "Look, don't fuck this up for me. Do you want me to tell Miles that you aren't cooperating?"

"No."

Antoine replies before hanging up, "You got until tomorrow."

Just when Sasha was beginning to soften up, she is reminded of her purpose, and having a real relationship with Carlos is just a figment of her imagination. Before getting back into character as Carlos' future soul mate, she sits on the edge of the bed confused and frustrated. She looks into her bedroom mirror and mumbles, "Get it together, girl. He's not worth your freedom." After her little pep talk in the mirror, she takes a deep breath and fixes her hair. Playtime is over; she needs to gain Carlos' trust now.

She playfully crawls. "Meow," she says.

"I never fucked a cat before, but I'm willing to give it a try."

"I fed you, now let me fuck you."

Sasha straddles Carlos and rides him like a porn star.

"Is it mine?" she asks.

"Yes."

"Say it."

"It's yours, and I'm 'bout to cum."

Sexually, Carlos is no match for Sasha. He would be so turned on by her adventurous nature that whenever they had sex, he only lasted a few minutes before popping. If this was a real relationship, Sasha would be sexually disappointed, but this is business. Afterwards, she walks into the bathroom, and returns with a warm rag. She wraps it softly around his dick, and cleans him off. Sasha knows that there is no better time to gain a man's trust than when his dick is in her hand.

Carlos grins. "What did I do to deserve you?"

Sasha squeezes his manhood with the warm rag. "You should keep some of your money here, instead of driving it all the way across town."

"I don't know about that," Carlos replies.

Sasha looks him in the eyes and lies through her teeth, "Everybody isn't out to get you, especially me."

Carlos smiles. "That's why I like you. You're the realist bitch I ever met."

Sasha playfully punches him. "Who you calling a bitch?"

Carlos holds her tight. "I always knew that you were down for me."

Sasha didn't expect this to be so easy and it only makes her feel worse. Her emotions swing back and forth and she is contemplating on telling him the truth or at least giving him a head start.

"Is everything alright?"

Sasha closes her eyes and exhales, "I think I'm falling for you."

"I know you love this dick."

"I'm serious, Carlos. There are some things I think you should know about me."

"I know all I need to know. You gotta phat ass and ya pussy smells like a fruit basket."

Sasha doesn't laugh.

"What's wrong?"

"You don't understand."

"Well make me, Sasha."

Just before she utters a word, Carlos' cell phone rings and he answers, "I'll be right there," he looks at Sasha. "I gotta go, but I'm coming right back."

Sasha just nods her head. Carlos has no clue that later is not an option. Sasha has twenty-four hours to rob him of everything, but she lets him leave.

"You promise?"

"Of course I promise," he says kissing her on the forehead.

\* \* \*

Later that night, Sasha sits in the kitchen staring at the clock. Every hour that passes, she is getting closer to deciding if she should come clean or run. She walks to the back of her closet and pulls out a white trash bag. Inside of the bag, is all the money that she received from Carlos. "I gotta get outta here." She frantically stuffs her bag with as much as she can. She doesn't want to leave Carlos hanging, so she grabs a pen a piece of paper to write a note. Before she writes the first word, she is startled by a knock at the door. She looks at the clock wondering if her twenty-fourth hour is up. She has no clue how Antoine is going to take the news, but she has to face it. Sasha walks to the door and opens it.

"Hey."

Sasha sighs with relief and leaps into Carlos' arms. "I'm so glad to see you."

"I was only gone for a few hours," Carlos says standing in the doorway holding a duffel bag over his shoulder, "You gonna let me in?"

Sasha pulls him inside and quickly locks the door.

"You alright?"

"Um...I –"

"I know you still wanna talk, but I need you to do me a favor. I got forty grand in this bag and I need you to hold it for me 'til I come back."

Sasha just stares. All her problems can be over now. She can either give Carlos' money to Antoine, or she can take it for herself and leave the city.

Carlos pulls her closer. "I'm giving you all my trust, so don't fuck it up."

Sasha can't even look him in the eyes. "I won't," she mumbles.

Carlos asks, "Is everything alright?"

"Yeah."

"When I come back we can talk, but I gotta take care of something."

Carlos leaves, and she locks the door. She opens Carlos' duffel bag and the most money she has ever seen is wrapped tight with rubber bands. She already has twenty-five thousand dollars stashed away, but if she takes Carlos' forty grand, she will have more than enough to disappear. Sasha paces back and forth, when her cell phone rings.

"Hello?"

"Where's the money?" Antoine asks.

"It's right here with me."

"How much?"

Sasha lies, "Thirty-grand."

"I'm on my way."

The last thing Sasha needs is Antoine and Carlos showing up at the same time. She takes ten grand from Carlos' bag and places it into hers. Every second that passes, her fears become more of a reality. While planning the perfect escape, her cell phone rings again.

"Where are you?"

"I love you, Sasha. Everything I got, I wanna share with you."

No one has ever said these words to her, not even her father. All the men that Sasha has been involved with were greedy, no-good men. All they wanted was her body, but not Carlos.

"Are you high?" she asks.

"No, I wanna share everything I have with you. I want you to be my girl."

Before she can respond, soft knocks riddle the front door. She grabs the money, cuts the living room light out, and hides in the closet.

"Do you love me?" she asks.

"Yes, I do."

Sasha cries, "I'm so sorry for how I treated you."

"Whatchu mean? You're the best thing that ever happened to me."

Sasha holds the duffel bag tightly to her chest and whispers, "You deserve someone better than me."

"All I need is you, Sasha."

While Carlos tries to convince Sasha that his love for her is real, Antoine's knocks turn to bangs.

"Open the fucking door, Sasha. I know you in there," Antoine yells.

Antoine walks to each window trying to get a glimpse of her. He looks through a small slit in her bedroom blinds, but all he can see are scattered clothes on the floor. He walks around back and bangs on the window.

"What was that?" Carlos asks.

"Ah…my next door neighbor, they've been arguing all day."

"You don't sound ok. I'm on my way."

"No. I mean, I'm ok, so take ya time."

Sasha hangs up the phone, covers her face and muffles her cries. She crawls to her bedroom and sees Antoine's silhouette lurking around. Sasha is terrified, and she knows it's just a matter of time before he breaks in.

"God, please help me," she begs rocking back and forth.

An immediate peace comes over her. "Thank you, Lord." She peeks out, looks down her hallway, and slowly stands to her feet. She takes her first step onto her squeaky wood floors and her front door bursts open. Sasha runs back into her bedroom and tries to open the window but she is so petrified, she doesn't have enough strength to flip the latches. She feels Antoine's steps getting closer.

"Where the fuck are you?" Antoine yells, "I'ma kill you, bitch."

"Shit. C'mon, c'mon." she says trying to coach herself up. She unlocks the window, tosses the duffel bag full of money, climbs through and places her back against the apartment building wall. Antoine kicks open her bedroom door and destroys everything in his path. He flips over the mattress hoping to find stacks of money. Instead, he sees a small black book, but Antoine didn't come here to read, he came for the money. He doesn't have much time so he pulls her dresser drawers to the ground.

"Fuuuck!" Antoine yells at the top of his lungs.

Sasha clutches the duffel bag tight and buries her face into her arms to muffle her sounds. All Antoine has to do is peek his head out of her bedroom window and she is dead. Breathing heavily, Antoine scans her bedroom one last time. He looks straight ahead and sees a closed window facing her backyard. He looks to the right and notices the curtain swaying back and forth from the wind. He walks over and snatches the curtain, but his only visual is the side of another apartment building. He tries to open it to get a better look, but it is jammed. "Dammit," he shouts while peeking out of the window.

Sasha closes her eyes and prays that Antoine isn't smart enough to check the other window and her prayers are answered. She hears his footsteps walking down the hallway and then her front door slams. Sasha buries her face into her arms for so long that she forgets that she is sitting outside. The reality of her decision has finally caught up to her.

Twenty minutes later, Carlos pulls up to the front of Sasha's apartment and notices all her lights are on, which is rare. He parks, walks to the front door and sees that the lock has been broken. He grabs his gun and softly pushes the door open just enough to peek in with his right eye. The house is destroyed.

He pushes the door further and aims his gun. "Aye, Sasha, you in here?" he asks stepping over a broken lamp.

The sound of Carlos' voice never sounded so sweet. Carlos walks down the hallway with his gun cocked and ready to shoot whoever shows their face. "Sasha!" he shouts.

"I'm right here."

"Where?"

"I'm outside."

Carlos throws his gun onto the bed, opens the window, and sees Sasha crying. He extends his hand, but she is too terrified to move.

"It's ok, it's just me. Grab my hand."

When Carlos realizes that Sasha is holding onto his duffel bag, he knows this is the woman for him. He isn't sure of what happened, but he knows that Sasha made sure that she kept her word and his money safe. He grabs the duffel bag and tosses it into the bedroom. Sasha climbs in and collapses into his arms.

Carlos looks around the wrecked bedroom. "What the hell happened in here?"

Sasha looks Carlos in the eyes. *I gotta tell him the truth.* "When I came home, somebody was in here and —"

"Did you see his face?"

"No, everything happened so fast. I just grabbed the money and hid."

Carlos stares into Sasha's brown eyes and he sees a woman in need of a man's security. He squeezes her tight and whispers, "Pack your stuff."

* * *

After destroying Sasha's apartment, Antoine drives to Miles' home and sits outside until he arrives. Miles walks to his front door and hears someone whistling to get his attention.

Miles walks over with a look of disgust on his face. "What the hell are you doing here? I didn't call for you. Have you lost your fucking mind?"

Obviously irritated, Antoine paces back and forth. "We gotta kill that bitch, Sasha. She's helping Carlos."

"If she wants Carlos, let her have him. Once I get your brother, Carlos and that silly whore won't even matter."

"What about me?" Antoine yells, "What am I getting huh? You promised if I —"

"Are you done?" Miles says.

Antoine clutches his fists. "Are we done? No, we're not done. Sasha is helping Carlos, and that wasn't part of the fucking plan."

"That wasn't part of your plan." Miles steps closer, "If I were you, I would get the hell out of my face."

Antoine takes a deep breath and steps back. "We made a deal."

Miles laughs. "A deal? Look, I know you want Carlos, but he is nothing compared to where you are going to go once I get Ramon."

"Well what are you waiting for?" he shouts.

Miles pokes Antoine in the chest. "Don't you ever question me, nigger. I will take you and your brother out."

Antoine hated when Miles used the word nigger so freely, but the truth is, he is Miles' little nigger. Miles places his arm around Antoine's shoulder and whispers, "You just make sure that money is there, because if it isn't –"

"It's there, I know it."

Miles lightly taps Antoine on the chin. "Be calm. You're about to be a very, very rich man. Now get the hell away from my house; you're bringing the property value down."

Antoine stands on the sidewalk and watches Miles walk into his home. He wants to drag Miles' naked body outside and hang him from that big oak tree that sits in the middle of his lawn, but all he can do is watch Miles' silhouette freely walk around. Antoine reaches into his pocket and lights up a cigarette, and a grin appears on his face. Right now he may be Miles little puppet, but when the time comes, Antoine is going to show Miles how a black man with power treats white trash.

* * *

The next day at 4:37 pm, Carlos drives Sasha to her old apartment to grab a few more things. The sun is high

265

and the sky is baby blue. Carlos unlocks the door and Sasha hesitates.

"Are you ok?"

"Yes," she mumbles.

"Look, I'll be right outside, and I ain't going nowhere. Just grab whatchu need and come back, ok?" Carlos opens his glove compartment, grabs his gun and places it into his lap. "Ain't nothing gonna to happen to you."

Sasha forces a smile to appear on her face. "Okay."

She walks toward her door and continuously looks back to make sure Carlos doesn't budge. She pushes the door open and steps over broken glass. She pushes open her bedroom door and her mind replays her escape. Sasha came back for something very important to her, her little black book that she kept under her bed. She continues to look until she finds it. An immediate sense of relief comes over her. She slips the little black book into her purse when she is suddenly grabbed from behind.

"Let go of me."

"I told you I was gonna getchu."

Sasha puts a fight. "Please let go of me."

Antoine pushes her onto the box spring and puts all of his body weight on top of her. "You forgot what side you on?"

"Get off me."

"Where's Carlos now?" he asks covering her mouth with his hand.

He turns Sasha on her stomach and unzips his pants. Sasha tries to twist her body out of danger, but Antoine

266

elbows her in the back of the head. "Where's the money?"

"I don't have it."

"Oh really? Let's see how Carlos feel about me fucking the shit outta you. Stop moving."

Carlos patiently sits outside with his windows up listing to music while Antoine is raping his woman. Sasha screams, kicks and punches until Antoine has had enough. While holding her down with his body weight, Antoine grabs the cord from the iron and pull it towards him. Sasha sinks her teeth into Antoine's left arm as hard as she can. The pain is unbearable, but that doesn't stop Antoine from grabbing the iron and striking Sasha in the head knocking her unconscious. Antoine lifts Sasha's yellow skirt, pulls her panties down to her ankles and rams himself inside of her.

"Take it, bitch," he demands.

He flips Sasha's motionless body over, spreads her butt cheeks and fucks her some more. Antoine has never raped a woman before, but there is something strangely sexual about fucking an unconscious body. Sasha has no clue that she is being taken advantage of, but if this was how it is going to go down, she wouldn't want to remember anyway. Antoine eventually cums, frantically pulls up his pants and escapes out of the same window that saved her life. Antoine knew he wasn't going to get any money from Sasha; he just wanted her to pay for betraying him, mission accomplished.

Carlos grows tired of waiting. *What the hell is she doing? I'm hungry.*

267

Too lazy to get out of the car, Carlos repeatedly calls her cell phone. The sound of her phone helps her regain consciousness and she sits up. Her head feels like she got hit by a truck and her thoughts are scattered. She knows that she and Antoine got into a fight, but the fact that she is alive scares her more than anything. She looks down and sees her yellow panties dangling around her right leg.

"That son of bitch," she says pounding her fist onto the hardwood floor.

Her memory is slowly returning and she remembers that Carlos is still outside waiting for her. She can hear her cell phone ringing, and she tries to turn her head towards the sound, but she's hit with a sharp pain causing her to put her hand on her forehead. "Ouch, what the hell is that?" Reaching with her other hand, she finally feels her purse, pulls out her phone and answers it.

"Hello?"

"Don't hello me. I've been out here like thirty minutes. What the hell are you doing?"

Sasha kicks off her panties, and stumbles into the bathroom to examine her face. "I'm coming," she says arranging her hair to cover up a wound on the corner of her head.

"You think I won't leave you?" Carlos shouts, "I ain't sitting out here all day."

Sasha has had enough of Carlos' bitching and screams at the top of her lungs, "I'm coming."

Under normal circumstances, a woman would notify the police and have Antoine arrested on site.

Unfortunately, the police are the last people that Sasha can call. Besides, trying to convince Carlos that being raped by Antoine is what caused her to take a long time would be impossible. Still weary, Sasha tries to act normal, but a blow to the head will distort anyone. She limps to the car, opens the passenger door and forces a smile on her face.

"I'm ready," she says.

"Where's your stuff? You walked in empty handed and you left empty handed."

"I came for my book, and I got it."

Carlos shakes his head. "We drove all the way across town for a book? You're selfish, that's your problem."

As bad as Sasha wants to cuss his ass out, she just closes her eyes.

# CHAPTER XII

Weeks after being raped by Antoine, Sasha tries to live a normal life as best as she can. Sasha doesn't know what rock Officer Miles or Antoine will climb out of, so she constantly looks over her shoulder in fear.

Even though it's just a matter of time before she runs into Antoine or Officer Miles, Sasha hasn't felt this happy in a long time. In the beginning of their relationship, Sasha loved to shop, party and be the center of attention but now, she barely wants to leave the house and whenever Carlos leaves her alone, she begs him to stay. Carlos thinks that Sasha is just being needy, having no clue that she fears for her life. Tired of sitting around and watching Sasha mope, he drags her to her favorite place, the mall. They walk around for hours and not once does Sasha pull him into one her favorite stores. Instead, she holds him close and nervously looks around. Carlos planned to spend a lot of money on her, but so far, all he's purchased are two cinnamon buns and a soda.

"We just walked passed your favorite store and you didn't even flinch."

"I don't care about that stuff anymore."

Carlos stops in tracks. "Hold on, you don't care about Gucci? Get da hell outta here. Do I need to check you into the hospital?"

Sasha smiles. "Don't get me wrong, it's very nice, but there's more to life than things. Sometimes there's this."

"What?"

Sasha squeezes his hand. "Spending time with you."

Carlos can appreciate Sasha's new outlook on life, but in the back of his mind, he's thinking, *She must want something big.*

They walk pass Kay Jewelers and Carlos pulls her inside. He leads her to the wedding and engagement ring section and Sasha finally gets excited. "Ooh, I like that one." she says.

The clerk pulls the ring out of the glass case. "This is a five-carat princess cut ring we just got in."

Sasha extends her left hand, while the clerk slides on the ring. It fits perfectly over her petite finger. "Whatchu think?" she asks.

"I think it fits you perfectly." Carlos places his arm over her shoulders. "I'm not ready for marriage, but this is my way of saying that I want you by my side."

"I was already by your side."

Carlos pays for the five carat diamond ring and even though Sasha isn't his wife officially, she is glowing as if she is. They leave the mall and drive to Ruth's Chris steakhouse to celebrate. Sasha stares into Carlos' eyes. She doesn't care if she spends the rest of her life in jail; she knows that she did the right thing. She covers his hand with hers. "I've never loved anyone as much as I love you."

"I have another surprise for you." Carlos pulls out an envelope and hands it to Sasha. "Open it up," he says smiling from ear to ear.

Sasha eagerly opens the envelope and inside are two first class tickets to Jamaica. "Oh my God. We're going to Jamaica."

"And we're leaving tonight." Carlos smiles, "I've been planning this for three weeks."

"Oh my God, are you serious?"

"Yup," he replies showing two first class tickets. "Our plane leaves in three hours.

"But I didn't get a chance to pack."

"We don't need luggage."

Sasha has never been treated this good before. She wants to tell Carlos everything, but if she does, her Cinderella story will end – so she continues to keep her little secret.

Just hours later, they arrive at the Sunset Beach Resort in Jamaica. The weather is beautiful and love is definitely in the air. Carlos pushes open the door to their hotel suite and the room is flawless with a beautiful view.

"I don't feel so good," Sasha says holding her stomach. "I think I'm 'bout to throw up."

Sasha runs into the bathroom and Carlos hears her gagging. He pushes the door open and Sasha is on her knees. "You ok?"

"Do I look ok?" she asks spitting out orange colored vomit.

Sasha has been feeling this way for weeks. Carlos escorts her to the bedroom and Sasha wraps herself in the sheets.

"I think I'm pregnant."

Carlos becomes fidgety. "Pregnant? Maybe it's the food, or maybe it was the plane. I knew something was wrong with –"

"Carlos, I think I'm pregnant."

Carlos doesn't know how to feel. He just became a soon-to-be husband and now, he might be a father.

"I'll be right back," he says, "We gotta get to the bottom of this." Carlos catches a cab to the nearest pharmacy and within minutes, he returns holding a pregnancy test. "Here," he says.

Sasha walks into the bathroom and pulls her panties down to her ankles. The thought of being a mother makes her feel complete, but how long is this fairytale going to last is the question that rattles her brain. She places the pregnancy test stick between her legs, and pees while Carlos paces back and forth.

"Hurry up."

"I'm trying," she screams.

While Sasha waits for the results, she stares at the mirror. *I'm not ready to be a mother*. Her reflection gives her no choice but to reflect on her life and she becomes deeply saddened. How can she possibly look her child in the eyes and raise him or her to do good when she has done so much bad? Sasha doesn't even know if she'll be alive long enough to see her child's first step. With her trembling hands, she picks up the pregnancy test and sees the '+' sign and almost faints.

Carlos tries to get inside the bathroom, but she locks the door. "Wait." Sasha sits on the toilet and tries to gather her thoughts. "I can't do it," she repeats until she cries.

"What is it? Am I a father?"

Sasha wipes away her tears, walks to the door and opens it. Kendrick stands in front of her, as Sasha buries her face into his chest and whispers, "I'm pregnant."

Fighting back tears of joy, Carlos holds Sasha. He has never had to care for anyone other than himself. For the first time, he understands what the word responsibility means. He doesn't even know his child's name and he's already in love. This type of love is new to Carlos but he knows this type of love comes with pressure. He begins to think about his hustling lifestyle and the thought of being incarcerated or murdered makes him paranoid.

Since he was a teenager, all Carlos thought about was hustling, buying new clothes, jewelry, and cars – but all of that has changed because today, at 9:30 in the evening, he is a father. Hours later, Carlos rolls out of bed and walks onto the balcony. He overlooks Jamaica's beautiful blue waters and dark clear sky, then closes his eyes. *Thank you, God, for blessing me. Forgive me for all I've done. I don't deserve to be a father, but give me the strength and discipline to do what's right, Amen.* Before returning to bed, Carlos wonders if he should call his mother, but he knows by now she is probably lying in her own vomit.

After four days in Jamaica, Carlos returns back to the streets of Bmore, but now he's hustling with a purpose. The money he earns from selling weed has been good, but Carlos is ready to take his hustle to the next level. Carlos was a strong believer in watching the signs, and to him, becoming a father was a clear sign that he was running out of time. His goal was to make as much as he can and get out.

One Saturday evening, Carlos and Ramon enjoy dinner at a five star restaurant in Washington DC.

"What's on your mind?" Ramon asks.

Carlos smiles. "Sasha's pregnant."

"Wow, congratulations my nigga." Ramon signals for the waiter.

The waiter walks over wearing a well-tailored tuxedo and bow-tie. "Yes, sir," he replies with great posture.

"We would like to order your most expensive bottle of champagne."

The waiter thinks about his fifteen percent gratuity and perks up. "Yes, sir. Our 1978 Dom Perignon costs eight-hundred and fifty dollars and it's absolutely delicious," he says as if he's actually tasted it.

"We need two bottles. My friend here is father."

"Congratulations, sir," the waiter says before walking away.

Moments later, the waiter returns with a bottle of champagne inside of an bucket of ice. He pops the cork and fills their glasses. "Let's toast," Ramon says raising his glass. "To family." Their glasses clank, but there still seems to be something on Carlos' mind.

Ramon puts his glass down. "I just spent seventeen hundred on two bottles of champagne, you better drink that shit."

"We don't have much time left." Carlos leans back on his seat. "Look at us, we're making money and enjoying life, but we know how this story ends. When will it all come crashing down?"

"I've been hustling for ten years, and I've never been to jail, so it can be done. You just have to be smart. I don't wear flashy clothes, jewelry and cars. I keep it simple and that's what kept me outta prison. Look at you, Carlos, everything about you says drug dealer."

Carlos shakes his head. "And I wanna change that, but we gotta make enough money to get out."

"So what's the plan?"

Carlos sits up and whispers, "Cocaine."

Ramon's body language changes and this dinner changes from a celebration to a business meeting. Before Ramon can respond, their happy go lucky waiter returns and refills their glasses. When he leaves, Carlos continues, "We can triple our worth if we sell coke. It's easy to conceal and it moves faster than weed. We can make enough to get out for good."

"That's your plan?" Ramon bursts out laughing. "Get out? There's no getting out of the coke game. The money is too fucking good. It'll come faster than you can spend it, but by then it's too late. I can't do it; I'm comfortable where I'm at." Ramon sighs, "I'm happy that you're a father, but don't let this shit cloud your judgment."

The waiter returns with their plates, and their conversation comes to an abrupt end.

* * *

Two months later, Sasha quietly rolls out of bed, while Carlos is asleep. She walks into the closet, grabs an iron hanger and tip-toes into the bathroom. She unwinds it until it's straight, and sits on the edge of the toilet with her legs spread open. "I'm not ready to be a mother," she says slowly pushing the dirty hanger into her vagina. She has no idea what she is doing, what to expect or what damage she is causing, but this has to happen. The further she pushes the hanger inside, she feels more guilt for lying to Carlos. "Lord forgive me, but I can't, I just can't." She cries twisting the iron hanger in every direction possible. After numerous pokes, she begins to feel a warm trickling sensation and then she hears a drop splash into the toilet water. Sasha looks down and sees blood. "It's working," she mumbles. She pokes herself again until she becomes dizzy. Sasha's toes curl from the pain until she can't take anymore. She slowly pulls out the iron hanger and her purplish blood runs down to her fingers and drips on the floor. She tries to stand, but a sharp pain strikes her in the stomach dropping her to her knees. "Oh my God," she says gripping the towel rack with her bloody hands. On her knees, she takes deep breaths when three knocks at the bathroom door startle her.

"You ok?"

Sasha grunts in pain. "Ah...yeah I just had to pee, and it hurts a little bit," she says placing the hanger in the trashcan.

"Is my baby ok?" he asks.

277

Sasha wipes away her tears. "Everything's ok. Go to bed."

Sasha waits for Carlos to leave, pulls down the towel from the towel rack and crawls to each spot of blood on the floor. "I'm so sorry, Carlos, you deserve better." The more she scrubs, the angrier she becomes at Miles and Antoine. "I hate you muthafuckas," she says under her breath while scrubbing as hard as she can. Sasha grits her teeth until her jaws ache. "I swear you're gonna pay for what you did." Sasha blocks out the pain and all she can envision is Antoine and Miles dying the worst type of death possible. After scrubbing the floor for almost fifteen minutes, she is exhausted and dripping sweat. Sasha leans up against the wall and her vagina feels like someone stabbed it with a knife. She crawls over to the sink and struggles to pulls herself up saying, "You can do it." After three failed attempts, Sasha finally stands and her reflection stares her in the eyes. She is so ashamed, that she cuts off the lights. Surrounded in darkness, her conscious attacks her, *Tell Carlos the truth, he loves you. Why'd you do this? You're a killer. You could never be a mother, and it's all Antoine's fault you're such a fucking liar. You deserve this shit, and you ain't nothing but a –"* The only way Sasha can stop these thoughts from running through her mind is to walk out of the darkness. Trying to not wake Carlos, Sasha slowly turns the knob and opens the door. She looks into the bedroom and Carlos is sleeping like a baby. She fights against the pain, straightens up her posture and takes small steps towards the couch. Every time she closes her eyes, she hears her conscience, so she just stares at the blank television until the sunrise.

At 7:38 in the morning, Carlos walks out from the bedroom. "Good morning, mommy," he says kissing Sasha on the forehead. "Everything alright?"

Her panties are cold from damp blood and her stomach hurts so bad that she can't move. *Please don't touch me.*

"I wanna show you something." Carlos runs back into the bedroom and returns with hundreds of dollars' worth of clothes for an infant. "I couldn't resist. I know we don't know what we're having, but I had to get it."

Sasha just stares at the clothes on the couch and her heart fills with hate. Sasha's eyes fill up with tears, but Carlos has no clue that these are tears of vengeance.

"I knew you were going to like it." Carlos holds up a shirt that says, 'Greatest Dad.' "I had to get it. Our child isn't going to need for shit, you feel me?"

Sasha looks at how happy Carlos is and she realizes that one man who shouldn't feel her wrath is Carlos. While Carlos continues to lift different colorful shirts in the air, Sasha takes a deep breath, inches closer. "I need to tell you something."

"I'm listening."

"I love you and I –"

Carlos' cell phone rings. "I gotta take this call."

Ramon yells frantically, "Yo, it's a bunch of fucking police cars outside my house." Ramon sees them running up towards his door. The officers kick down his door and rush upstairs. "Yo, call my brother. I –" Ramon screams before the phone disconnects.

Carlos sits with a blank stare.

"What happened?" Sasha asks.

"Ramon got locked up."

Sasha plays stupid. "Who's Ramon?"

"Ramon is Antoine's brother, and that's my damn connect. I gotta go, I'll talk to you later."

"Where you going?"

"To find Antoine," Carlos yells before slamming the door.

While Carlos drives recklessly through traffic, Ramon is being brutally forced to the ground. The officers push their knees onto his back and squeeze the cuffs until they are cutting his wrists. While on his stomach, Ramon looks around as three of the officers ransack his room.

"What's the charge?"

Miles places the bottom of his boot onto Ramon's face and pushes it into the carpet, "Where's the money?"

"What money?"

Miles kicks him in the ribs. "Don't play wit me, Ramon. Where's the safe."

"What safe? I ain't got no fucking safe." Ramon screams struggling to catch his breath.

Officer Miles kicks him again and Ramon can't take another blow. "Check the closet," he moans.

Two of the officers destroy the closet and pull out a gray box and place it on the bed. "Aren't you gonna give me the combination?"

Ramon braces himself, "I ain't giving you shit, white boy."

"I had a feeling you'd say that."

Ramon waits for Miles to beat the shit out of him but instead, Miles reaches into his pocket and pulls out a small piece of paper with numbers written on it.

Ramon bursts out laughing, "You gotta be the dumbest white boy I ever met, you'll never guess the combination. Only two people know it, and I ain't giving you shit."

Miles grins and turns the dial to number nine and it clicks, he then turns the dial to number one and it clicks. Miles turns the dial to number eight and it clicks one last time before Miles presses the button. Ramon's stomach drops like he jumped out of a plane. His eyes are wide and his heart is completely shattered. Ramon can't believe his own brother turned him into the police. Ramon buries his face into the carpet while Miles gives each officer their share of the robbery.

"Did you come here to rob me or lock me up?"

Miles grins. "Both."

"Y'all ain't cops. You got whatchu want, so just let me go."

"I wish I could, but a deal is a deal."

They pull Ramon to his feet and escort him to the patrol car, but before they shove him in the backseat, Ramon blurts out, "Tell my brother that I still love him."

"Aww, that's sweet," Miles replies, pushing Ramon's head into the back of the patrol car.

\* \* \*

Carlos finally arrives at Antoine's house and bangs on the door. Antoine opens and Carlos runs inside.

281

"Ya brother got locked up."

"Take ya shoes off." Antoine walks to the couch and finishes off his slice of pizza. "You want some?"

"Huh? Did you hear me? Ramon got locked up."

Antoine flicks through the channels on his television clearly not stunned by the news, "One monkey don't stop the show. Now, me and you can do business just like the old days. Ramon is gonna be fine."

"You must be high?"

Antoine stands up. "Nah, nigga, I'm more focused than I ever been."

Antoine has never raised his voice to Carlos, but he was finally in a position of power. A position that took him a lifetime to achieve.

"You knew about this shit?"

"He brought it on himself," he replies. "No more small-talk, if you wanna keep living the lifestyle that you've become accustom to, you've gotta go through me now."

Carlos clinches his fists. "You ratted on your own brother?"

Antoine steps closer. "You think you know everything, but you don't know shit, and you're right in the middle of it."

"What?"

"Ask ya bitch," he says with a sneaky grin on his face.

Carlos wants to wrap his fingers around Antoine's throat and watch him die, but he knows that the boys in blue are protecting him. He backs his way to the front door.

"This is your last chance, Carlos."

"Ramon is your brother. He raised you."

"He also kept me down, but them days are over and if you ain't fucking with me, you're gonna get ran over too. Period."

Carlos takes one last look at Antoine, opens the front door and leaves. He runs to his car, turns on the ignition and nervously speeds out of Antoine's complex. "What the fuck just happened? I must be dreaming," Carlos says looking through his rear view mirror to make sure he isn't being followed. *What the hell does Sasha have to do this?* Instead of parking in his usual assigned parking spot, Carlos parks in the distance and jogs over. With a hood over his head, he opens the front door, pushes passed Sasha and closes all the blinds.

"I can't believe this shit. Antoine setup his own fucking brother."

"Calm down."

"Nah, fuck that, and why is your name coming out of Antoine's mouth? He told me to ask you."

"Ask me what?"

Carlos puts his hands over his face. "I don't know. What the fuck is going on, Sasha?" Carlos stops pacing and stares at Sasha. "You know what? It was real ironic how you just so happen to show up on my birthday."

Sasha wanted Carlos to find out, but not like this so she lies, "It was a coincidence. He told me that his friend was having a birthday party. What are you saying, Carlos; that I had something to do with Ramon getting locked up?"

Carlos can feel that he is on to something, but the pieces aren't fitting together. "I don't know, why would he bring up your name?"

Still in pain, Sasha struggles to stand to her feet and walks over to him. "He's trying to fuck with your head, Carlos." Sasha touches her stomach. "Did you forget that I'm carrying your child? Why would you say that me?"

Carlos gives Sasha a hug. "You're right, I'm sorry. I just don't know what to believe, everything is fucked up now."

Sasha looks Carlos in the eyes. "Let's just take what we have and leave."

"And go where? I don't have enough money to just leave. Besides, we can't go on the run while you're pregnant."

Every time Sasha thinks that she is in the clear, she is reminded of how much of a liar she has become. Deep down, she wants Carlos to know the truth, but she is too afraid. Sasha is all Carlos has and she is also the reason for all of his confusion. While Carlos looks for answers to this misplaced puzzle, Sasha buries her face into his chest. Sasha realizes that the only way she's going to get their life back is by getting Miles and Antoine out of the picture, but first she has to clean up one more lie.

"I didn't want to tell you this, but there really isn't a good time."

"I can't take no more good news, Sasha. What is it?"

"I had a miscarriage."

Carlos gives Sasha a hug while she musters up a few fake tears. Carlos is disappointed, but he is not as hurt as he thought he would be. When things were going well, being a father was the motivation that he needed to change his life, but Ramon's incarceration changed everything. The last thing Carlos needs right now, is the responsibility of taking care of another life. He doesn't even know if the police are going to kick down his door next or who he's going to buy his product from. Carlos believes this may just be a sign from God that they are not ready to become parents. He doesn't know that his child was killed, and he never will.

* * *

Six months later, Miles introduces Antoine to Carter and he practically becomes a success overnight. Antoine climbs up the ladder of success and the further he goes; he is no longer doing business with the 'corner boys.' Antoine no longer has time to chase after Sasha and Carlos. Since the beginning, Sasha and Carlos were always just pawns. He now mingles with the upper echelon of society and conducts business with individuals who import large amounts of drugs all over the east coast. He's made it, and gained a position that Ramon and Carlos would have never reached. Antoine purchased a six bedroom single family home in Essex and he spoils himself to the finer things in life. After taking over a quarter million dollars from Ramon, Carter encouraged Miles to resign from the police force. Carter's encouragement didn't come in the form of a pat on the back, but a gun to the face. Carter was tired of Miles' unpredictable nature and decided that his services were no longer needed. Miles knew that once he introduced Antoine to Carter that it was just a matter of time before he was killed or caught up in some orchestrated scandal, so he took Carter's advice and plans to move to Canada, but for now, Miles still lurks around the city manipulating his underworld ties.

* * *

Ramon has been incarcerated for eight months and it hasn't been easy. Carlos makes sure that Ramon has enough money on the books to get whatever he wants, but jail is still jail. The food is horrible, the inmates are on edge and the environment is despicable. Time doesn't exist behind these walls but he has plenty of time to think about his life. Ramon has never been incarcerated, but he learns that anything that happens on the street will be heard behind these jail house walls. Ramon has heard inmates talk about murders, robberies and drug transactions before they happen on the outside. Ramon heard plenty of stories of how Antoine was living a lavish lifestyle and if he wanted to, he could have Antoine killed without leaving his cell, but Ramon loves his brother too much. Inmates would brag when their 'hits' from jail made the news like it was some sort of honor and in jail, and it is. Ramon was living in hell, but at least he has a place to sleep and eat. After the raid, Ramon lost everything and his brother gained the world, but Ramon tries to make the best of it.

Instead of a queen sized bed, he wraps himself onto a cot with filthy sheets. Instead of holding Tynisha's butt at night, he holds his sheets and dreams of being in-between her legs. Tynisha has always been loyal to Ramon and she makes sure she visits him regularly. In jail, how a man's woman looks says a lot about who that man was on the streets. Whenever Tynisha visited Ramon, she made sure that she wore skin tight pants, high-heels and shirt that showed her perky breast. Three times a week, Tynisha mailed Ramon love letters and naked pictures of her spreading her pussy open. Ramon doesn't have long to go, but these are the things that keep him sane, but all of that changes one afternoon.

Ramon finishes a game of spades and walks towards the pay phone. Using the phone while in Jessup Correctional Institution (JCI) has caused many fights that ended in bloodshed. Ramon picks up the pay phone, but before he can dial the first number, a short stocky nigga named Tommy walks up behind him. Tommy is in prison for aggravated assault and serving four years. Tommy is tatted from head to toe with gang signs and he's built his reputation with his fists. Ramon turns around to face Tommy and he can sense that shit is about to get ugly.

"You need something?"

Tommy clutches his fists. "I heard ya brother is a snitch. If he a snitch, what that make you?"

Ramon grips the phone tight. "I ain't no fucking snitch."

A crowd gathers around and Ramon knows that he has to fight even if it ends in death. Ramon looks around sees Tommy's friends inching closer. *Shit.* Ramon keeps his composure.

"Aye, Tommy, Antoine is his own man, and I ain't got nothing to do wit that."

"Shut da fuck up."

"I don't want no trouble, Tommy."

"I didn't ask you that, nigga."

Tommy steps closer and Ramon swings hitting Tommy in the face. Ramon tries to put up a fight, but within a matter of seconds, he is jumped and brutally beaten. Tommy spits out a small razor into his hand and cuts Ramon across the face. "Fuck you, nigga." Tommy yells slicing him again. Ramon thought he had friends, but as he gets tortured, he sees his so-called friends staring. Moments later, the correctional officers rush into the room, but all the inmates scatter leaving Ramon in a pool of blood. They pull Ramon to his feet, but he can barely stand. His face is sliced from his forehead to his chin and his orange jumpsuit is covered in blood.

Days after being beat, Ramon returns to his cell, but he isn't the same. Every night, he sharpens the end of his toothbrush against the wall until it becomes a deadly weapon. When he first arrived, he slept on his stomach, but now he sleeps on his back with his toothbrush tightly gripped in his hand. Ramon is ready for war.

Ramon knows that the only way he is going to get respect from the other inmates is to put Tommy in a body bag. Ramon knows if he attacks Tommy, his gang will kill him – so he waits for the right time. For a week, Ramon stays to himself and keeps a close eye on Tommy. Their cell doors open, Ramon jumps out of his bunk, grabs his toothbrush and walks towards the door. The correctional officers lead the inmates outside and

Ramon stands in the distance. He takes a deep breath and prepares himself. *You gotta do this shit.* The hour of recreational time ends. The inmates form a line and Ramon positions himself a few men behind Tommy. The correctional officers escort groups in one at a time, and he waits until Tommy is standing by himself.

Ramon walks up, grabs Tommy's head and slices his neck. "Bitch nigga." Ramon grunts. Tommy falls to the ground holding his neck and no one says a thing. Ramon falls to the back of the line and drops his toothbrush to the ground. The correctional officers rush over and try their best to stop Tommy's neck from gushing blood. Ramon keeps his head straight enjoying the sounds of a tough guy moaning in pain.

Tommy survived the stabbing, but instead of going back to his cell, Tommy was transferred to another jail. Those who saw Ramon 'put in work' respected him, but that wasn't the last time Ramon had to fight because of his brother's actions and reputation.

\* \* \*

Monday afternoon, Carlos waits inside JCI's visiting room. Ramon walks out wearing a bright orange jumpsuit. His beard is thick and he has a long scar on his face. Ramon sits down and his eyes tell the story of someone who has been at war.

"Damn, nigga, what happen to your face?"

"It's nothing."

"I see you put on some weight. How you holding' up?"

Ramon sighs. "As long as you keep money on my books and Tynisha keep sending me naked pictures, I'm good. She's a good girl."

Carlos leans in closer to Ramon. "Antoine –"

Ramon bangs his fists on the table. "I don't wanna hear that nigga's name."

Carlos whispers, "Just give me the word."

"I can't."

"Why not? You in jail looking like Scarface, and he on the outside acting like he Scarface."

"How can I look my mother in the eyes after killing her youngest son? Killing a stranger is easy, but killing your family is pure fucking evil. I can't do it." Ramon looks off into space. "Every dog has its day, that's what he told me."

Carlos didn't just come here to see how Ramon was doing, he came to talk business. "What about that 'thing' we had to take care of? I need it, I ain't making no money."

That 'thing' that Carlos is referring to was a large shipment of weed that would have been a huge moneymaker for them both, but Ramon's incarceration changed everything.

"That was months ago, and these niggas ain't fucking wit' me while I'm in here." Ramon places his hands over his face, "You better start thinking about your exit, or you're gonna be sitting right here next to me."

"What I'm supposed to do?"

Ramon stands. "Go legal. Look where I'm at. If this ain't enough motivation, they got plenty of space for you."

"Go legal? We're hustlers, this is what we do."

"You sound stupid. My brother put me in here, so what do you think a stranger will do?"

Ramon signals to the guard that his visit is over. With empty eyes he stares at Carlos and grins. "This ain't where you wanna be my nigga."

All Carlos can do is watch Ramon disappear into the concrete jungle. Carlos isn't broke, and he is doing enough to keep his lights on and food on the table, but he knows this won't last long.

The same day that Carlos visited Ramon in prison, Tynisha hears three knocks at the door. She rolls over and looks at the clock. "It's 11:38 at night, who the hell is this?" she says wrapping her body in a purple robe. Before walking downstairs, she opens her blinds and sees a grey Maseratti parked out front.

She walks downstairs and opens the door. "Whatchu doing here?"

Antoine stands in the doorway holding two bags of Chinese food. "You hungry?"

"What the hell are you doing here?" Tynisha tries to close the door, but Antoine stops her.

"Let me in so I can explain."

"There ain't shit to explain. Get the fuck away from my house before I call the fucking police."

Antoine chuckles. "Trust me, that's the last thing I'm worried about."

"Move, Antoine."

"No, just let me in so I can explain." Tynisha realizes that Antoine is not going to leave, so she steps back and Antoine walks inside. He takes off his jacket and sits on the couch.

Tynisha stands with her arms folded "Don't get comfortable, nigga, whatchu want?"

"I just wanted to make sure you were ok."

"Do I look like I'm ok? Who's gonna pay these bills while Ramon is in jail? I can't take care of his shit and mine."

"Ramon can't do shit for you in prison, and you know it." Antoine walks over to Tynisha and forces her to walk into the wall. "You need to worry about yourself. Who's gonna take you shopping and keep you looking pretty, huh?" Antoine pulls her closer. "Don't be stupid. Let me help you."

"Stop, Antoine! You know I love Ramon," she screams.

"You don't love Ramon." He reaches into his pocket and pulls out two large knots of money, "This is what you love, now take it."

Antoine pins her against the wall, grabs her wrists and forces a kiss on her neck. Tynisha puts up a fight, but he grabs her tighter so she can't move. Tynisha stops resisting and Antoine opens her robe. Antoine falls to his knees and places her right leg over his shoulder. He kisses her inner thighs and works his way to her panties.

She stops him. "What about Ramon?"

"I'll worry about him."

Tynisha runs her fingers through his dreadlocks and pushes his face into her trimmed bush. Her robe drops to the ground while Antoine unbuckles his belt. Tynisha faces the wall and hikes her ass in the air. Antoine rubs his dick against her clit and she flinches from excitement. Ever since Ramon's incarceration, she has been pleasing herself, but right now her body can't deny the touch of a man. Antoine pushes himself inside of her and she feels like a virgin.

"Fuck me."

Antoine pounds harder. "Tell me it's mine."

"It's yours, ahhhh, it's yours."

"Say my fucking name?"

Tynisha loved being told what to do, "Antoine. Antoine." she screams, "Harder."

"Ahhh fuck, I'm cumming," she moans.

He picks Tynisha up and carries her to the couch. "Ride that dick, baby."

Tynisha moans, "Cum inside my pussy."

"I'm cuming."

"Cum inside me."

Antoine digs his fingers into Tynisha's back and fills her up with his semen.

\* \* \*

A few weeks after Carlos' visit, Ramon sits in his cell when his name is called. Ramon jumps down from his bunk and walks toward the Correctional Officer.

"You got mail."

Ramon smiles, since getting mail is always the best part of his day. He snatches the letter and walks to his cell. Whenever he got mail, he would find a secluded corner and read. Words have never been more important to Ramon, especially a love letter from Tynisha. Tynisha always sprayed the envelope in her favorite perfume. He holds the letter to his eyes, but her scent is missing. Ramon has read so many of her letters that he can practically hear her voice, but this time something feels different. After reading the emotionless letter, Ramon checks to see if there are any pictures and they're aren't. "Fuck." Ramon mumbles before balling the letter up. The one thing that gave him a piece of mind was tainted. "You bitch." Ramon's mind races and his cell block walls tell him things that make his stomach turn. Every night, he envisions Tynisha getting fucked and he can't take it.

The next day, Ramon gets a visit so he takes a shower and gets dressed.

"Who coming to see you?" Ramon's cell mate asks.

"It's my girl, but she got some explaining to do, you feel me? Something ain't right."

"The only thing we can't control from jail, is these bitches. That's how it goes."

Ramon buttons up his orange jump suit and waits to be escorted to the visiting room. While following behind the correctional officer, all Ramon can think about are the million and one questions he is going to ask. Ramon looks through the bullet proof Plexiglas, but he doesn't see Tynisha. *She's always on time.* Ramon sits down and gets comfortable. Seconds later, Ramon sees a distinguished gentleman wearing a black suit, and red tie. Ramon squints. "What the fuck," he mumbles.

Antoine sits down. "Wassup, Ramon?"

294

Ramon sarcastically claps his hands. "Whatchu trynna get me killed? If I would've known that all you had to do was snitch on me to reach your full potential, I woulda turned myself in." While Antoine crosses his legs and exhibits perfect posture, all Ramon can think about is choking him the fuck out. Ramon is filled with adrenaline, and becomes so angry that his knees shake. "You wanna be me so bad that you had to get rid of me. You'll never be me, nigga. You're a rat, and you're gonna die like one." Ramon bangs on the table. "Every dog has his day."

Antoine adjusts his arm to show his twenty-three thousand dollar custom Breitling watch. "Tell me, how does your cage feel?"

Ramon grits his teeth. "Fuck you."

Antoine shakes his head. "Fuck me?" Antoine reaches into his pocket and pulls out an envelope, and slides it on the table. "Tynisha said hi," he says before walking away.

Ramon yells, "You think you safe, nigga? Every dog as has its day, muthafucka." The correctional officers quickly surround Ramon so he calms down. Before leaving, Ramon grabs the envelope. His cell doors open and Ramon walks inside. He has no idea of what's inside of this envelope, but he can't resist. He rips open the envelope and inside are two pictures of Antoine and Tynisha on a beach obviously having the time of her life. Ramon balls up his fists and punches the concrete wall as hard as he can.

# CHAPTER XIII

With Ramon behind bars and Antoine controlling most of the weight being transported into the city, Carlos' money begins to decline. He only has a hundred grand saved and he is beginning to feel the pressure. It has been months since Sasha spoke to Antoine or Miles, and Sasha has finally built up enough courage to come clean. She would rather lose everything than continue to live this lie.

While sitting at home watching television, Sasha blurts out, "I need to tell you something."

"Wassup?"

*You can do it,* she reminds herself while taking deep breaths. "It's about Antoine."

Carlos turns down the television and sits up. "What about him?"

Sasha distances herself just in case Carlos loses his damn mind. "A while ago, some fucking racist cop pulled us over. Antoine had a gun and drugs on him, but instead of locking us up, we worked for him."

"Whatchu say?"

Sasha pleads, "This was before I knew who you were, and I was too scared to go to jail."

A still confused Carlos shakes his head as if he is living in a bad dream. "So that's why Antoine brought your name up." Carlos stands. "You muthafuckers been playing me from the start."

Sasha cries, "I didn't know I was gonna fall for you. I'm so sorry."

"You knew about Ramon too, didn't you?" Carlos yells. "You don't fucking love me. I would've done anything for you."

She grabs Carlos hand. "I'm sorry."

"Getcha fucking hands off me."

"I can make it right, Carlos, just give me a chance."

Carlos paces back and forth. "Give you a chance? You lucky I don't fucking kill you right now." Carlos grabs her by the arm and forcefully leads her to the bedroom. "You don't mean shit to me. Get the fuck out." He opens the closet and rips her clothes off the hangers. He clinches his fists and raises it high. "What was the cop's name?"

Sasha flinches, afraid for her life, but this is the only way she can begin to rid her life of ruthless lies and deceit. She places her hands over her head and mumbles, "A cop, white cop."

"Was his name Miles?" Sasha doesn't respond, so Carlos slaps her in the face, "Tell me!"

Sasha cries, "Yes."

Carlos is so distraught that he can barely breathe. All this time, he has been nothing but a pawn and now everything around him is crumbling. Carlos' anger quickly turns into a deep dark loneliness that reminds him of how his mother treated him. The pieces are finally coming together, and Carlos unclenches his fists and steps back.

"Am I next?"

"What are you talking about?" Sasha asks.

"Ramon is locked up, so I must be next. How could you do this to me?"

"I don't work for them anymore. I chose you over them and my freedom." Sasha continues to cry, "I don't wanna lie to you anymore." Sasha blurts out, "They raped me."

As bad as Carlos wants to feel sorry for her, he simply can't. Instead of listening to her sob story, Carlos runs into the bedroom and frantically grabs his money and anything that would trace back to him. Sasha stands and follows Carlos into the bedroom. She attempts to talk, but Carlos is too occupied with getting his shit.

"Don't leave. We can get through this."

"Bitch, if you putcha hands on me again, I'ma knock you out. You worked for a cop, so we can never be anything."

Sasha grabs Carlos' arm and Carlos pushes her as hard as he can. Sasha falls onto the dresser, breaks the glass mirror and cuts her hand. Sasha looks Carlos in the eyes and she can see the hate. Sasha doesn't want him to go because she may never see him again, but she knows that if she tries to stop him, he may kill her. Carlos scans the room one last time before leaving out of the back door. Sasha collapses on the floor and cries for hours. There was no turning back and there are no more lies to tell. Miles and Antoine ruined her life before it began and she needs to get it back. Sasha wraps her bloody hand, reaches into her purse and calls Miles.

Miles sees the number. "What this bitch want?" He answers, "Hello?"

"I have something that you and Antoine need."

"What could you possibly have that I need? Where have you been, sweetheart? I resigned from the police force, and I'm done." Miles hangs up. Seconds later his phone rings again and it's the same number. "Look, I told you I'm done –"

"If the right people get their hands on what I got, you won't make it passed Washington, DC you bitch."

Miles holds the phone. *Did she just call me a bitch?* He hasn't seen Sasha in a while and he wasn't used to her having so much courage, but she has his attention. Miles checks his watch. "Can you meet me at the Marriott in thirty minutes?"

"I'll be there in fifteen," Sasha says before hanging up.

Miles puts his phone down. *What do this bitch got up her sleeve?*

Sasha realizes that she will never be able to fix her relationship with Carlos, but she is happy that she no longer has to live a lie. Sasha was going on the run. She grabs her money, her little black book and gets dressed. She walks to the front door and hanging on the wall in the foyer is a picture of her and Carlos. "I love you," she says before opening the door and leaving.

Sasha zips through traffic and all she can think about is getting rid of the cancer that started it all. Sasha pulls her little black book from out of her purse. "I'ma show you how it feel to get it extorted." She grips the steering wheel feeling empowered. "I gotcha life in my hands now muthafuckas." Sasha knows that she got Miles and Antoine by the balls, but she still fears that she won't make it out alive. Sasha just wants to be left alone and she feels like this little black book will keep Miles and Antoine off her back for good. Seventeen minutes later, Sasha pulls to the front of the hotel. She walks inside and standing behind the desk is the same smart-ass receptionist from before.

"Back again?" *I knew you were a hooker.* "Welcome back, can I help you?"

Sasha walks passed the receptionist desk. "Don't say another word to me, bitch. I know where I'm going."

She catches the elevator to the eighth floor, walks down the hallway and stands in front of Miles' suite. The last time she was in the Marriott, she was raped. She knocks and Miles opens the door with an unusual smile on his face.

He leads Sasha to the suite's sitting area. "You want something to drink?"

"Don't fuck wit me, Miles."

Miles reaches under the hotel bed and pulls out a black duffle bag. He unzips it reaches inside and grabs stacks of money and throw onto the bed. "I'm rich, Sasha, so I don't have time to fuck with you. Now, what do you have that I need to see?"

Sasha reaches into her purse, pulls her little black book and tosses it on the bed. Miles picks up the book, flips through the pages and his eyes widen. This small booklet the size of Sasha's hand contained the names, the locations, and how much money Miles made from robberies and extortion. During Miles' meetings he

300

would brag about how he was the king of streets, but little did he know, Sasha was taking notes that connect him to murders and illegal activity with high ranking corrupt cops like Carter. As Miles flips through the pages, he can see his trip out of the country fading away. Miles knows that if this book gets into the wrong hands, he will be on the run from dirty cops and major drug distributors.

Miles squeezes the little black book. "You little bitch." He grits his teeth. "How much will it cost to make your little black book go away?"

"I want all of it, and if you ever step foot in this city again, I'll make sure that Sergeant Carter gets a copy."

"Be reasonable."

"I am being fucking reasonable. I didn't have to come here."

"You don't really think you're gonna walk outta here with all this money, do you?"

Sasha grins. "That's the plan."

When Miles realizes that Sasha means business, he loses his cool, "No one is gonna believe some little black bitch over me. I'm the fucking law."

"That's not what this little black book says."

Miles walks over to the duffel bag filled with cash and grabs it. "That little black book can't stop me from beating you to death."

Sasha reaches into her purse, pulls out Carlos' gun and aims. "What about my little black gun? You think this will help?" she asks sarcastically.

Miles drops the bag and walks towards her and Sasha cocks it. She raises it higher. "People like you don't just go away. You need to be put away. Now, move away from the bag."

Miles stares down the barrel. "If I wanted to kill you, you would be dead already," he says inching closer. "You can't kill me, you'll never get away with it."

Beads of sweat form on Sasha's forehead. She has never used a gun before so even though she is the one holding it, she is not in a position of power. Miles' gun is lying under his jacket, and all he needs to do is buy a little more time, "Calm down," he says inching closer, "I'm sorry for all the things I've done."

Sasha closes her eyes and squeezes the trigger. The impact pushes Miles into the wall. His eyes widen from shock and she pulls the trigger again. Miles grabs his chest, and takes short steps towards her, so she squeezes the trigger again. He finally falls to the ground and Sasha enjoys hearing him cry from the pain of the burning bullets moving throughout his body. Miles tries to speak, but he doesn't have enough strength. Using her cell phone, Sasha calls the front desk.

The clerk answers, "Front desk, how can I help you?"

"I heard some loud bangs and I'm sure it was gun shots."

"Gunshots?"

"Yes, I think it's coming from the suite at the end of the hall."

"Ok. Just relax, I'm sending someone now," the clerk replies.

Sasha grabs the duffel bag, and to avoid being spotted by the hotel cameras, she arranges her hair so it covers her face. Sasha walks down the hallway and keeps her eyes to the ground. The hotel's security rush towards her and she freezes.

"Are you ok, ma'am?"

"Yes, I heard some gunshots, I just wanna get outta here," she replies.

"Ok, ma'am, just go to the nearest exit."

Sasha jogs to the elevator and waits for it to arrive. She looks out the window and sees police cars pulling up to the entrance of the hotel and she panics. The elevator dings, she steps inside and it slowly takes her to the main lobby. The doors open and the lobby is filled with police officers.

Sasha pretends to be frightened. "I think someone got shot," she said.

"Everything's going to be alright. Just get to safety," the officer replies.

Sasha squeezes through the crowded lobby holding a large duffel bag. She walks outside and sees police cars and yellow tape everywhere. Her car is only twenty feet way, but it looks like a mile and the closer she gets, the more anxious she becomes. She finally reaches her car, unlocks the door, and leans her seat back as far as she can.

"Oh my God," she says looking with amazement.

Sasha turned the beautiful five star Marriott Hotel into a crime scene and she was far from remorseful. Sasha has never killed anyone before, but in her mind, she did the streets a favor and if she could remove Antoine, she would. Sasha doesn't have much time, but she refuses to leave until she sees his body covered with white sheets. The hotel's main entrance doors open and Miles' body is rushed to an awaiting ambulance. "Are you fucking serious?" Sasha becomes so angry that she wants to run towards the ambulance and shoot everything in sight. Sasha bangs on the steering wheel until her hands hurt. "I killed you. I fucking killed you." She cries hysterically. Seconds later, Sasha grabs her purse and dumps all her items onto the passenger seat. "Where's it at? Please tell me I didn't do what I think I did. Shit." Sasha frantically pats herself down looking for her little black book when it hits her. When Sasha grabbed Miles' duffel bag, she dropped the little black book onto the floor. "Oh my God," she says covering her mouth in disbelief.

That little black book was her trump card and the one thing that would keep her alive. Sasha would trade all the money in the world to get it back, but it's too late. The news crew arrives to the scene so Sasha doesn't have time to dwell in her failures so she wipes her tears, puts the key inside the ignition and slowly drives out of the parking lot.

\* \* \*

Carlos drives an hour away from the city and books a room at the Sheraton hotel. Mentally drained, he throws his bag full of cash on the floor and flops onto the bed. "I knew I shoulda killed that bitch." Carlos mumbles. "Think, Carlos, think," he repeats hoping the answer to all his problems will appear. "I need a fucking drink." Carlos gets out of the bed and walks over to the refrigerator containing overpriced miniatures of liquor. He grabs five miniature bottles of Tequila and empties them into the glass. He swallows the liquor, lights up a cigarette and walks over to the window. He pulls the shade to the side, just wide enough to see one eye and peeks out. It's completely quiet outside, but Carlos envisions a barrage of cop cars coming to end his reign. He thinks about that long scar on Ramon's face and he comes to the realization that if the cops do come, they're gonna have to kill him. Scared to go home, all Carlos has is the money in his duffel bag and the clothes on his back. Carlos stares at the four way intersection. "Fuck it, if they coming, then they're coming," he says closing the blinds. Carlos' mind is moving a one hundred miles per hour so he cuts on the television to break up his thoughts. The first thing he sees is Sarah Plies from Fox-45 news.

Sarah reports, *"I'm standing here at the five star Marriott Hotel in Downtown Baltimore. Tonight, a bizarre event took place in one of the luxurious suites. Officer Miles a well-respected officer was brutally gunned down in his hotel suite and is in critical condition."*

Carlos stands to his feet. "Oh shit."

Sarah Plies continues, *"The detectives have also found a little black book that contains information about multiple robberies and killings throughout Baltimore City. The detectives are not allowed to give me all the details of the case, but sources say that Sergeant Carter Mantelli is said to be the ring leader of a gang of corrupt cops throughout the city. Unfortunately, we do not have a clear picture of the shooter, but the suspect is said to be an African American female standing at five foot three, one hundred and twenty pounds. I'm Sarah Plies reporting live for channel twenty-five news."*

Carlos stands speechless.

Six degrees of separation is an understatement in Baltimore City and it's inevitable that they will all meet again.

To be continued